Ambiguous

LESLIE McADAM

Copyright © 2022 by Leslie McAdam

All rights reserved.

No part of this book may be reproduced in any form or by any electronic or mechanical means, including information storage and retrieval systems, without written permission from the author, except for the use of brief quotations in a book review.

Special edition cover design by RJ Creatives and interior design by Champagne Book Design.

Love is for other people, not for me.

At least that's what I believed, until I met *him*.

Julian Hill.

The most famous rock star on the planet.
A music god with untidy hair and the voice of an angel.

I'll never be anything but out,
and he has very good reasons to stay in the closet.

After all, every move he makes is dissected, critiqued, and posted on social media, so he just wants a little privacy.

I understand that. Truly.

But no one makes me feel the way he does,
and I'm pretty sure he has feelings for me as well.

Which is inconvenient since his record label hired me to sue him.

I should've sorted things out before I kissed him.

Oops.

Ambiguous is a forbidden mm rock star romance about a fashion-forward singer who hates labels of all kinds (except for clothing), a dapper attorney who already has a (fake) boyfriend for a very good reason, and the possibility of love saving the day.

Author's Note

The record approval process depicted herein has been manipulated for narrative purposes. It's not intended to be anything other than fiction, as is everything else in this book—except for the love between Jules and Sam. That's real.

Content Warning: Portrayals of bigotry based on sexuality and gender expression/identity, as well as various phobias (including claustrophobia and chapodiphobia).

Ambiguous

One

Jules

"Jules! Jules! Jules!"

Hoisting my guitar, I duck into the strap and sling it over my back. When I open the greenroom door to head to the stage, the volume increases like I've removed earplugs.

"Jules! Jules! Jules!"

Speaking of which, I dig in my pocket, fish out the in-ear monitors, and insert them. They're custom-made for me, with black rhinestones on the outer edge.

While I'm stopped in the hallway, I scan my body. Do I feel it?

Yeah, I do. I'm ready. *Let's do this.*

Grinning, practically skipping, I race through the bowels of the Forum, passing crew dressed in all black with ID tags around their necks. I wave and acknowledge them as I pass and hear "Good luck," "Knock 'em dead," "Break a leg."

They spur me into being even more excited about the show. Someone snaps a photo of me with their phone. That'll be on InstaTwitFaceTok in a moment, no doubt.

Julian Hill backstage with a rakish grin.

My pulse pounds, and I run the last few paces toward the stage.

I can hear the roar of the crowd getting louder and louder. Then it crescendos into an all-encompassing shriek, like everyone out there plugged into an amp.

The house lights must've turned off.

Now, it's nothing but anticipation—for me and for them.

Everyone—literally every paid ticket holder—is here for me, but I can't help but wish for someone who wants me in a quieter way. Someone I could cuddle up to after the show. Someone I could confide in.

Although I need to be grateful for the fans. I don't know what I'd do if they went away.

I shake my head. *Stay focused, Julian.*

I ready myself to climb up and walk out on stage. No one can see me in the dark except the crew, one of whom has a red-covered penlight to show me where to go so I don't trip on a stair.

Goose bumps race up my spine, and the hairs on the back of my neck stand on end.

This is the best part—or one of the best parts—besides actually singing. This time *right now*, before it all begins. Yes, it scares me. But therapy has helped me train my anxiety to stay in its lane. I've learned to love this moment when I don't know what's going to happen next. When the performance is open to all possibilities.

I'm free.

Oh, of course we have a set list, but I don't know what's going to happen beyond that. Some nights a streaker breaks through security to run across the stage, and others I get beaned in the head with a banana.

That's rock 'n' roll … or whatever you want to call the kind of music I play.

Mitch begins to beat out a rhythm, the stage still in darkness behind the gauzy black curtain, and the sound of the crowd somehow increases further in volume. They know the show is beginning, and the vibrations of their shouts and claps soak into my skin, skittering through my body until I can't take it anymore.

Deep breaths. I bring my guitar around to my front and grin at Loren.

"Go get 'em, kiddo," they say.

I blow a kiss and climb the stairs, then bounce onto the stage in the darkness, the drums still increasing in intensity.

A huge indoor arena extends before us just beyond the curtain as I linger beside a wall of amps. I can feel the music surging in my body: not just what the band is playing, but what I'm going to create.

Everyone's here. We're thumping. Pulsing. Radiating energy.

After meeting my eyes for a quick check-in, Stu picks at the strings, and a deep bass joins the drumbeat.

A roadie plugs in my guitar. I give it a strum, knowing the crowd can hear it, and am rewarded with another massive round of squeals and applause.

I glance around at everyone and nod.

We're ready.

The curtain is whisked away and lights flood the stage.

I step out, dazzled, so I can dazzle them myself. I can't hear a thing but the music in my ears, and it's overwhelming.

I absolutely love it. This moment. This jolt of adrenaline.

It makes everything else in my world vanish, so all that exists is *now*.

Shading my eyes with a hand, I survey the shapes in the darkness before us. I stand at the mic, stare down my fans, grin, and launch into the opening song.

Two

Sam

I SLIDE ON MY DARK BLUE SUIT JACKET COMPLETE WITH POCKET square—old-school style, but it screams *Lawyer!*—and grab my briefcase from the back seat of my car.

Century City has a reputation for having the most cutthroat lawyers in the state. I'm not sure I fit in. But the firm's name looks good on my résumé, and the opportunity to work on major nationwide initiatives that matter to me helps me deal with the rest. Mostly.

I take the garage elevator down to the ground level and cross the landscaped path to a high-rise office building, flashing my badge to security and weaving through the construction. I'm used to the dust. Someone's always remodeling or upgrading, with particleboard cordoning off areas and quilted moving-van-style blankets padding the elevators. Four people get in the car with me as I take it to the thirtieth floor.

"Morning, Sam," Bruce, our receptionist says, when I walk through. He's a Parisian macaron of a man, with satiny dark skin and no hair, wearing pastel from head to toe. Somehow, he pulls it off, managing to look like the chicest person to ever live. "Terrill asked for you. He says he wants you in a meeting at ten."

I assume it's music related, which is a perk of working here. I love discovering new artists. I spend my days drafting and negotiating entertainment contracts, because we represent most of the major American record labels. It's common for recording legends to stroll our halls, which is kind of a rush. Still, since this is LA, I have to act like I'm too cool and don't notice their presence.

I nod. "Thanks for the heads-up."

In the break room, I pause to brew a K-Cup. Then I make my way to my boss's doorway. He's on a call. He waves me in, and I sit down in a client chair, listening to him yell at someone … at eight fifteen in the morning.

Did I mention I'm not sure I like working here?

But. *Think of the special projects. Think of the reach. Think of the opportunities.*

I sip my coffee and wait, taking in his desk piled with papers. I restrain my shudder. How does he get anything done?

When he sets down the phone, he gives me a once-over, his nose wrinkling. He's made no attempt to hide the fact that my sexuality creeps him out. He didn't ask for me to be assigned to his division. He thinks I barely earn my keep. Given his attitudes, I'm amazed he's civil to Bruce—although Bruce's competence shines through, so perhaps that explains it. Or maybe he knows Bruce wouldn't put up with his asshattery the way I do.

"Lighthouse Records has asked us to explain to one of its artists the penalty terms of the agreement he signed. His laziness is hurting their bottom line."

"So it's time to get tough?" I hide my grimace. This is my least favorite part of the job: threatening others with breach-of-contract lawsuits. But there's only so many pro bono hours I'm allowed to log, even if that's my main reason for being here.

He gives me a toothy smile. "Exactly. They figure if they can scare him, he'll put out."

"Fine. Who is it?"

"Julian Hill."

That stops the forward motion of my thoughts, and I blink. Julian Hill is one of the biggest stars on the planet, and he has a reputation for being Tom Hanks–level kind. Why the hell does he need lawyers to read him the riot act?

Also, he's my best friend Emily's crush. I'll be able to taunt her for the foreseeable future with this one—if meeting him isn't confidential.

"What's he done?"

"Hasn't recorded diddly squat for his new solo album, and the label's about to drop him or sue him. This is his last chance. They want you and me to explain his obligations to him and babysit him until he finishes. Make him accountable. Document progress. That sort of thing." His phone rings. "I'll have Devin email you the contract." He waves me away.

I nod and go to my office. I set down my briefcase and coffee, hang up my suit jacket, and adjust my bow tie, my neck stiff.

Conflict and unpleasant meetings are part of this job. It's not the first time I've had to lecture the talent. Even famous talent. I spend the next hour reading the contract and highlighting all the penalties that will go into effect if Julian Hill doesn't get his act together and record the album he's contracted for.

When it's time for the meeting, Terrill stops by my office, and we proceed to the medium conference room. Julian is sitting at the end of the table, slouching like a rock god king with his legs stretched out to one side. His expression suggests he's in charge, even though he's the one ostensibly in trouble. Next to him sits an older, dark-haired person with short hair and long, sharp, black nails.

Julian takes my breath away. While I've met plenty of celebrities, with him I feel this hit to my solar plexus. I freeze, because he's so hot it's too much to process.

Dark, perfectly mussed hair. Dark brown eyes. Tan skin.

His black pants are painted on, highlighting his lanky form. He's wearing heeled black boots with chains on them and a loose, lacy, unbuttoned blouse and piles of long pearl necklaces. Rings on every finger click as he fidgets. His Adam's apple moves as he drinks from a bottle of water.

He started with a boy band a decade ago. And, while I listen to plenty of pop music, I've intentionally ignored him just to piss Emily off. I'm mature like that sometimes. I'm not sure why I even started that—she and I love a lot of the same music and go to concerts together whenever we can, but at some point I decided he was just too cheesy, and then it became a *thing*. Julian is now on his own, the only one from his original group to have a successful solo career.

Of course I've heard his music. I'm generally aware of him, because I live in a condo in America and not under a rock cut off from communication with the outside world.

I've just never put his songs on voluntarily. Now I wish I knew more about him.

The table's been set up for the meeting with bottles of fancy water and carafes of coffee. Readying himself for introductions, Julian sets down his water and stands up.

I walk over to shake his hand, and it's like it happens in slow motion. One second I'm standing, and the next my toe hooks on a chair leg and I go flying. My flailing wrist manages to knock his open bottle of water from the table, and I take him down to the floor in one fell swoop, splashing water all over him as I go.

He lands on the industrial carpet with an "Oomph," and I end up sprawled on top of him.

Heat singes my cheeks. *Oh shit, oh shit.* I won't blame him if he pulls a diva fit after I ruined his clothes. They're next season's Gucci.

I start mentally updating my résumé.

"Oh my god," I whisper, fumbling up to the table to grab a stack of paper napkins from the coffee service while struggling to get off of him as fast as I can.

Julian frowns, and then he jackknifes up to a sitting position, forcing a laugh. His now-wet shirt leaves little to the imagination, revealing the shapes of tattoos scattered all over his chiseled torso. I kneel at his feet and start wiping his pants, only to realize that, yeah, I'm trying to dry off the crotch of a Grammy-nominated recording artist.

"Oh my god," I repeat. "I'm so sorry."

I can't stop dabbing at his crotch.

With a white napkin.

That's leaving shreds of wet lint.

On his dark designer pants.

I'm making it *so much worse*—and my reaction to him is getting worse, too. Partly because there's a bulge underneath that zipper, and it's not small. Like, not *at all* small. Partly because he smells amazing—like maybe rum and vanilla—which makes my body hum and my cock wake up.

Even though I don't live my life as a train wreck, apparently it can get derailed in one second flat.

But all those thoughts vanish when his brown eyes focus on mine. His irritation has been shut down, and now I see resigned amusement in his expression. He smirks and runs his fingers through his hair, then puts a large paw on my hand, stopping my movements.

"It's no biggie, mate. I'm used to people dousing me in water, though security usually keeps them from touching my junk." Julian Hill has this honeyed British accent, the kind that makes anything he says instantly respectable. I can see the media training click in place, and he gives me the broadest smile I've ever seen. A famous smile. He stands up, his pants soaked and covered with the napkin fragments from my attempt to fix my gaffe. I yank my pocket square out of my jacket and make one last-ditch effort to clean him off, realizing too late that I'm on my knees while he's standing—and this position is perhaps worse than covering him like a blanket. He again puts a hand on my wrist, which is still on his zipper, takes the pocket square, and looks at me with those soul-searching eyes. "There's no harm done. You didn't hurt me. Water will dry."

I swallow hard and am officially starstruck, which isn't something that happens to me very often.

When I get to my feet, I'm looking at him straight on. He's within an inch or so of my six foot one. Hard to tell with his heels, but I might be taller than he is. He's about as lean as me, too, although I think he gets that from running around a stage rather than the way I do it.

I toss the napkins in the closest trash can and stammer, "I can't believe I did that. Can we get you some, uh, new pants?" I wince.

"That's not necessary. I'm Jules. Jules Hill. It's a pleasure to meet you." Like he needs to introduce himself.

He holds out his hand, and I take it. I can tell he's a guitarist by the calluses on his fingers. His grip is perfect, not too strong but not limp, and it's somehow comforting.

I manage to say, "S-S-Sam. Sam Stone."

Dear sweet baby Jesus, Mary, and Joe Jonas. I was taught how to properly introduce myself before I started school, but you'd never know it now.

I need to come back to reality. Julian Hill is making me feel all sorts of out of sorts. I need to escape from him and his magnetism.

Julian's still holding my hand, and I can't seem to look away from his face.

Someone clears their throat.

"And who else do we have here?" Julian lets go of my hand and looks over my shoulder, and I remember that he and I aren't the only two people in the room.

In the country.

On the planet.

I glance back and see the expression of horror on Terrill's face. Because I fucked this meeting up before we even got to the introductions.

I'm so fired.

With a grim glare at me, Terrill steps forward and shakes Julian's hand. "Terrill St. Martin. I'm the managing partner. My colleague, Sam, has been assigned to your matter."

Please, whoever is the god of music—Apollo?—find me and pull me out of this meeting with whatever transport you have. If it's Apollo, I think you have a sun chariot. Take me. Or zap me. Either way, please put me out of my misery.

Jules maintains a genuine smile and gestures to his companion, who's wearing a neutral expression. "Pleasure. This is Loren Brooks, my manager."

Loren slides off a messenger bag, stands, and shakes Terrill's hand. "My pronouns are they and them."

Terrill grunts.

"Mine are he/him," I say.

"As are mine," says Julian.

We all nod, and yep, it's still all the awkward.

"Have a seat," Terrill says, gesturing to everyone to take their places.

Julian sinks back down into his chair, which looks like a throne with him on it.

I'm counting the fact that he hasn't complained about sitting in soggy pants as a major win.

Only now I'm thinking about his soggy pants and wondering whether the water soaked through to his underwear, because wearing wet underwear sucks. Although a rock deity probably goes commando.

Then I wonder why I'm thinking about his underwear.

Then I'm thinking about what I felt under the napkin.

Then I wonder if he's straight.

Then I blush hard.

Then I remember my training, *for Taylor Swift's sake*. Lawyers are taught to think on our feet. To come back from being down. To fight.

I need to pull myself together.

Campaigning for my grandfather, I've been trained to compartmentalize. To put pesky feelings and deep embarrassments off to the side.

So, while part of me thinks it will be an absolute miracle if I make it through this meeting with a job and without being struck down by the god of music, the rest of me toughens up.

I'm a professional, dammit. And I can act like one.

Three

Jules

Oh, my giddy aunt, I'm not sure whether Sam Stone is the most hapless individual I've ever met—and as I've sung in front of hundreds of thousands of people and done heaven only knows how many meet and greets, that's saying something—or the most adorable. People do tend to get fazed around me. I just didn't expect the solicitor to be that way. Given how cute he is, I think I'll let his accident fade into the past.

Between his innocent demeanor and unintentional sexiness—he's a Ronan Farrow lookalike with turquoise eyes, golden blond hair, and pale, lucent skin—I can't look away.

Or stop thinking about how he nearly gave me a wank by accident ... although if he's to inspire me to write faster, that's one way of going about it.

He's a handsome distraction in the middle of fun things sure to come, like being threatened with getting dropped by my label and having my reputation shredded into tatters while the suits claw back every penny they've ever paid me.

Not that my mind leaps to doomsday scenarios.

The record company apparently thinks this ethereal being is one of the heavies who'll make me quiver in my boots and start stammering, *Yes, it will be done, overlords.*

He did make me quiver, though. His hand felt *great* on my knob. Now that we're all settled at the table—physically in place, that is; I'm not feeling the least bit settled emotionally, and I'm hyperaware of the cutie in the bow tie—I listen to Terrill, the scowling partner, tell me how I'm about to be responsible for repaying advances the record company's made against the new album and will need to cough up not only that money but also lost profits if I can't craft a new album out of empty air instantaneously and also make it sell a trillion units by yesterday.

As one does.

His spiel is exactly what I'd expected, although hearing it out loud and not just in my head does drive home the point.

When Terrill takes a deep breath, I smile. "Please let Lighthouse know that I'm aware of my contractual duties, but I don't want to put out an inferior product. You can't rush a good thing, and art is particularly hard to rush. If they'll just hold on—"

"All artists have to make something. You signed the contract, and you need to deliver on it. You just need to do the work," he growls.

Loren puts a hand up, but I don't need their help right now. I knew Lighthouse Records was going to hold a university-level class on "This is the way the real world works," just for me.

I turn to Loren. "It's fine. They have a right to get the work they're paying for." Then I address the rest of the room, wanting to assure Sam in particular. "I'll make the album. The tour is over, and I only have the Fly by Night show left. I'll have time to spend in the studio."

I just hope what I come up with will be good enough.

Because no matter how many songs I've sung, how much I've written, how many times I've performed, I always feel anxious when starting a new project.

And afraid that I'll lose my entire fanbase by, you know, being myself.

"Two months," Terrill sneers. "You have two months to deliver."

I furrow my brows. "That's impossible—"

"If we gave you two years, you'd take it. You'd be like a goldfish expanding to the size of your aquarium. You have two months, and that's final. Otherwise you'll be in breach of your contract."

Like I don't already know this. Like I haven't beaten myself up every day since signing that contract, because I haven't been able to write. I remind myself to keep a level head. I didn't even bring my own attorneys to this meeting because I didn't want to escalate matters. I just want to solve the problem.

Sitting back in my chair, I survey the room. Terrill's cracking his knuckles. Sam gazes at me, his eyes searching. Loren's unnaturally silent, which means they're about to go ballistic. It's time to express my underlying concerns. "I don't know if I'll be able to create something excellent in that period of time. It has to be fresh. Exciting. I don't want to repeat myself."

Terrill scoffs. "The record company *wants* you to repeat yourself. Chart more hits. Make something as popular as your last album."

Like that's simple to pull off.

I glance at Sam, who has been watching the volleys between Terrill and me like we're playing a particularly worrisome spectator sport. He opens his mouth and licks his lips. I'm momentarily distracted by his soft, pink tongue.

Fuck me sideways, he's cute.

"I'm sure Julian has been trying," Sam says. While he's addressing his boss, he's looking at me, those Caribbean blue eyes sincere. "I imagine being creative on demand is difficult. I have an artist friend who tells me deadlines are rough." He smiles at me, an expression that manages to be both sheepish and conciliatory at the same time. Like he's still stressed and embarrassed but wants to do his job. "If I can help you in any way to get this project done, please let me know."

Will his "help" be spilling things on my trousers? But that was an accident, already forgiven.

Before I can decline Sam's offer, the boss looks at him as if he's suggested they give up the law and start a band themselves. "Julian's been in the business long enough to not require coddling."

"Every artist needs support," Sam says, flashing me another smile.

He's supposed to be demanding I fulfill my contract, and instead he's sticking up for me. Being kind.

I like his kindness.

Loren nods fiercely. "If you tell an artist they can't waste time and have to create, they'll waste even more time worrying about being creative. Jules just needs to focus on writing, and he should be able to do that now that the tour's finished. Don't worry."

"Do you have a place to write?" Sam asks me.

"I have a studio at my house, yeah."

"Is that conducive, though? Do you need to go somewhere else? A mountain cabin or—"

My heart melts. He's being persistent in a polite way.

I like his politeness, too.

"Julian Hill doesn't need a vacation," Terrill barks, apparently not content to have us figure this out without his input. "He needs to get his job done."

"But this kind of creative work is difficult, I imagine," Sam insists. "Julian has extraordinarily high pressures because of the fans' expectations."

Sam's baby face distracts me from realizing he has a backbone of steel.

If he keeps this up, he's going to become my new favorite human being.

Sam turns to face me fully. "We represent the record company, and they've asked us to enforce the contract. But it seems to me that the way to achieve that isn't with threats, it's with encouragement."

His boss looks disgusted, and it dawns on me that Terrill is toxic to everyone, not just those he's supposed to yell at on behalf of his clients.

But if I'm reading Terrill right, he thinks Sam is weak because he's not swearing at me and playing by the alpha male rule book.

Funnily enough, *because* Sam's not playing by the alpha male rule book, I'm more willing to cooperate.

I lock my gaze on his boss. "Sam's right. I can get the job done, now that I have the right environment and incentive. I don't want to breach the contract, and I'm not going to. Go ahead and tell Lighthouse you threatened me and I was properly contrite. I am. I'll get cracking on the record."

However the hell that's going to happen.

"Excellent," Sam says, brightening.

Loren nods. "This is a good start." They turn to Terrill. "You don't have to beat up artists as if they're adversaries. You can treat them like human beings."

Terrill still looks miffed. "Sam, monitor the situation. Mr. Hill, you need to be in contact with him on a consistent basis. We will give you Sam's business card and expect you to send regular progress reports."

"I'll give Sam my mobile number," I say. "I can just text him. What's your number?" I catch Sam's wide eyes and rethink this. "Or—Is that okay?"

Sam blinks at me. "Uh. Sure." After a moment's hesitation where he goes bright red, he recites the number. I enter it into my mobile and send him a text.

Jules: Hey

I watch him type back, and then my phone buzzes.

Sam: I received your text, Julian.

Okay. Sam Stone has officially become the most darling human being I've ever met. When I glance up at him, he looks like he can't believe he just texted me. I don't think he's intimidated by me, though. More like I'm pushing him out of his comfort zone. I very much like the idea of keeping in contact with this lovely.

Loren stands up. "Are we done here?"

"Yes. I understand what I need to do." I shake Terrill's hand. Then I shake Sam's, holding it just a beat too long because I like the way it feels in mine.

We leave, but I find myself wanting to come back.

Four

Sam

It's been hours since I left work, but I'm still not over meeting Julian Hill. My body shivers as I remember the feel of his long, slim body under mine. That rich voice. *That bulge.*

But I'm feeling supremely guilty I haven't told my best friend I met her crush. If I wait much longer, she'll disown me.

I grab my phone.

> **Sam**: I need to tell you about the celebrity I met today at work. Unlike the last one, it's someone you'd want to meet.

The last celebrity I met was a singer who was fresh out of rehab and got a starlet pregnant while in the process of divorcing his wife.

> **Emily**: Who? Tell meeeeeee
>
> **Sam**: JH

I brace myself. My phone lights up with a call. I answer it but hold the phone away from my ear, expecting an earsplitting shriek.

She surprises me. There's silence. Complete and utter silence.

"Hello?" I try.

More silence.

I look around for a weapon, feeling the need to defend myself even though she's not in the room. Like I'd actually go after her with a weapon.

"Em?" I try again.

"Sam Stone," she says in this steely, quiet voice, "are you telling me that you met, in person, in the flesh, in real life, no kidding, Julian Hill?"

"Um, yes." I gulp.

"Ohmygodohmygod," she breathes. "Did you touch him?"

My cheeks heat. "Actually …"

"Did you shake his hand?"

"First I shook his dick."

Now I get the shriek I was expecting. "You did *what?*"

"I was a fumbling dipshit and tripped and spilled water on him. Then I tried to clean it up and ended up stroking him through his pants. It was"—*delicious*—"embarrassing."

Emily bursts out laughing. "I am so fucking jealous of you I might turn myself inside out. Do you know how many *millions* of people want to do what you just did?"

"It was a complete accident. I'm lucky I didn't get fired. Or reprimanded. Jules acted nice about it, though, so my boss didn't say anything afterward."

"You need to tell me every single thing."

"I can't tell you anything that would breach client confidentiality."

"Then tell me every single thing you can." She sounds like she's gritting her teeth a bit, which, okay, it's not like she doesn't know I can't talk about client secrets. "What was he wearing? What did he say? What did he smell like?"

"He wore Gucci and pearls, he has a really sexy accent, and he smells like rum and vanilla."

Silence. Then, "Seriously?"

"He smelled great," I admit. "Like you want to lick him."

"Do you understand now why I've had a crush on him forever? Oh my god, you have a crush on him, too, now," she accuses. "You do, don't you? You've never said anything positive about him since I became a fan. I bet you've been suppressing this for years, Sam. *Years.*"

I let out a very loud sigh. "He's your favorite, not mine. But after meeting him? I can see the attraction."

"Tell me everything."

I put her on FaceTime. Hazel eyes watch me, framed by straight dark hair.

By the end of me telling her everything not confidential or private, she sighs contentedly. "You're the envy of the entire Jules Hill fandom, you know that?"

"I can't be the envy. No one's going to know about it. You can't tell anyone."

"Absolutely not." Her horror registers, loud and clear. "This was one of those special moments that will go down in history as the best day of your life."

"Well, I don't know about that—"

"It will be. Mark my words. You will measure time by BJ and AJ. Before Julian and After Julian."

"Most people will not think 'Before Julian' if I say 'BJ.'"

Emily laughs. "Let me bask in the reflected glory of your brush with greatness."

"He's just a man. I'm not going to put him on a pedestal."

"But can you see why everyone adores him?"

"Yeah," I admit. "I can see how there's something about him that makes everyone fall in love with him. Not that I believe love is such a big deal," I add hastily, wincing as I think of Asa.

She rolls her eyes. "I know you're the cynic, Sam. But us normal people, we believe in love."

"Love's a cop-out. It's a plot device."

She gasps and holds her crossed hands to her heart like she's Snow White. "How dare you say that."

"Oh, give it up, Em. All the worst movie endings are the ones where love is the answer to all the problems. Book endings, too. *A Wrinkle in Time?* She saves her brother by *loving* him? Give me a break. *Interstellar?* For fuck's sake, do something original."

"Most people think both of those stories are highly original," she retorts.

"Just ... love is not the strongest thing in the universe, okay? It's simply not."

"Wow. You feel very strongly about this, ironically. What is the strongest thing, then?"

"Diamonds, I think."

"You're *so* unromantic," she groans.

"I don't need to be romantic," I argue. "It's pointless. When love shows up as a solution in those movies, it means the author didn't have a better idea. It's the easiest resolution. Sure," I scoff. "Love will save the day. Whatever." You could probably see my eye roll from the moon.

Emily's quiet and gives me a look.

"What?" I ask, feeling even more defensive.

"I've always known underneath that perfect veneer you're a fighter. Scrappy. Independent. But now I think you're a lover, too." She rubs her hands together. "Oooh, boy. I'm gonna have so much fun seeing the moment when you get out of denial and fall in love. Call me, okay? I want to be there."

"Whatever," I mutter. Then I give her a smile. She smiles back, and I know all is well. I decide to change the subject. "Cute color," I say, pointing to her olive-green sweater. "It's very pea soup."

"Goes with this." She pans the camera down to show me her pearls, shorts, fishnets, and penny loafers, then gives me a red-lipsticked smile full of teeth.

"You look like grandma got run over by a goth."

She beams. "Aww, thanks. And thanks for telling me all about JH. I gotta go, but I'm gonna have nice dreams tonight."

I open my mouth to say goodbye, but she stops me. "Sam? Are you sure you're okay? It's a big deal to meet a celebrity like him."

"Pshaw. I've met plenty of huge stars."

"But not him. He's special."

I think about the way his thighs looked in those tight pants and the way his shirt showed a lot of skin yet was still covering him up—at least, until I dumped water all over it. "I'll admit, he was interesting."

And the sexiest being I've ever met.

"Are you going to start listening to his music now?"

"Haven't I absorbed enough through osmosis?"

"I dare you," she says. "I dare you to deep-dive into him and see if you don't feel something."

I sigh. "Okay."

"I'll let you go. Thanks for spilling your guts about him. I won't tell anyone."

"I know. I trust you."

"Okay, love you."

"Love you, too, Em." We hang up.

I never said I *can't* love people. I just don't need romantic love, and it certainly can't solve all problems.

It's more likely to fuck you up for your entire life.

Five

Jules

I CROSS MY JEAN-CLAD LEGS, HOOKING THE HEEL OF MY motorcycle boot into the rung of the director's chair. I've spent most of the day trying to focus and, like, *be present*, but I'm at the point where my mind's as numb as my arse and I'm liable to say something off script.

That could be fun.

Or it could cause a riot on Twitter.

The blue curtain draped behind me forms a plain background, over which they'll surely superimpose a logo of the YouTube show. I'm hot under the lights in this stuffy, soundproof room, which is set up for interviews of the Lighthouse artists. Since our tour is over, this is publicity for the Fly by Night music festival happening next week in the California desert—a competitor to Coachella. Karen, the interviewer, is a cute, tiny, perky Chinese American woman wearing piles of contour makeup. She's my last stop on today's press junket.

Giving my best, most sincere smile, I lean forward, sure the camera is catching every expression that runs across my face. The shoulder of my oversized T-shirt slips down, showing a few more tattoos. I slide it back up again, my black pearl bracelets jangling on my wrists and a skull necklace thumping my sternum. "My fans are the best people in the world," I say. "They deserve every piece of me I can give them."

My accent sounds more pronounced when I'm around Americans.

Vowels don't come out of my mouth the same way as theirs, like my words need to pass through gauze before being spoken aloud.

"Gotta love the fans," she says, giving me a commercially appropriate smile full of white teeth.

"I *adore* them," I correct her, mock sternly. "I wouldn't be here without them. The past ten years have been astonishing. But you know the history …" I shake my head, smiling. "All I am is because of them."

"The Hillions *are* legendary." Karen's referring to the nickname for my fans, a play on my last name. She hesitates, and it's a studied, practiced pause, because she then cocks her head to the side in a studied, practiced move. "Have you ever read the fan fiction about yourself?"

"Some, yes. Nowhere near all of it. To be frank, I have to keep off my mobile because it can be too much—social media, Google alerts, and the fanfics." I give her a cheeky grin. "I've been told fictional me is often put in, shall we say, *sexually compromising* positions. Bit strange to read that about myself." I twitch my fingers, and my rings clink together.

"I'm sure it is." Karen blushes and fans herself with her notecards. And I can tell the flavor of fanfic she's read about me—the kind where I'm engaging in some rumpy-pumpy with another man. Or a werewolf. Or a T. rex shifter.

In some fics, though, I'm paired with real people—like my ex-bandmates—even if those hookups never happened in real life.

At least not as far as the public knows.

Reading my reluctance to gush about fictionally shagging Regé-Jean Page and the entire Pittsburgh Penguins hockey team—all at the same time—the interviewer changes the subject. "What's next, now that your world tour is over?"

Contractual obligations. My stomach swoops down like I've hit a sudden drop on a roller coaster … until I think of Sam Stone and his adorable smile. "After headlining at Fly by Night, we'll be taking time off to work on the new album."

The one that's two years overdue.

"Your new *solo* album?"

Ambiguous 23

"Yes." I square my shoulders.

"If it's a solo album, why do you say 'we'?"

"Darling," I purr. "I can't do this all on my own." I gesture around as if we're about to get stormed by hundreds of musicians and producers from just behind the blue curtain.

"But you're, well, *you*." Her confusion seems genuine, but in this business you never know who's acting and who isn't.

I shrug. I never argue with interviewers, even if they try to provoke me. *Especially* when they try to provoke me. I inspect my yellow-painted nails. They're rough, short, and wrecked from playing the guitar.

Then I look up again. "It's a group effort."

The actual heroes are my support system.

"One of the most loved rock stars in America and Europe, and you don't take credit—"

"I like to give. Give love. Give music. Give my all." I uncross my legs and slump back, reaching over to the glass of water on a side table and taking a sip.

"And we adore you for that." There's an awkward pause, and in it, I can see the hearts in her eyes. Karen's a fan, and she's been holding in her excitement for this interview.

I'm flattered. I raise an eyebrow and wait.

She refers to her notes for the first time since we started. "What would you call your music genre these days? When you started with the Paradise, it was pop, but then with your first album, you transitioned to folk. It seems like you've transitioned again to rock. Some of the songs are hard rock, and some are more soulful. How do you characterize it?"

"It's just music, love," I say lightly, although this topic irks me no end. "Up to the label how to describe what I do. I just do it."

This is the fourth time I've answered this question on this press junket. Journalists seem to think artists can't try something new.

But I'm not going to be pigeonholed into any one thing.

Karen turns to the camera. "We're here with Julian Hill, British rock star, formerly of boy band the Paradise. And I must say, he's even kinder in real life than you can imagine." She turns to me. "You have a reputation for being so nice. Don't you get tired of it? Don't you ever just need to lash out at someone?"

"Never. What do I have to be a twat about? Nothing." I grin. My long legs need to stretch out, but I can keep from fidgeting for a few minutes more.

She bats her eyes and reaches out to touch my forearm. "Seriously. Do you ever have a bad day?"

Days when I get called into a solicitor's office aren't grand. Unless there's a cute man there, of course.

"Absolutely. But that doesn't mean I have to take it out on someone else. Especially not a fan."

"Fans want to know: who is the *real* Jules Hill? Can you tell us a secret about him?"

Always with the secrets. Why anyone would bother knowing the kind of aftershave I like is beyond me.

It's not like I'd ever tell them my true secrets.

I shrug one shoulder. "He's a simple chap." I close my eyes, shake my head, and chuckle. "Wait, I hate talking about myself in the third person. Makes me feel like a git."

She gives me an obligatory laugh and encourages me with a hand gesture to keep talking.

"The secret, the real truth about me is no secret: I'm just like everyone else. The only difference is I like to sing, and I get to perform. I'm grateful for how far I've come. I spend my days just trying to keep a good thing going."

Even if it kills me.

Karen nods, then adopts a flirty look. "Do you have a special someone in your life to keep it going with?"

I don't know why the face of my new friend, the attorney, flashes in my mind.

I pause.

"Lots of special some*ones*. Like you." I reach over and graze her wrist.

She blushes again. "Are you ever going to get married, Jules?"

"If the right person comes along."

Again, why am I thinking of *him*?

Then a look comes into her eyes, and my stomach drops again. Uh-oh. I can tell by not only the look but the time—the interview's just about over—that she's going to ask something I don't want to answer.

That I'm not going to answer.

"A final question, because I'm sure all your fans want to know. If you were to get married, what gender would that person be? Or are you open to more than one possibility?"

There it is. The media loves to dig into my sexuality. Something about me having all the fangirls but wearing ruffles and frocks and jewelry makes them wonder. Makes them lust after a definition. Makes them ask the rudest questions. And the fan fiction feeds into it, portraying me as shagging everyone (and everything).

But seriously, my sexuality is the most pedestrian thing about me. It's also the most private, and I want to keep it that way as long as I can. Which is easy when I'm not dating anyone.

I can't really date anyone.

I glance over at Loren, who's giving me the signal to leave.

Giving my most media-friendly smile, I lean toward Karen. "I appreciate your interest in the subject, but it's not something I talk about. Thank you so much for having me today." I give her a wink and stand, finally freeing my arse from the uncomfortable director's chair.

Karen opens her mouth to ask another question, but Loren stands in front of her, effectively ending the interview, saying, "I think we're done for today. Was that your last question?"

She nods.

I stand and give a slight bow, my hands pressed to my chest like I'm praying. "It was lovely to meet you all. Thank you for taking the time to talk to me." I shake hands with Karen, who seems surprised that I give her a smile after I refused to answer her last question, and then with the cameraman, boom operator, producer, and all the other crew standing around.

Loren rolls their eyes, because we need to get moving, but the crew often get ignored, even though they do all the work. Me shaking hands can give them a story to tell for the rest of their lives—not to be arrogant about it. It's the least I can do.

After a few selfies—with Loren checking their phone repeatedly for the time—we leave the PR tent and head for the white van that takes me to my next appointment.

Six

Sam

"SAM!" MY MOTHER CALLS FROM THE ENTRYWAY. "There you are!"

It's a beautiful, sunny day in San Marino, and we're at some huge verdant bungalow estate that's decorated in an explosion of red, white, and blue.

Taking a deep breath, I paste on my smile. I have a slight headache. "Hey, Mom."

She gives me a hug, knowing that people are watching and we're being photographed. My father's off to the side, talking with a few reporters. We're headed toward a party full of dressed-up people eating passed hors d'oeuvres and sipping champagne cocktails. Some of whom are famous, either entertainers or politicians, and some of whom are the plus-ones. I'm pretty sure they each paid $5,000 for the privilege of attending this shindig. She steps back to inspect me, but I know I'm flawless. "Is Kurt coming?"

I nod. "He'll be here."

"Wonderful." She beams at me. "Go say hi to your grandfather. He's around back. Remember to take pictures for the ad campaign once Kurt's here."

I follow the bunting-clad railing on the wraparound porch, punctuated by American flags flying in the gentle breeze, and locate California's top Democratic state senator—who also happens to be my grandfather—in front of a team of reporters in the backyard.

He lifts his chin as he sees me coming and puts on his huge politician smile. The one that makes me feel conflicted, because I know he loves me … but he also uses me. I'm the token gay, after all, here to prove that even though Fred Stone's an old-school middle-aged White man, he's honestly into the liberal causes California Democrats support. I give him street cred.

Lingering on the sidelines for a moment, I wait for him to gesture for me to come to his side. When he does, I approach all jolly smiles, like we're buds from a 1950s sitcom. "Hey, Pop-Pop," I say, shaking his hand.

He puts an arm around my shoulder and faces me to the cameras. "Everyone, I'm sure you all know my grandson Sam Stone. Because of him and his partner, I've dedicated my life to ensuring California leads the way for LGBT rights."

"Dedicating his life" is pushing it. I restrain an eye roll.

Oh, he cares about the cause, and he loves me, sure. But he *needs* me—for votes—as much as he loves me.

Still, he's family, and I care about those votes, too, so I open my mouth and say the words I've been trained to say by his speechwriter. "I'm very proud that my grandfather is supportive of the gay community." I smile and get my picture taken, my bow tie and suspenders feeling tighter than usual. I answer a few questions, stand by my grandfather while he does the same, then excuse myself to go find my "boyfriend."

I don't have a boyfriend. Never again.

But that looks bad. Which, yes, is a judgment steeped in heteronormative prejudices. So while I combat those, I have a friend who's also gay and coincidentally related to the Democratic leader of the state assembly. She and my grandfather long ago made up the fiction that Kurt and I are dating.

It works, because neither one of us does relationships.

An image of Julian Hill comes to me, together with a memory of the way his body felt under mine. Like he belonged there.

Not sure where that thought came from.

Anyway, Kurt and I are very good at posing for the camera,

reciting sound bites, and then leaving each other alone to go about our own lives.

Kurt texts me that he's almost here, so I return to the front of the mansion, where he emerges from a black town car. Smiling, I approach and dutifully give him the safe peck on the cheek and hug that are expected of acceptable gay men.

Yes, I spend my life putting up with other people's ideas of how I should behave, but it's for the greater good.

Kurt's a graphic artist, the kind who designs junk mail, but he's passionate about government policies. He makes political posters in his free time.

I want to make the world a better place for LGBTQIA+ people and stop legislation fueled by hate—like taking away health care for trans teens. I will do anything to keep some kid in an intolerant society from suffering that prejudicial crap. And Kurt's the same way, so he's as on board with this pretense as I am.

"Hey," Kurt says, brown eyes shining, his dress shirt and slacks well tailored. "Glad to see you, sweets."

"Likewise." I squeeze his shoulder.

Our friendship has kept me grounded and able to play this charade. Kurt and I both wish our relatives' politics went further than lip service and a few sponsored bills. Our relatives "care"—but they also "care" about global warming, taxes, immigration, schools, health care, and myriad other causes. Kurt and I want to improve queer rights so badly that we're willing to play this dating game to have as much access and visibility as we can ... even though we're just buddies.

Buddies who have maybe blown each other a few times when fundraisers got interminable.

Still, I wonder what it would be like to have an actual partner at these things—one who cared about the issues as much as me, but also cared *about* me.

Ha. That'll never happen.

I take Kurt's hand and tug him into the party, where we're soon surrounded by women in high heels and salon-styled hair who want us to be their best friends who dispense fashion advice and opine on style. Kurt's better at it than I am, but I do all right. He flirts and laughs and hooks his chin over my shoulder, causing more than one person to go, "Aww, aren't they the cutest?" We see other activists like us, doing the circuit to help our respective causes.

Eventually we get pulled aside for a photographer to take our pictures for some PSA ad campaign.

Kurt and I are the poster boys who don't cause any trouble. We follow all the rules and are ever so grateful when legislation comes down—sponsored by our relatives. Legislation that generates more votes for them in the future.

This is how I spend my weekends. Taking pictures at political fundraisers because I support my family and fight for rights.

No matter what.

When I finally get home, it's late, and I'm bored. I search on my laptop for one of Julian Hill's live concerts and find a recent show. Now that I've felt his warm skin and seen his face in person, watching his performances is far more appealing than it was before I met him.

Jules cradles the microphone, closes his eyes, and sings. I unmute the video, and his strong, rough vocals blast through the speakers. He exudes a prowling confidence as he stalks about the stage. He's magnetic, a glorious rock star all the way.

I'm struck by how much emotion he pours into this song. The only phrase I can use is he's giving it his all—not a cliché; it feels like there'll be nothing left of him once he finishes—and he hits high notes and carries an impossible vibrato and okay, *damn*, the man can sing. It isn't just hype.

This is why he's on the cover of every tabloid: underneath the sexy man who I assume dates supermodels lies a base of astonishing talent.

I'm not usually interested in famous people. They photoshop their appeal, say controversial things to get attention, and boost their "talent" with digital modifications and makeup or plastic surgery.

Not this guy. None of the packaging matters when he sings live.

Well, the packaging is nice.

But with one song—one song that I truly listen to, rather than just humming along at the grocery store—I morph into a fan.

Jules Hill doesn't need Auto-Tune. He barely needs a band or a microphone. He could carry the show on his narrow hips.

He's a solid performer.

It's only when a YouTube ad cuts in that I realize I haven't blinked for a really long time.

When the concert resumes, I'm still mesmerized, and I watch him sing four more songs.

But then the show stops. "Hold it," Jules says into the microphone, holding up his hand. "Sorry, sorry," he says in his melodious accent. "We need to get some help here. Can we please allow security and medical staff through?" He's gesturing to someone in the crowd.

The camera shifts to focus on a commotion below him, someone being held up by her neighbor, head lolling to the side. Maybe she's passed out. Jules gets down and sits on the edge of the stage, his long legs dangling off the side, reaching for the girl as security personnel keep other people away. His voice becomes hushed and soothing. "Shh, darling, it'll be okay. We'll get you some help." Then he sets down the microphone and says something only she can hear.

The audience quiets, respectful, while a stretcher arrives. Jules watches to make sure the girl exits safely, then blows her a kiss and leads a round of applause. "Best wishes to you, love. Feel better." He climbs back on stage, dusts himself off, and looks out into the crowd. "Thank you, darlings, for your patience. We can't have any of you hurt. This is a safe place. Forgive me for stopping. We'll start the song over from the top, shall we?" He catches the drummer's gaze and nods, and they launch into the song again.

Wow. Who does that?

So many people don't care about anyone else or would think something like that wasn't their job. But apparently not him.

I'm impressed as I watch the rest of the concert. Then, because I can't help myself, I check out the comments section.

ERMIGAH I LURV HERM

Look at his rings! On all his fingers! Look at him, people!

Hill hair is goals.

When he did that thing where he stuck his hip out? Omg I died. Did anyone else die? Are we meeting in heaven now?

Did you hear him talk about his sex life in that interview? Or how he didn't? He didn't answer the question. That's because he's totally bi. I think that's so hot. I mean, he dates girls, but he has to like boys too, don't you think? Like this comment if you agree.

And *this* is why I've ignored Julian Hill for a decade. There isn't any room to like him, because so many people already do. Although, to be honest, I've probably ignored him more to tease Em than for any other reason. Now all those excuses fall apart.

Simply stated, his performance enthralls me.

Also, do those comments have a point about his sexuality? Is he really gay? Or pan?

Could he ever be interested in someone like, oh, me?

Wow. With him my thoughts really go on a speedy train to Not Gonna Happen. Which is somewhere between Get a Grip and Knock It Off.

When I go to bed, I drag my laptop with me and do a deeper search for Julian on YouTube.

Besides his songs, one of the first videos is "How Jules Hill Is Different from Every Other Celebrity."

I click, because I have to. I justify it as research. Maybe I could bill Lighthouse for this.

Yeah, no. This is just curiosity.

The video starts with a very famous celebrity, about Jules's level, getting water thrown at him on stage. The celebrity angrily clicks his mic into the stand, demands a towel, then screams, "That's it, assholes! Show's over," and stomps off.

The next clip shows Jules, midsong, being doused with water from someone's bottle. He throws his arms back, like some kind of Jesus figure. Even though it's live and recorded on someone's cell phone, he looks like he's in a spontaneous music video being drenched in the rain. He turned something annoying and intrusive into something sexual. Beautiful. Captivating.

Amazing.

The compilation video keeps going. Tons of clips of paparazzi trailing celebrities and provoking them to anger. Then a very wan Jules asking politely if they wouldn't mind please letting him enter his hotel because he was quite exhausted and needed to get some sleep, thank you.

A fan asking for a hug from one singer who just said, "No," and walked past. Jules getting asked for a hug and stopping, smiling, and giving the fan a hug. Then standing there hugging ten more fans and taking a selfie with every one, all with a huge grin on his face.

Jeez.

I sit back when the video stops. I'm aware that it picked the worst moments of those stars and compared them to Jules's best moments. No one can be on 24-7, and we all have bad days. But there seems to be something gentle that's essential to Jules's personality, a basic human decency and appreciation of where he came from and where he is now. He expresses it in every action, being gracious and friendly and fun.

No wonder he's so popular. No wonder the world is in love with him.

He's someone you're bound to fall in love with—if you believe in that sort of thing.

I'm not naive, though. I start searching for "Jules Hill mean." "Jules Hill fighting." "Jules Hill worst behavior."

The worst thing I find is him being followed by a pap. He doesn't engage, doesn't yell or make a rude gesture. The only words he says on the entire video are to point out a curb so the pap doesn't trip.

He can't be for real.

Still, having seen him sing, met him, and cyberstalked the skeletons in his closet to learn he apparently has none, I don't know what to think. I don't know what to make of these warm feelings.

He *is* for real.

I should stop my weird searching, because it feels invasive and creepy.

But it's irresistible. I do a risky search for "Jules Hill kissing" and find him jokingly kissing a late-night host and sweetly smooching fans on the cheek. No images of him kissing anyone on the beach. No making out in clubs. No tabloid photos of him caught with anyone.

Oh, there are stories about the people he's dated—basically a list of every single, young, famous female out there, from singer to actress to heiress—but who knows whether any of that is true, and none of them seem to last long.

Jules is an enigma.

Whatever his private life may be, it seems that it can't be found. So perhaps it's something he keeps very hidden.

Which only stokes the fascination.

Embarrassed and sick of myself, I turn to his official channel and start watching his music videos and live performances.

I see videos of him crooning. Rocking out. Being soulful, funky, pop-y. His voice can be husky and raw or sweet and falsetto. It can ring with sincerity and emotion. I stare and stare and become even more of a Jules Hill fan.

Emily's never going to let me live this down.

But despite his very real musical talent, it's the man himself I can't seem to ignore. The rough-voiced, sexy-as-fuck famous person.

Who's also my job assignment.

On Monday, after a run-in with Terrill where he demands to know whether Julian has made progress on the album, even though it's been only five days, I sit at my desk with my computer monitor glaring at me, daring me to send an email or do some actual billable work. Or make progress on the charity project the firm hired me to spearhead—monitoring the status of anti-LGBT+ legislation nationwide and developing plans to counter it.

Instead, I chew on my Bic Clic Stic—custom imprinted with the firm name—and panic.

Office noises lurk in the background: the soft bleeps of phones ringing, voices, clicks from computer mouses and keyboards.

All of it ordinary.

And yet I'm tasked with the extraordinary: "encouraging" megastar Julian Hill to create a new album by, like, last week. How short a leash should I keep him on? Is he doing well on his own?

How do I get him to go faster?

My stomach goes sour, like the coffee I drank was battery acid.

I'm a lawyer, not a lyricist. I'm not even a music critic. I don't write anything but legal contracts. A decade of piano lessons and a fondness for a wide variety of music won't help me here. Even if he sang me all his new songs, I wouldn't know if they were any good. Or, more important to my client, if they will sell.

His number burns in my phone contacts. Given my new respect ... oh, hell, *fascination*, being able to text him is a temptation. Emily wasn't wrong when she said millions of fans would envy me. But I'm not sure how to play this. I have access to him for a purpose, which puts me in a different position.

My gut—roiling as it is right now—tells me sending daily texts asking, "Are you done yet? ... How about now?" won't be effective. Judging by the way external pressure gets to Kurt in his creative field, I think it would make Jules go into a shell and never want to come out.

How do I do my job? How do I encourage him to get the work done and be accountable without feeling like he's being manipulated—or compromising his standards.

I start a text.

> **Sam**: I wanted to make sure you're doing okay with the album.

Um. Boring.

Why is this business of interacting with other human beings so hard?

Especially with a human being who is so … so … in demand and yet still so kind.

Without thinking about it further, I hit send. I don't know a better way to write it, and I feel a bit stiff, but I guess I'm the formal one. Kinda funny since he's the one from England, land of protocol.

I can see that he reads it immediately—*holy shit*—and that he's typing.

Holy shit, again. My heart thumps.

> **Jules**: Thanks for checking in, Sam
>
> **Jules**: All good

His soothing text does nothing to calm my heart rate, as much as I want to pretend it feels natural to chat with Jules Hill.

> **Sam**: I feel like my work and my gut feelings are in conflict. I'm supposed to be checking in on you moving the album along, but if I put pressure on you, that's just going to cause you undue stress. So, how do I support you but still keep us on track?

I hit send.

Is using the word "us" wrong? *Shit for the umpteenth time.* I mean *us* in the generic sense, like us, the music label and him. But it sounded like I want a relationship.

I cringe. I should not be allowed to text. I only err.

> **Jules**: Kind of you to ask
>
> **Jules**: Nothing yet, but I hope for a break thru soon
>
> **Sam**: Me, too. And not just because it's my job.
>
> **Jules**: If all of your texts are going to be as kind as this one, I think you're fine to just ask how it's going
>
> **Jules**: Or I can tell you
>
> **Jules**: Once I've got something new done
>
> **Sam**: Please do. I'd love to hear all about it. Actually, I think the creative process is magical. There's some alchemy going on that I don't fully understand.

Jules: <Smiley emoji> Then I'll let you in and see how the wizard works

Jules: Only I don't use a wand

Jules: Well, not that kind of wand

Jules: Shit, that was inappropriate. Sorry

Sam: Don't worry. And yes, I would love it if you showed me.

Sam: The songs, I mean.

Sam: OMG never mind.

Sam: I'm just worried about interrupting your process.

Jules: Relax, Sam. You're no interruption. I'm happy to have you along for the ride

I fixate on that word, "ride," remembering how he felt in my hand. And wondering if he felt anything, too.

Seven

Jules

THE OCEAN BREEZE TANGLES MY HAIR, AND THE SUN BEATS down on my bare shoulders as I pace on the uppermost balcony of my beach house. It's late in the afternoon on an utterly gorgeous day, but I can't take the time to enjoy it, because I need to get a song written. Or ten.

I stare out at the Pacific Ocean.

Okay, music. Come to daddy.

The music does not, in fact, come to daddy. Perhaps because it knows that's not my kink.

Slinging myself into a sleek patio chair, I pick up a pencil and doodle in a notebook.

What the hell am I going to do? It's been a long day of me plunking away on a piano and a guitar, with nothing to show for it.

I look up. No one's on the beach. Maybe a ramble would help. I'm not jailed here.

While I relinquished my anonymity the moment I became famous, a perk of making a lot of money is that I can buy privacy. This house is at the upper end of Malibu's twenty-something-mile coastline, and I bought the lots on either side. There's no one to the north for miles. The property is also away from the highway, so for the most part, I can avoid being bothered by the paparazzi. The security system and the guard at the gate help, too. By state law, anyone can walk on the beach, but since it's a bit of a hike to get to it without crossing private property, it's usually pretty quiet.

I race down three flights of stairs, grab a baseball cap and sunglasses, and exit to the beach below.

The sand's hot, so I go to where it's wet and let the fingers of the tide lap at my feet. A seagull caws overhead.

Could I write a song about the beach?

Ugh. Overdone.

I stare at the sea. *Okay, sea, deliver me a song.*

The sea does not, in fact, deliver me a song, so I keep walking.

In the past, songs have come to me as downloads from the universe, revving to be heard. Now I feel like a stalled engine. No flow. Nothing.

There has to be something to write about. I dig my toes into the sand.

Rock. Pebble. Sand. Seaweed. Bird. Bird shite. Ocean.

None of that feels like the emotion I need in a song. Maybe I just need to keep walking. Maybe something will come to me.

Please, something. Come to me.

My mobile chimes in my pocket. I glance at it. It's Colin.

I glance up at the sky. *Not quite what I was asking for.*

However, latching on to any available distraction is the part of the creative process known as procrastination. I'm familiar with it, since I've been in it for several years. I answer my phone.

"Colin," I say. "Hello."

"Jules." I hear him clear his throat. "Um, hey. How are you?"

He's stalling. That's never a good sign. "Just fine."

"Good, good." A pause. "And record sales?"

"They're fine, too."

"Excellent."

The line is silent. I sit down on my bum in the sand next to a bulbous strand of green seaweed, all of me focused on him. "Can I help you with something?" Being the protective older brother is an ingrained habit.

He sighs. "Natalie's thrown me out."

Things seem to always be tough for Colin. I rub my hand down my face. "I'm sorry to hear that."

"And I don't have a place to stay."

I pinch the bridge of my nose and close my eyes.

What I want to say is, *You're an adult, and that's not my problem.* Or *Haven't I bailed you out of enough situations?*

"What are your plans?" I ask.

"I was kind of hoping I could come and stay with you. If you don't mind," he stammers.

I'd never turn him away. Not with our upbringing. Nor the guilt I feel about where each of us is today. "I don't mind."

"Really?"

"Yes." I want to tell him that I like my privacy and to get a hotel, but given the size of my house, I don't want to be a bellend.

"Okay, I'll see you soon. I'm almost done packing."

I shove my phone in my pocket and stare out at the never-ending ocean, still unsatisfied and now slightly peeved. Standing, I pick up a pebble and throw it as far as I can.

The conversation didn't give me anything except a distraction from my songwriting process. Whatever that is. It's like that joke about the Holy Roman Empire: not holy, Roman, or an empire. My songwriting process has no songs, no writing, and no process.

I keep walking up the beach.

Sand. More sand. If I write about rough sand, though, I risk sounding like *Star Wars: Episode II*. Better not go so literal.

Not like I'm writing anything right now, anyway.

Mary had a little lamb.

Once upon a midnight dreary.

There once was a man from Nantucket.

I sigh. When I was with my old band, we collaborated on our songs, messing around in the studio for weeks on end until we came up with lyrics and music we all liked. Now I'm on my own—my current band members are great musicians, but they're not songwriters—and I'm not really in touch with the other Paradise boys.

I dial my best friend, James Winterthorn. He's known me since before everything and now lives in California, too, although he's up the coast a bit.

"Mate," I say, "what do you know about writing songs?"

"Not a thing."

"Hmm." I scratch the back of my neck. "You're no help."

"What's going on?"

I sigh and stare at the water. "I'm a bloke on the beach being forced to write."

"Sounds like a rough life."

I deserve that remark. "Sod off. Wanker."

He chuckles. "You could start there."

"With a wank?"

He sputters. "No! Well, I dunno, maybe that would be a good idea. But I meant, start with complaining about being forced to write."

I tilt my head and think about it. "That sounds annoying."

"So don't whinge on about it. Just say what it feels like. That you're more than a tool to make other people money. That you wish they'd treat you like an individual and not a commodity." I can hear his shrug over the phone. "It'd be a 'fuck you' to the label."

My head starts nodding before my voice can catch up. "You're brilliant."

"I know."

"I have a thought. Oh my god," I say in a rush. "Sorry, James. I want to capture this idea before it evaporates."

"Fine," he says. "I understand. Anything else I can help you with?"

"Not now," I say. "I think you've given me something. I'll call you later, okay?"

"Glad to be of service."

We hang up, and I begin pacing and talking into the recorder, lyrics and ideas about selling myself to the machine that just wants to monetize me. I don't know how long I'm out on the beach. By the time I head back to my house, I have the outline of something that might work.

I linger outside, thinking of Sam and his backbone and kindness.

Then I reread his texts, starting with the first from the other day.

> **Sam**: I received your text, Julian.

Five words. So amusing.

I think I have a crush.

And a silk cloth that I somehow ended up with after our meeting. Part of me wants to make up an excuse to contact him, but I want to be able to go to him with progress on the album.

That gives me another song idea. One about being scared to contact someone I like because I don't have anything to say. When I've captured the concept, I key in the gate code and go back inside, grateful for Sam's assistance as well as James's.

Two begun. I grab a bottle of water and go into the studio. Then I sit down and hit record, trying to round out what I've thought of on the walk. After years of no progress and so much heartache, I'm writing songs, finally.

I remain in there for hours, absorbed in the work, developing music. It's not until after midnight that I realize I'm still in nothing but my shorts and haven't eaten anything in a long time.

And all the while, I'm thinking of Sam Stone. Before I can stop myself, I text him.

> **Jules**: I'm actually making progress on the album
>
> **Jules**: I don't wanna jinx it, but I wrote two songs today
>
> **Jules**: Couldn't wait to tell you
>
> **Jules**: Sorry you're probably asleep
>
> **Sam**: No, I'm up.
>
> **Sam**: That's wonderful! I'm so glad. But it's late. You should probably take a break, shouldn't you?
>
> **Jules**: I do need a break
>
> **Jules**: My eyes are as dry as sandpaper from staring at the sheet I'm scribbling on and the laptop and the keyboard. My fingers are needing a break from the guitar, too.

What I really want is to ask if whatever I'm feeling about him is as one-sided as my logical mind tells me it must be.

Does he feel it, too? Or am I making something out of nothing?

>**Sam**: You need to take care of yourself. While there's a deadline, yes, you can't hurt yourself over it, either.

His concern makes me melt. People like Loren watch out for me, but in general, no one is watching to make sure I don't sabotage myself.

>**Sam**: I shouldn't say this, but deadlines are artificial.
>
>**Sam**: I mean, I bet you could sweet-talk your way into an extension if you had a significant portion of the work done.
>
>**Jules**: That means I have to get a significant portion of the work done
>
>**Jules**: And also you have more faith in my ability to, as you say, sweet-talk
>
>**Sam**: I am fairly certain you could sweet-talk anyone. Even me.

That makes me grin at my phone. Oh, Sam. What I want to sweet-talk you into, you have no idea.

>**Sam**: All I'm saying is, you need self-care to create. Get some rest. Make sure to eat. Don't get dehydrated.
>
>**Sam**: Sorry, I sound like your mom.

That brings a lump to my throat. He doesn't know what happened to my mum.

>**Sam**: Forgive me for overstepping.
>
>**Jules**: I like it when you overstep

I don't want to be a pest. But ... after all, I have an article of clothing that belongs to him. I'm sure returning it is the polite thing to do.

Eight

Sam

At my desk, I reread my text conversation with Julian from last night. Does he like me? I thought he was being a little flirty in his texts, but maybe I'm reading something into it. Was I being too forward when I said he could sweet-talk me into anything?

My office phone buzzes from reception. "You have a visitor," Bruce says.

"I don't have any appointments today."

He pauses. "He says he doesn't have an appointment, but he wanted to give you something."

"Who is it?"

"Julian Hill."

My heart starts beating erratically. Really? He came to see me? "Okay. I'll be right there," I choke out.

Trying to act nonchalant, I take a deep breath and stroll out to the reception area.

I wish I could think of something to call him other than "rock god," but that's what he is. He's leaning against the wall, brown hair artfully tousled. He wears dark gray jeans so tight I can see his kneecaps, a dusty rose dress shirt—five buttons undone, displaying dark tan skin and those tattoos—and a black velvet blazer. His shoes are shiny black Chelsea boots that have little flowers embroidered on the ankles.

Fuck. Me. He's *glorious*.

When he sees me, he gets this sweet, delighted look on his face before he schools it quickly.

But that look makes my week.

I'm aware that we have an audience, although Bruce is the utmost in discretion. But even he can't pretend he's not interested in Julian. A clerk walks by and does a double take, then scurries away.

"Hey," I say, walking forward and shaking Julian's hand. I stutter out a laugh. "Managed to do that without tripping this time."

"Well done, mate." His expression turns sheepish. "Sorry to drop by, but I was in the neighborhood and wanted to return something to you." He fishes in his pocket and pulls out my striped pocket square.

"Oh, you can keep it," I say.

He smiles, then leans forward and whispers in my ear, delicious scent and sweet breath tickling my skin. "Maybe I wanted an excuse to see you again."

Gooseflesh erupts all over my body at the idea that he was thinking of me. I turn to Bruce. "Is a conference room available for us to use for a few minutes?"

Bruce keys his computer and shakes his head slowly. "Sorry, no. A big mediation's using them all."

"That's okay," I decide. "I can just take you to my office." I turn to Jules. "If you want to come, that is."

"Absolutely. Lead the way."

Conscious that *Julian Hill* is following me down the hall in this office environment where he's so out of place, I pass by gray cubicles and attorney offices until we get to mine. It's a junior office, but nice enough.

Jules lingers at the door, taking in the one file that's out on my desk. He grins. "You're a tidy sort, eh?"

"Being neat soothes me," I say. "I can't function when things aren't tidy."

"Makes sense." He looks at the diplomas on the wall and, beside them, the abstract painting of two men embracing. "That's beautiful."

"Thanks. My friend Kurt painted it." Then I remember my manners. "Want to sit?" I gesture to the client chairs.

"Sure."

"You can close the door behind you, if you want privacy."

He nods and does so. Now I'm well aware that I'm once again in a room with this man for whom I have an overwhelming attraction.

Only this time we're alone.

Making a quick decision, I take the chair next to him instead of sitting behind my desk. His eyes widen, and I say, "This is a chat, right? We don't need to be so formal."

"Right. Thanks."

Sitting this close was a tactical error, though, because our knees practically touch and it feels so, so intimate. I have to say something before things get awkward. "How's the writing going?"

"I've finally got a few songs—"

There's a knock on the door, and it flies open before I can respond. Terrill stands there, ready to say something. But then he sees Jules and stops short.

"Can I help you?" I ask. "We're discussing the Lighthouse Records matter."

"Uh, right. Yes. Fine. When you're done, come see me."

I'm 99 percent sure he simply didn't like my door being closed. He's made it pretty clear he disagrees with my pro bono projects, and because my desk isn't piled high the way his is, he thinks I don't take my job seriously enough.

If only he knew how much I stress about it all.

Still, I'm pleased that he caught me working ... if "working" is the right term for talking with Jules. It hardly feels like it, since he's so yummy. Billable. But yummy.

Terrill does an about-face and closes the door behind him. Jules looks at me with amusement. "What would happen if you were doing something compromising?"

My eyes bug out. "I'm never doing something compromising, so that's not a relevant question."

"I don't know," he says slowly. "I think there might be some fire underneath that bow tie."

"Perhaps." I grin. "You really can keep the pocket square." Then I start stammering because I remember that he has the clothing budget of a large corporation. "Not that you need it. It's hardly your style. And besides, I'm sure you can get whatever clothes you want."

He shrugs. "True, although I don't want to take anything that doesn't belong to me. It's a talisman, though."

"It is?"

"After meeting you, I started writing songs." He looks me right in the eyes, and I can't look away. "The album's got a good start. Because of you."

"Then you definitely should keep it."

A moment passes where neither of us says anything, but it's not uncomfortable.

"Two songs down, then?" I finally ask.

"Going on more."

"I'd like to hear them sometime. It seems like the music is flowing."

Julian smiles. "Music is my favorite thing in the universe, and when it's just me and the guitar, it's the easiest, too. But when we start talking about money and sales and merch and all that, I go cross-eyed. I have to put all that out of my head and just focus on the songs." He chuckles. "Seeing you, funnily enough, doesn't remind me of sales and contracts. It reminds me of music and things I actually like doing."

Somehow, I hear that as meaning I'm something Jules wants to do, and I like that idea so much I can feel my ears go red. I cough, trying to get my brain back into reality mode. "Uh, I'm glad to hear that." Tilting my head to the side, I reach out and touch his hand. His skin is warm and soft, and he doesn't draw back, which makes me think my guesses about his sexuality are on point. "That things are going well, I mean. But if you'd like some help with this album, I imagine Lighthouse would be willing to provide someone for you to work with. Like, a collaborator?"

"I know the label has resources, and there are so many songwriters just waiting for a chance. But I want to be able to do this on my own. If I'm going to sing the songs, I want them to be ones I wrote."

"That makes perfect sense."

"Thanks." His dark eyes catch mine. "You're easy to talk to." He stands. "I'm sure you need to get back to work. I'll leave you to it."

"I'll walk you down," I say. "I was going to get some lunch in the basement."

He stands and follows me back out to the elevators.

Nine

Jules

I walk with Sam to the lifts. When one opens, we get in it by ourselves. I glance around. "It's like a padded cell."

Sam shoves his hands in his pockets. "I'm sorry. They're doing construction. I think they line the elevators so they don't get damaged when they move supplies and equipment."

"I see." I eye it warily. The entire space is covered, except for the area with the buttons. "The one I came up in was normal. This one feels like someone's great-aunt decorated. She got into quilting and didn't stop."

He chuckles. "The one across the way's all done in crochet and doilies, you know. And there's one with sequins. You must have missed it on the way up."

I laugh despite myself.

The doors to the lift close, and he presses the button for the lobby. It starts to descend rapidly, triggering that dipping feeling in my stomach. I reach for something to hold and grip a bar under the padding.

We judder to a sudden stop and both throw our hands out to stabilize ourselves. The doors don't open.

"Um," he says, glancing around. "This is weird. I wonder if they're doing maintenance."

"Fuck," I say, not able to come up with a different word. My heart is racing. I'm not fond of lifts to begin with, but having one stop like this is hellacious. I'm starting to sweat.

I've been in lifts around the world, from the fanciest high-rise hotels to places with questionable construction and electricity. I was trapped once before, and it took six hours to get me freed. Flashbacks of the darkness and the terror I felt are sweeping over me in waves.

Sam hasn't noticed my distress yet, still glancing around the metal box as if it will give away its secrets. "Do you think they stopped it because of the construction?" he asks. "I bet that's it. It will restart in a moment. Do you want me to call?"

I can't answer.

He pats his pocket and pulls out his mobile. His words feel muffled, but I make them out. "Bruce. It's Sam. We're in the elevator, the one on the northeast corner, with the construction padding. And it's not moving. Could you please call building management and find out what's going on? Thanks."

I'm not sure what the person says in response. Everything feels gray and dim.

"Are you okay?" he asks. He pauses, and I'm so out of it I can't look at his face. But I can hear the change in his voice. "You're not okay, are you?"

"Not really."

My legs feel weak, and I'm aware enough to be pissed off that this is happening but not aware enough to control what I'm doing.

A warm hand is firm on my shoulder, and I lean into it, pressing my cheek to his skin. Everything is spinning, but Sam feels reassuring and solid.

Something's buzzing, and I'm not sure if it's the lift or if it's just inside my mind.

The air thickens, and I feel a wave of nausea.

"It's going to be all right," he murmurs.

I open my mouth to say something, but nothing comes out. My throat is dry, and I try swallowing.

"I'll talk you through this. Come sit down."

Those hands grip my biceps and pull me to the ground. I'm dizzy and unsteady.

"I never," I croak. "I never—"

"I'm here, Jules. I'll help you." In a moment, the wall is supporting my back and my arse plops onto the floor, my knees drawn up to my chin. Sam slides down next to me, a lean line of warmth. He throws an arm around my shoulders, and I can feel the soft scrape of wool—his suit jacket—against my neck. "This okay?"

I nod, not able to do much more. Not sure how he knows I need the grounding. Not wanting to move. Having him right here feels better than just about anything.

His phone vibrates, and he shifts so he can answer it, removing his arm from my back. "Hello?"

I can hear the person on the other side telling him that they know we're in here and are working on the lift and will get us out as soon as they can. He hangs up.

Then he grabs my hand, and it feels as natural as could be. His voice is soothing, and it breaks through the fog of my fears.

"I'm sure we'll start up again in a moment," Sam says. "We'll be fine. We just need to keep it together until they get things sorted out."

"Your voice," I whisper. "Please. Keep talking."

"I will. Um. So … it can't—won't—last long. This has happened before to people in this building, and they get out. Maybe an hour or two."

I inhale sharply.

"I'm sorry," he whispers. "Do you want me to call anyone for you?"

I shake my head. "No. I don't want this to become an international incident."

"I don't think there's anything else we can do right now except keep calm. Here. Let's both get more comfortable." Sam eyes me, likely noticing that my unbuttoned shirt and blazer don't restrict me the way his clothes constrict him.

He slides off his jacket, tugs at his bow tie and pulls it off, then undoes the top button of his shirt. He sets the bow tie down on his knee, and I finger it.

"Take it," he says. "It's okay." I feel the navy blue silk between my fingers. Between his calming voice and sitting down, I start to breathe. "Stay with me. Just take one breath after another."

The lights flicker. And then they go off, and we're alone in the dark.

"Seriously?" Sam asks, a frustrated bite in his tone. "*Seriously?*"

But for some reason, being in the dark makes me forget that I'm trapped in a metal box—well, not *forget*, exactly, but it doesn't constantly remind me, either. I lean against him, inhaling his scent, and it's the sexiest thing I've ever smelled.

That scent grounds me even more. It's not overwhelming at all. Unless your nose is right near his skin, you'd never notice it.

And no, it's not ironic that I care what his aftershave is, when so many people ask about mine.

"Do you wear Tom Ford?" I ask.

"What?" I hear a smile in the way he says it.

"Is that Oud Wood?"

"Yeah." Sam's voice sounds scratchy. "How did you know?"

"It's my favorite. I don't wear it because I'm, uh, sponsored by a different brand. But I love it."

"Oh." He hesitates. "Thanks."

We sit for a moment, and I can feel my heart rate slow down. I take a few deeper breaths, and something inside me loosens.

"Want me to turn on my phone for a light?" He shifts against me. I like his solid presence next to me. I play with his tie some more, the soft silk comforting, like a childhood blanket.

"Actually, being in the dark is easier. Then I can pretend …" I trail off, not wanting to focus on the fact that we're still in a tiny metal container dangling however many floors off the ground. "Just, can we keep it this way?"

"Sure, Jules." And the way he says my name makes me want to weep. So does the fact that he reaches out, fumbles around, and grabs my hand again. "This okay?"

"Yes. Please don't let go. Sorry."

"Don't apologize. Hold my hand as long as you like." He hesitates. "Or until the cameras show up. I don't want Jules Hill to be caught holding some guy's hand. They'd probably think I'm with you." I can feel heat radiate from him. "Sorry, that was the wrong thing to say."

I take a deep breath. "It's true. And funny." Then, because I can't help myself, I ask, "Are you … do you hold guys' hands often?"

"Yeah." Again, there's a smile in his tone. "I'm gay."

"Oh."

My mind is calm enough to be thankful he's not asking me the same question. Because right now—while trusting this almost-stranger in the dark—I might answer him.

We sit quietly until Sam asks, "How come you're not afraid to be mobbed by fans, but a largish box with four walls scares you?"

"Dunno. It's not like fears are rational. Maybe I don't trust machinery. Though it's not lifts themselves. I use them all the time. It's being stuck in one." I exhale. "Your voice helps."

"Okay, then. I want you to listen and focus on relaxing your body. Can you do that?"

"Yeah," I rasp.

Sam starts chattering about how he's an only child and his family is in politics and what his favorite foods are and what he likes to watch on television. I can tell he's just saying anything he can to keep talking, and I appreciate it more than he knows.

"… and I spend my evenings doing yoga."

This makes me snort. "You do?"

"I do."

We sit in silence for a moment, but it's more companionable. I'm not as panicked. And I admit another fear.

"Lately—for the last two years, actually—nothing I've written has felt right. It's felt … banal. Nothing that I would consider good enough to put out for the public. I'm not a perfectionist, but nothing I've created has had the emotional impact I want. Not until you inspired me."

He pauses, then in this sincere voice says, "You'll get it done." As if it's as simple as that.

And maybe it is.

"Thanks."

After some time, another buzzing noise sounds, and the lights go back on. We both go to stand up at the same time and bump into each other.

"Sorry," I mutter.

He reaches over and squeezes my hand again. "Don't worry about it."

The lift lurches down, and I barely keep from wrapping myself around him like a vine on a tree. I manage to limit it to clutching his hand and leaning my face against his shoulder.

Chuckling, he holds my hand tight as I bury my nose in his neck. "Hey. It's fine. It will—"

The car jostles to a stop. When the doors open, we quickly separate and discover we're on the fourth floor, where we're greeted by a gentleman in a hard hat wearing a tool belt.

"Sorry about that," he says. "You can get to the parking garage from this level if you go over the bridge, and those elevators are running."

"Thanks," Sam tells him before turning to me. "I'll walk you out that way and then use the stairs to the basement."

I nod. I'd been expecting to have to deal with paparazzi, but the tech's the only person around. I pull out my phone and text my driver, who meets me where we exit.

Sam walks me to the idling car. He slips his hands into his pockets, his jacket folded over one forearm, and studies my face. "Are you going to be okay?"

"I'm fine." I smile. "Thanks for your help today."

"You're welcome." He reaches out a hand, and I shake it.

I like the way his hand feels in mine.

I stare into his gorgeous eyes, full of sincerity and kindness, and realize how lucky I was that he was in the lift with me today. Of all the people on the planet, I was trapped with the one who treated me the exact way I needed to be treated.

He fidgets under my gaze. "Well, I guess this is it."

I nod. "Thanks again for keeping me from losing it."

"I'm happy to have helped."

I get in the car. As it pulls away, I can see him, even though he can't see me with the tinted windows.

At home, I go to change my clothes and realize I still have his bow tie in my pocket. I'm starting to build a collection of his accessories.

Like a creeper, I sniff it, and I'm flooded with memories. But not of the panic I felt; of calmness.

Taking it with me, I sit outside by the pool with an old acoustic guitar. I start picking out a tune, just messing around, wishing I could have Sam Stone in my life for more than business.

Ten

Jules

A FEW DAYS LATER, I'M ON THE PHONE WITH JAMES AGAIN.

"How is it going with your brother?" he asks.

"He's barely emerged from his room. I don't know what to do except make sure he's got a roof over his head and food in his belly."

"He's always been like that, though. Even I know that."

"I just wish he would be more open to talking out whatever's bothering him. When we were growing up, it was just me and him against the world."

No one but us knows our entire history. Not even Loren. And I'm going to keep it that way. Sometimes, though, I think if only Miss Poole from that horrid place in London could see us now.

Three-story beach house in Malibu, with the most upscale furnishings imaginable. Eight cars in the garage. And this is just one of my houses around the world.

James knows the most, given how long I've known him, which is why I trust him. With anyone else, it's hard to know who likes me for me, and who's looking for a free party or to get famous by proximity.

"You're eons away from the care homes."

"All because I got lucky on a talent show … and he didn't."

"I'd hardly call it luck."

"It was. But I can't rely on luck to write this next album. I just have to lock myself in the studio."

"So you're calling me to waste time?"

I laugh. "I don't call conversations with my best friend a waste of time."

"They are when you have a deadline. Go on. Write."

We hang up, and I do.

After I finish another song, I emerge for a lunch break and find Colin in the kitchen, eating a sandwich and playing on his phone.

We nod at each other. He hasn't volunteered anything about his wife, and I haven't wanted to pry. I also haven't asked him how long he's staying.

"Are you doing okay, Colin?"

"Fine," he grunts.

"Anything I can help you with?"

"No."

I take a deep breath. "Okay, well. Let me know if there's something I can do."

After I gulp down a glass of water and heat up a meal in the microwave, I go back into the studio and lose myself in the work.

At the end of the day, I text my new favorite person.

> **Jules**: I'm super happy
>
> **Jules**: I sketched out a few more songs
>
> **Jules**: You helped

My phone pings in response.

> **Sam**: How did I do that? I mean, I'm glad if I did, of course.

I grin, and my heartbeat goes all wonky. Even without seeing the contact name, I would've known by the full sentences and punctuation that it's from Sam. My hands fly over the phone.

> **Jules**: I got inspired by you again

Specifically, by that accidental hand job. Not that I'll tell anyone that's what the song is really about.

And the other one about quiet and darkness, then suddenly motion and movement, accompanied by a tidy man in a bow tie.

Jules: A few more songs and I'll go to the studio with the band

The little three dots keep showing, and I leave the studio, head up the stairs, and end up in my room, where I see the bow tie on my bedside table—this emblem of the man I have a schoolboy crush on. I flop on my bed.

A text comes through.

Sam: I'm glad you're making progress.

Jules: It's going so great

Jules: Want to come over after I get a few more songs done? In maybe two weeks?

Jules: You can check up on me and I can feed you dinner

Then I pause. What if the way Sam is with me is just an act? He seems adorable, but in reality he's a prickly and sadistic sociopath?

Yeah, Jules. That seems likely.

What *is* likely is that in the real world, this charming man would never be arsed with the hassles of being with me. And me pursuing something with him is going to be painful.

Still, though. I can't give him up. I *absolutely* want to spend more time with Sam.

The pause before he answers kills me, because those three dots appear and then disappear. And then appear again. Finally, when my stomach is in knots and I'm wondering if I should text back and say I was only joking, I get:

Sam: Okay.

I laugh out loud. Really, Sam? Was that so hard?

Speaking of hard.

How many times since we met have I stroked off to memories of his tight arse and strong jawbone? His kissable lips.

Sam Stone has the softest-looking skin I've ever seen, and I want to lick him. That's bad, right? I'm probably not supposed to lick my lawyer.

Well, he's not *my* lawyer.

Then again, I *am* a rock star. It gives me some degree of license to do whatever the fuck I want.

What I want is him. Since our first interaction in that Century City conference room, the hour or so I've spent with Sam has given me more song material than I've had in months. And it's more than creative inspiration.

I just want more of him. I can't get him out of my brain.

> **Jules**: When I get more done, I'll text you dates that work. Okay?
>
> **Sam**: That sounds great.

My mind starts wandering to the kind of menu I'd serve him. Maybe ordering from a local restaurant instead of having my personal chef make something. I don't know. I just want Sam to like it.

I feel like I'm planning a date—only the date is at my house with a dapper lawyer who's supposed to be making me do my work.

Sounds normal.

Eleven

Sam

IT'S BECOMING ROUTINE FOR ME TO GET REGULAR TEXTS FROM Julian, and I like it a lot. Like the ones from last night:

Jules: I'm taking a break for the night, but songwriting is going well

Sam: Excellent! I love hearing that. What are you going to do for a break? Go to the gym? Get a massage?

Jules: Probably stay in my bedroom in my underwear while eating crisps and going down a YouTube rabbit hole of some topic I didn't know I was interested in

Jules: After I exhaust the TikTok offerings

Sam: <Laughing face emoji> At least you're honest.

Jules: Don't tell me you've never fallen in there only to emerge an hour later not sure why you're watching a group of children playing Ozzy Osbourne on percussion

Sam: I LOVE that video. It's one of my comfort videos.

Jules: Me too, actually

Jules: What else is a comfort video

Sam: The trailer for season three of Skam. The original Norwegian television show, not the remakes.

Jules: Hold, please

Jules: Holy shit. That's the most incredible thing I've ever seen

Sam: I know, right? If the day is rough, it never ceases to cheer me up.

His reaction to a bunch of guys in a locker room having a water fight in their underwear makes me pretty sure I understand his sexuality. We chat a while longer, trading our favorite links that have nothing to do with my work or his. And for the next couple of days, whenever I'm particularly irritated with Terrill's nonsense, I find myself pulling out my phone and scrolling back through a conversation with one of the world's most recognizable celebrities. A conversation that never fails to make me smile.

Which is all quite difficult to translate into a progress report for my client.

It's the weekend, so I'm in a penguin suit, as required, for a family function. The Loughty Chandler Hotel is spectacular, all Belle Epoque grandeur. A landmark that's hosted royal weddings and heads of state.

It's huge, but private and discreet. The perfect place to host a fundraiser.

We're in a chandelier-festooned ballroom, and servers circulate with trays of appetizers. I recognize two actors, a well-known director, a supermodel, and a bunch of political types.

I just showed up as directed. I didn't even bother asking what the event was for, specifically.

I arrived a bit later than I usually do to these things. The room is buzzing with excitement. Maybe Pop-Pop is going to announce new legislation or something. At any rate, I'm here.

My grandfather stands in the middle of the room, wearing a sharp suit and flashing his signature grin. He holds up his hands, and everyone quiets down, hanging on his every word.

I wonder what Julian is doing right now. If he's writing another song.

What would happen if he came with me to one of these things? No one would pay attention to my grandfather, that's for sure.

"Friends, welcome," Pop-Pop says. "I'm pleased to make an announcement I'm sure you've all been waiting for."

I haven't been waiting for any damned announcement.

The jostling media horde, however, apparently was, judging by their cameras, microphones, and handheld recording devices.

"I'm pleased to let you all know that I've thrown my hat in the ring to be California's next governor. And Melissa Delmont is running for lieutenant governor—I hope we'll have the opportunity to work together to lead this great state."

Kurt's mom.

Save me Cardi B.

I'd heard talk about this possibility at family dinners for years and years, but I didn't know it was going to be this election cycle. I plaster on a smile, knowing there are cameras everywhere.

Good thing I like my "boyfriend." Because it looks like we are going to be spending a lot of time with each other.

I eye Kurt across the room, and he comes over and squeezes my hand. "Did you know?"

I shake my head. "Did you?"

He wraps an arm around my waist and holds me close, whispering in my ear as if he's nibbling on it. "Only this morning. I can't believe they've been working on this forever and didn't tell us. Governor is a huge difference from legislator."

"You ready?"

"No. But at least I have a friend."

I smile and kiss his cheek. A camera clicks near us. "Right."

But I can't help thinking how my life is going to change during the race … and beyond, if Pop-Pop wins. California's economy is massive—I think it's between India's and Germany's, if it were separate from the US—and the decisions the governor makes often resonate far beyond the state's borders. There's no doubt I'm going to be having my picture taken a lot more. And have even less time to myself.

"How come I haven't seen you as much lately? I had to do one of these without you," Kurt asks.

Shrugging, I grin, thinking of Jules. "You know how my work gets. And have you been following the restroom legislation that's being proposed in …" I natter on about my real passion and hold Kurt's hand as the reporters turn to us asking for a statement. We smile and offer our support for the candidates.

This must be a small fraction of what Julian Hill deals with on a daily basis.

I can't imagine what it's like to be him.

Twelve

Jules

My eyes sting with the aftereffects of camera flashes, amoeba-like bursts keeping me from seeing the luxe hallway clearly. But my band steers me in the right direction, and together, we navigate to the correct part of the Loughty Chandler Hotel.

I'm not really into making appearances for appearance's sake, but I make an exception every year for this event, given that I'm a sponsor.

"I love this hotel," Lizzie breathes, her hand in Janice's. They're my backup singers. The other members of my band are here, too. Stu and Mitch grin at me as Stu takes off his sunglasses. We're all decked out for the occasion. I'm in a tuxedo, only I'm wearing a black shirt instead of white, and I've got on piles of white pearls, because I like a bit of androgyny. Even Loren's dressed up in a shiny black jacket and black tuxedo pants.

I look around. I've been to this sumptuous old heap before, but it still impresses, the intricate light fixtures and velvet curtains palatial. It could be boudoir-ish, but it isn't. It's just … distinguished.

We're shepherded into a ballroom with dozens of tables, all decorated as for a fancy wedding, and find our way to the table in front. "You'd think that they'd let me choose a seat," I whisper to Loren. "I'd prefer to be out of the spotlight at this."

"There's enough star power here to light up Manhattan. You're diluted."

I look around, spotting a few A-list actors, Grammy winners, and politicians. "Perhaps." I grin. "Then maybe I don't have to stay for the whole thing."

"You never have to stay for the whole thing. But," their eyes are sincere, "I appreciate you coming."

This charity is Loren's special baby, an organization for homeless LGBTQ+ youth. Loren was helped by a similar one when they told their parents they were enby and it didn't go well. Once I learned the story, I made sure to donate generously. Especially since I met so many kids like Loren when I was young and rootless.

That said, I'm really not one for schmooze fests. I get enough of those at backstage meet and greets.

"Always happy to help," I say, hooking a glass of champagne from a passing waiter who does a double take when he sees me. I grin at him.

Loren shrugs. "After dinner, there's a band. Stay for a while, then leave."

"Deal."

I leave Loren and say hi to a few people I know, both in the music industry and filmmaking, and make sure to thank the organizers. After an hour, it's time to sit down for dinner and the charity auction. Frankly, I'd rather have a burger than the nouvelle cuisine they're serving, which is about six bites of foam.

A couple of tiny courses in, I need a break and escape down the hall.

When I emerge from the loo, I bump into my new favorite person looking suave in a tuxedo. I grab his arm to steady myself, and he blinks at me, startled, before a smile spreads across his face.

"Sam! What a pleasant surprise. I didn't think I'd see you until our dinner!"

He tilts his head to the side. "What are you … Why are you here?"

"Attending a charity fundraiser. You?"

"My grandfather has an event." His cheeks pink, and I want to pull him close and give him a hug. There's something about Sam that draws me to him. Makes me want to shelter him from everything—even though I know he doesn't need help, since he's, you know, a competent lawyer.

But maybe lawyers need support, too.

"What room are you in?" I ask, wanting to keep talking with him.

"Over there." He points. "Where is yours?"

Now it's my turn to point.

"Cool."

A group of people walk by who I know vaguely, and one of them taps my shoulder. "Hey," I say, smiling, but I really want to talk to Sam, not be dragged into other conversations. I lean in and get a whiff of his aftershave. "Want to go for a walk?"

Sam looks worried. "I'm supposed to be, you know, seen."

His eyes shift to where his grandfather is framed by the open doors to a ballroom, and I get the picture.

"Do you ever feel that he's, well, kind of using you? I mean," I add hastily, "I shouldn't assume. Maybe you love these events."

He presses his lips together. "That's complicated. It can get old. But it's my duty."

"To your family?"

Sam's shoulders hike up. "Not only to my family, although if you ask me in public, that's what I'll say. But to the queer community."

"What do you mean?"

"As a gay man in the US—and one from such a prominent family—I have an obligation to be visible. To help others feel confident enough to be their true selves. To fight against injustice wherever I can. To be a positive role model."

"No, you don't."

He gives me a look. "Of course I do. It's like voting. People have died to have the right to vote. And still, so many Americans don't bother. Standing up for LGBT rights is the same. My life is easy because of other people's struggle and sacrifice. I owe it to them to continue their work."

I draw in a breath. "Wowzers trousers. There's a lot to unpack there." Rubbing my jaw, I say, "Walk with me. We can come right back, but you're entitled to a reprieve, at least."

Sam relents. "For a few minutes. Just let me text and say where I'm going." He pulls out his phone, types for a moment, and then returns it to his pocket.

Down the sumptuous corridor, large double doors lead out to the warm evening. The hotel has expansive private gardens with teak benches. Outside, we start walking in the moonlit night. No one's around. Music floats out from a band in one of the ballrooms.

"I get what you're saying," I say, a small jolt of nervous energy running through my body with how I'm going to phrase this. But I trust Sam. "I mean, yes, lots of people all over the world still don't have the same rights you and I have. But I'm not going to adopt some guilt for being born in the right country or being alive now instead of a generation ago—or simply for being me. I can't help those things, and I don't have to prove a damned thing to anyone."

Sam stares at me. "I *always* have to prove myself."

"Haven't you already done that? You went to law school and are a licensed attorney."

He shrugs. "That means I worked hard in school. Big deal. I'm an adult now and need to pull my weight."

"Well, okay," I say slowly. "But you don't have to live your life for others. You can do things *you're* passionate about."

"I'm passionate about gay rights. I have to speak up, and being visible as part of my family helps what I do carry more weight. Since I'm not famous in my own right, I have to accept certain limitations in exchange for that extra visibility. Unlike someone I know ..."

"Ouch. I'm restricted in the way I act as well."

"True. But you can get away with more than the average person."

"Get away with?" I smirk. "What exactly do you think I'm getting away with? Aside from the record contract ... which I'm not shirking, by the way."

"I assume you have wild parties and ... things."

"What, like orgies? I can assure you I don't. I'm actually quite boring."

Sam puts a hand on his hip. "Now *that* I don't believe in the slightest."

"Mostly, yeah." I lean into him, my voice quiet. "If you must know, there was a phase when I had a lot of escapades that involved non-disclosure agreements. Or, well, professionals."

An eyebrow is raised. "I can't believe you just told me that."

"I can't believe I did, either. But it seemed safer to use a professional than to find someone random."

"I understand. It makes the rest of us wonder if we could ever compare, though."

I laugh. "Are you thinking you'd want to be a part of the comparison?"

He sputters, and oh, heavens, I adore making him blush.

"I'm only teasing." I lower my voice and murmur into his ear. "And I haven't done that in years. With professionals, that is. Not tease."

Sam gulps. "Good to know." The band inside shifts to a slower tune. "We should get back," he says.

On an impulse, I grab his biceps, feeling his strength. Yum. "Stay a moment more. They won't miss us." I lower my voice. "And besides, they're dancing inside. I don't know how to ballroom dance, and it always makes me feel awkward to stand around while everyone else spins and twirls."

He rubs the back of his neck. "I could show you. I mean, if you …"

"Yeah?"

"Do you want to?"

I smile. "I very much want to dance with you." His smile back makes my heart rate increase.

"Okay. Let's dance, then. I can teach you a few steps, although I'm sure you're a natural dancer, given how you move on stage."

"You've seen that, have you?"

"Not in person. Only on YouTube. Come on."

While I want to know more, I usher him to an area with a few square feet of concrete, where we can move but won't be disturbed.

As he directs me to put one hand on his waist and the other on his shoulder, I realize this is way more romantic than I bargained for.

And I kind of wanted it to be romantic. But we're two men in tuxedos in a garden in the moonlight—fairy lights hung in the trees and a band playing—and we're about to dance.

It isn't just how good he looks or smells, but how he feels next to me.

This man belongs in my arms.

No wonder our grandparents and great-grandparents spent so much time dancing. It's sexy as fuck to be this close. My cock is noticing our proximity and likes it very much.

I see sparkles in his eyes—maybe from the fairy lights—and he swallows hard.

"Okay," he says, his voice raspy. "On the count of three, you take one step back with your left leg, and I'll take a step forward. One, two, three."

I do it, and he moves with me.

"Then take one step to the side, this way"—he taps my leg—"and bring your other foot to meet it."

We move together.

"Take one step forward. That is, you go forward, and I go back." We do. "And then repeat."

This time I cock it up, and we crash into each other, chest to chest. I grab him to keep from toppling over.

A laugh bursts out of me. "Not ready for *Strictly Come Dancing*."

"Keep going. We can do this. Now, we repeat."

I nod. "Shall we do this from the top?" We return to the position we started from.

"Yes. One, two, three," he says. I step backward, he steps forward, and we carefully move to the side, and then we switch.

"We did it!"

The grin on his face is infectious. "We did."

The music keeps going, so we continue this simple pattern, and all the while I'm feeling his solid, warm body next to mine, clad in luxurious fabric.

Why did I ever think this was a good idea? Because all I want to do is kiss him.

So maybe I should.

We dance, and for every smooth movement we have one where we bump into each other and laugh.

As the music swells, I look into his eyes, which heat up and melt simultaneously when they see mine. His lips part, and I take that as an invitation. I lean in—

A door from one of the ballrooms opens, and the music's volume increases, along with the sound of voices heading our way.

We break apart. "And, uh, that's how you do the box step," he says, clearing his throat.

"Cool, cool." I smile at him. "Thanks for teaching me."

"You're welcome." He looks at me, and we both stand there a moment.

"Shall we go back inside?"

"Yes, we should. But before we do, can I ask you something?" he says. "You don't have to answer. And I promise, whatever you answer—or if you don't answer—stays with me."

"Okay." I can't keep the wariness out of my voice.

"I don't know how to ask this. You know I'm gay. And you just danced with me. And you did say something earlier about *our* rights. So I wanted to know if you, um. If you ever … liked men, like that."

My heart starts beating fast. "That's not a question I answer publicly, because my sexuality is my own business." Kind of like my personal history. My voice drops. "But yes, I find men attractive. Certain ones, at least, especially those who douse others in water."

"Oh," he says. And it's the cutest "oh" I've ever heard. Like he's processing what I just said and what it means.

Still, knowing his stance on being out, I feel defensive. I keep my voice even. "I wear whatever the hell I want and have sex however I like, because I think both are fun and both are expressions of myself. End of story. But I don't talk about it, because it's my business. I don't go down the street demanding that people show me their genitals and tell me what kind of genitals they prefer to rub against."

"When you put it that way, I feel bad for asking."

"You, dear Sam, may have been asking for a personal reason. No?"

"Yeah," he says, his voice husky. "I may have a vested interest in your answer."

"And that's entirely different. I trust you to not add it to my Wikipedia entry."

"I won't."

A song starts forming in my head about that feeling like you're in a tailspin, when you're falling for someone. And how scary that is.

"Sorry," I say. "Just thought of a lyric. Do you mind?"

I pull out my phone and take a few notes.

I look up at Sam when I'm done. "Something about being near you makes me want to write."

"That's a good thing, isn't it, given my job?"

I nod and smile. "It is." I gesture to the open doors leading into the hotel. "Shall we?"

"Sure."

We walk back inside.

"What's next for you?" Sam asks.

"The Fly by Night festival. Even though we wrapped up the tour, we added that on as a one-off."

"Oh! That sounds like fun. My friend Emily was trying to get tickets, but it's sold out."

I grin and pull out my phone again, type quickly, and hit send.

Sam tilts his head. "What did you just do?"

"Backstage passes will be couriered to your office Monday morning."

He presses his palms to his cheeks, trying to hide a smile. "You really don't have to do that."

"I know. But maybe you can help me with the album more if you've seen a live show. You haven't, right?"

"Right. Emily has."

"Then you both shall go. If you like, that is," I say, suddenly feeling like I've assumed too much.

"She will flip," he says. "Thank you."

"You're welcome."

When Sam goes to shake my hand, I pull him in for a hug. For some reason, I'm finding it hard to swallow, and I hold in a breath.

When we break apart, I touch my throat. "See you."

"See you."

I go back into the event I'm supposed to be attending. The ballroom is now darkened, and people are watching a presentation on all the good the foundation does.

I slip into my seat and lean over to whisper in Loren's ear, "Saw my new favorite person."

They tilt their head. "The attorney? He's here?"

"He is. He's at a different event."

"It's like you're orbiting each other."

"Kinda, yeah."

"Hmm. Well, he works for the other side, don't forget."

"I like to think of it as collaboration. Plus, he's my muse."

"Whatever you say, Jules."

Thirteen

Sam

After we get searched by security, a woman in a black T-shirt scans my phone and nods at the lanyard around my neck. I wait for Emily off to the side while they check her ticket.

We're in this hot, vast desert space of open skies and crowds of people.

They've made it as comfortable as it can be with covered areas. The stages have little to no shade, though, so both Em and I are wearing hats.

I'm not very good at dressing down, and I stick out in a pink polo shirt and shorts. Emily's more in her element in a long hippie dress. I should be dining at a tennis club in Palm Springs. She belongs at Burning Man.

Em hooks her arm in mine. "This is *amazing*!"

All I can think about is Julian. I haven't told her I danced with him. After all, he's her celebrity crush. She knows way more about him than I do. I could grill her for details.

But the feelings I have for him are more delicate, and I don't want to talk about them. I hide them under the cloak of my interaction with him being work-related, but in reality, I'm picturing his beautiful face in the moonlight at the hotel and wondering if I should have kissed him. If he was going to kiss me. Or if we were going to drag each other to some room there and do very naughty things to each other.

"This place is glamorous, in a dusty way," I say, to distract myself from my thoughts. The attendees exude a sheen of youth and look good in tattoos and band T-shirts and skimpy things. I glance down at my Top-Siders and feel older than I am.

"I'm so glad you invited me along. Because I would have killed you if you didn't."

"I know, although you've seen him in concert before."

"Backstage passes are another level."

"True." I look around. "What do you want to do first?"

We walk past hordes of pretty people having their significant others take videos and pictures of them, like it's more important to prove that they were here than to actually be here. We look at some of the booths and listen to the music, which is in the format of band after band after band on numerous stages. We find a shady place to sit and people watch for a while. Concertgoers pass us with plastic cups of beer, and I don't think I've seen more stoned individuals in my life.

In short, this event isn't my thing.

"I stick out, don't I?" I say, tugging at my shirt. Several women in cowboy hats and short shorts saunter by.

"In a good way. You're you."

I see a group of shirtless guys shotgunning beers. "It must be fun to be able to let everything go for a while and not worry about something getting into the news cycle or social media."

"I'm sure you could take your shirt off without jeopardizing marriage equality."

I shake my head. But a grin tugs at my mouth, because I actually wouldn't mind doing it.

"Fine." She sighs. "I'm just trying to get you to loosen up—"

A guy holding a plastic cup stops and stares, then tugs on his friend's shoulder and points at me, slurring a little. "You're that guy!"

Tilting my head, I look at them. "Which guy?"

"The guy in the ads. About Pride. Some new, um, thing."

"Oh, yeah. That's me." I rub my face.

"Can we get a picture?"

I shrug. "Sure." There are tons of celebrities here, but they want a pic with me? Fine.

I smile for the camera and shake hands, and they go on their way.

"Guess being recognized *is* something for you to worry about," Emily muses. "I thought you were exaggerating, but maybe you aren't. I forget how you're a member of a dynasty. I just think of you as Sam."

"It's only going to get worse, with Pop-Pop's campaign."

"Are you okay with that?"

"It's not like I have a choice."

"Oh, you always have a choice," she says. "You just don't want to make the hard one."

I decide to let whatever she's talking about go.

As the day goes on and the crowd gets drunker, we pass couples making out, some getting really hot and heavy, especially as the sun starts to set.

She gives me a quick squeeze. "Want to get a drink?"

We've been monitoring our alcohol consumption, not wanting to get sick in the sun. But it's now darker, and since the air is still hot, a beer sounds good.

We get in line at a rainbow-flag-bedecked booth to buy a drink, but before I get to the front, someone runs into me with a full cup of beer.

Cold, smelly, sticky liquid runs down my front and pools in my shoes.

"Oh god, I'm so sorry, dude," a man slurs.

"No worries," I say, thinking of how Julian handled me doing practically the same thing. Though at least that was clean water. "It can happen to the best of us."

My polo shirt is soaked, so I take it off and put it in my back pocket. I'm toned from all the yoga. I just don't usually flaunt it. But if I'm going to cut loose, this is the place.

"Looking good there," Em says, trailing a finger up my abs and licking her lips exaggeratedly. "I mean, six-packs aren't only for drinking. And you've got some pretty nice pecs. Just sayin.'"

"Shut up." I blush.

Emily and I have been best friends since the first grade. We kissed in high school, which cemented for me the fact that I was gay. But she's good for my ego, even if she'd throw me over for Julian Hill in a heartbeat.

"I'm serious." She eyes me. "Judging by what you've told me, if our friend JH sees you like this, you'll be even more inspiration for him."

I redden, and it's not from the heat of the day. "Maybe."

We buy our drinks and make our way through the crowd. Now that I'm shirtless like half the men here (and some of the women), I feel like I fit in. Like I'm less buttoned-up, preppy Sam and more of a … partygoer.

The edges of this festival are loosening up—and it already was a free-for-all. While there is security and medics and all sorts of safety equipment, it's also the most fun I've had in a long time.

I sip the beer, which tastes wonderful, and Em and I get tacos for dinner. I check my phone. "Jules is on in a half hour. Should we go find him?"

She puts her hands on her hips. "Like you have to ask."

We walk by group after group of chattering teenagers wearing Julian Hill shirts, which gives me the oddest possessive feeling, like *No, kids, he's mine*—even though he's not—and make our way to the main stage, where we show our passes to security. Wandering around the darkened area, we try to be unobtrusive until I see a familiar face.

"Hey," Loren says, shaking my hand. "Um, nice outfit."

"Sorry." I cringe, automatically flexing my stomach muscles. "My shirt got soaked, so I had to take it off."

"No one minds seeing you like this. Just, you look different than you did in a suit."

"No kidding." I laugh and rub the back of my neck. Then I remember my manners and gesture to Em. "This is my best friend, Emily, who is a major fan. Em, Loren, Julian's manager."

"Nice to meet you." They shake hands. Loren looks around.

"Jules is getting ready. Why don't you watch the show from the side, and when it's over I can take you back to his dressing room?"

Emily looks like someone gave her ten years' worth of birthday and Christmas presents at once. "Ohmygod."

I start, "We don't have to—"

"Yes, we do." Emily glares at me. I hold up my palms.

She grabs my hand, and we walk over to the side of the stage, where the crew is busy checking equipment. Loren points out folding chairs we can use, and we sit, watching the show get ready onstage. Down in the pit, people start to backfill behind the diehard fans who've been waiting at the front all day.

The sky's now totally dark, although portable lights on generators are set up all over the place, like streetlights.

"All these people want access to him," Em says. "What they'd give to have him pay attention to them for five seconds." She shoves my shoulder gently. "And you've been one-on-one with him."

I have to tell her. "I danced with him," I say in her ear.

She turns away from the activity and faces me, eyes wide. "Danced with … *him?*" With her head, she gestures to the backstage area where Jules is surely hanging out.

I nod. "I'm sorry I kept it from you. It was at the hotel, the night Pop-Pop declared for governor. He was there for a charity thing. We went out into the garden and talked." I stare at my hands. "It was special."

"Oh, Sam. He's been my crush for a decade, but that's just fantasy. Whatever is happening between you and him is more than okay with me. I mean, access to all this"—she waves her hands around—"is every fangirl's dream. I never thought I'd know someone who'd actually have a chance with him. I can't wait to see what happens next. I can't wait to meet him. Am I really going to get to meet him?"

The thought makes my body prickle.

Just then, I hear, "Hey, Sam. You made it." I swivel my head. Jules is standing there. My skin seems to have become aware of him even before I did.

My heart starts pounding. Fuck, he looks good—as usual. He's wearing striped, skintight pants and a loose black shirt with ruffles. He has jewelry piled on, and his hair is an artful mess.

I stand up, but don't know whether I should shake his hand or hug him—probably not that, given that I reek of beer—so I settle for wringing my hands and waving.

He eyes me up and down. While I should feel self-conscious that I'm basically only wearing shorts and a hat, I don't. *Thank you, plank pose.* He gives me a smile and turns to Emily. "Hi—Emily, is it? How are you?"

I glance over at my bestie to see the color has drained from her face.

"You know my name," she whispers.

"Of course," Jules says warmly. "A friend of Sam's is a friend of mine."

Emily is practically vibrating next to me. "It's so nice to meet you. Thank you for the tickets. I can't believe I'm actually meeting you."

"The pleasure is mine." I feel like he's going to say something more, but Loren calls him. "Sorry, gotta go. See you after the show." He winks and strolls away, his ass unbelievably attractive in those pants.

Emily is trembling. "I can't get over how Julian Hill is *right there* and he *knows* you."

"Me neither," I admit. I'm feeling flustered, too. Because it's one thing to see him in my space—my office. Or all formal at an event.

But this is his turf. We're here to watch *his show.*

The bustle on the stage stops as the last-minute checks are completed. The musicians walk on all at once and take their places. Down on the field, the crowd roars its approval.

Before Julian walks on, he looks over at me and smiles. I wave, feeling dorky. He laughs and runs to the microphone.

The concert starts. It's raucous and energetic and all noise. Earplugs help.

Watching from the wings, though, the event is indescribable. If

I thought Julian was powerful coming through a laptop screen, it's nothing like watching him command a whole stage.

The whole *outdoors*.

He's prowling and interacting with the audience. Singing low notes and high. Holding a note for so long I grow faint.

But the way he moves.

The way he looks over at me every once in a while and winks.

Holy Biggie Smalls.

I'm … starstruck.

I wish it were only Jules and me and no one else around.

Sam

After the show, as promised, Loren shows us back to Julian's dressing room. It's gotten chilly, and Loren brings me a tour sweatshirt, which I put on.

I'm amazed they remembered, with everything else they must be responsible for.

As we approach the dressing room, though, Emily eyes me thoughtfully, nods three times, and stops. "I must."

"Must what? Come on, don't make Loren wait," I say.

She shakes her head, then leans over to whisper in my ear, "Look. My best friend has a chance at getting together with my favorite rock star. I am not getting in the way of this. You shall owe me for life, and I will feast upon your stories at the end. Just call me the matchmaker."

OMG she's the *best*.

And all sorts of feelings flood my gut.

Loren looks between us. "If you don't want to meet up with him …"

"Oh, he does," Emily says, and pushes me forward.

She steps back and watches Loren knock on the door. No one answers, so they open it, and I step in.

"Wait here," Loren says, so I enter the small dressing room, which only has a few things in it. I sit on a couch.

Em gives me a finger wave and turns to Loren. "Can I meet Stu and Mitch? Maybe Janice and Lizzie, too?"

They smile. "Sure. Follow me." Loren closes the door, leaving me in Julian's space.

There's water running in an attached room, which I assume is a bathroom. Not wanting him to be caught unawares, I call out, "Hello?"

"Sam?"

"Yeah, it's just me. Em went with Loren to go meet your band members."

The door opens, and a waft of steam comes out … along with Julian Hill wearing nothing but a towel.

My heart goes to my throat, and my dick surges to life.

All those tattoos are right here on that sexy chest, tan and defined and so gorgeous. His hair is wet, and a drop of water runs down his forehead before falling on his collarbone and then tracing a path down to his brown nipple.

"Sam?" He tucks in his towel with a smile. "Lovely to see you. Sorry about," he gestures down his body. "I get sweaty onstage."

"No worries." I go to stand. "I can leave."

He holds up a hand. "No, don't. Stay. Please. One sec."

He grabs a bag and takes it inside the bathroom, then comes out a few minutes later in black jeans, a white T-shirt, and bare feet, his toes painted a deep purple.

I could get used to that sight.

Jules settles next to me on the couch, his knee up on the seat so he's facing me. I'm distracted by how beautiful his face is—not model perfect, but he has vibrant eyes, cheekbones set at a high angle, and full lips.

I have to force myself to blink. "Thank you so much for letting me come. I really liked watching you perform."

Jules's grin is huge and genuine. "Did you? It was a good show. The band sounded tight."

"It sounded wonderful to me."

"Thanks," he says shyly. "I sang some of those songs for you."

My tummy does this little wiggle, and I finger the wristband of the hoodie Loren gave me, feeling much warmer than I was a few minutes ago. "You did?"

"I did. You've been my muse these past few weeks, Sam."

"Wha-what does a muse do?"

"Be himself." The way he's looking at me, it almost seems like he's going to lean over and kiss me, and I find myself staring at his mouth.

I nod and gulp, then take a deep breath and smile. "I can do that. Be myself, that is." I chuckle. "At least when I'm not playing the fool by tripping and falling into you. Though maybe that was being myself, too."

"I dunno. I liked you doing that. Bit different than the way I've met other people."

That makes me laugh, and the nerves have gone.

The moment when I thought he was going to kiss me is gone, too.

"I bet you meet all kinds of people."

Jules's expression goes thoughtful. "I do meet all kinds, and there are so many more who feel like they know me because they track me on social media."

"That must be weird. And amazing, in a way."

"But if I look too closely at my follower count or streaming statistics, I can get really depressed. Because why did those people unfollow me? Was I not enough for them?" I open my mouth, but he holds up his hand and continues. "When I see them live, I can see the looks on their faces. I can tell that this is working. And it gets me away from some of the fears."

"Julian, with a huge following like yours, there are always going to be people coming and going. You have to recognize that."

He nods. "I do, but I get scared that they're all going to leave if I give them the smallest reason."

I tilt my head. "I don't think that could happen."

"It's just how I feel."

Tapping his hand, I say, "Hey. Your feelings are valid. But they aren't based in fact. You have tons of rabid fans who will stay with you as long as you keep being yourself and keep giving them something to listen to. What are you working on now?"

He grins and starts talking about an idea for a song, and I listen, loving how passionate he is when he talks about creating art. I'm not artistic myself, but hearing him? It's the coolest.

I lose track of time as we talk. When there's a knock on the door, the frustration on Julian's face is palpable, and frankly, I feel it, too.

Loren walks in. "Have you satisfied the lawyer and all he needs?"

"Not even close," Jules mutters, and I stifle a laugh as we get up.

We meet up with Emily, and Jules takes time to talk with her before we go. I can tell she's filling up her tank of stories by the way she watches every move he makes. Loren hands him a Sharpie, and he signs our backstage passes and presents Em with a bunch of merch.

"Best day ever," Em whispers, after Jules gives her a hug.

He hugs me, too—a bit longer than her, I think, but I could be mistaken.

We say goodbye, and Emily and I head back to our hotel in Palm Springs to pass out for the night.

After showering off the stale beer, sunscreen, and sweat, I feel more like myself again. I lounge on my bed in pajamas while Em gets cleaned up. She emerges from the bathroom clad in the oversized T-shirt she just got, her hair wrapped up in a towel.

"You're going to sleep in that, eh?" I gesture at Julian's larger-than-life face on her chest.

"For the rest of my life. I can't believe you *know* him. I can't believe I *met* him. I'm just thrilled he's even more awesome than I hoped. You can fan worship someone and then meet them and it's a disappointment. But this wasn't."

"He's pretty cool," I say.

"You need to spill. What did you guys talk about? Did he put the moves on you? Did you kiss him?"

I laugh. "No to those last two questions." And I tell her what I can remember of our conversation. Except the parts that feel too personal. I can keep secrets, even from my best friend.

At the end, she sighs happily. "Emily Stevenson, Jules Hill

aficionado extraordinaire, gets to not only meet the man himself but have her best friend get closer to doing the horizontal cha-cha with him."

"Uh, no. We did the box step—not today—and it was while standing."

"Whatever. I'm taking credit for you having more time alone with him." She yawns and crawls under the covers of her bed. "I am going to dream about this day for the rest of my life. And you have a chance with him!"

"Hardly, E."

"*Pfft*. You do."

I smile into my pillow. "I love you."

"Love you, too. But if you don't kiss him sometime soon, I may kick your ass."

"Ha."

I curl up in my bed and fall asleep fast, dreaming of a towel-clad singer crooning only to me.

Fifteen

Jules

The day Sam is coming to dinner, I pace around the house. I've spent the week writing new songs.

A *lot* of new songs. And the reason for those songs will be here soon.

Thankfully, Colin said he would go out tonight because I told him I have an important business dinner. I'll have the house to myself.

My heartbeat quickens, and my pulse pounds in my throat. I grab a drink of water, then race to chug it down as Sam's car slides past the gate and crunches up the drive. After checking to make sure my hair isn't doing something ridiculous, I fling open the door and walk outside to greet him. I know I'm supposed to play it cool, but I can't wait to see him.

He drives a very clean Audi—an electric model, because of course—and he has on a nice dress shirt and slacks.

And fucking hell, he looks good, albeit a tad nervous.

It makes my heart happy.

Sam Stone glints in the sunlight, prettier than any human has the right to be. His eyes are just so blue and his hair is just so blond. And he's a rare natural blond, I can tell from the rest of his coloring, while I'm the brooding Brit with the dark hair and dark clothes—even if I'm often boiling hot in LA.

I resist the urge to grab him. Instead I walk over and hold out my hands. "Hug okay?"

"Suh-sure," he stutters. And then he wraps his arms around me and holds me tight.

Oh, god. He feels so, so good against me.

He smells like sunshine and Tom Ford and something I've been missing in my life.

I want to kiss him.

"I have to admit," he says, "I wasn't this nervous the first day of law school when I got called on in contracts class by a professor straight out of *The Paper Chase*."

"What's that?"

"An old movie law students watch."

"And why are you nervous? It's only me."

"I don't know what I can contribute."

Contribute…

Oh, that's right. I'm supposed to play music for him. I got distracted about Sam coming over for dinner and forgot that this is presumably related to work.

Time to refocus.

"You contribute by being you," I say. "You're refreshing. Come inside. I'll give you a tour and show you the studio. I can play you what I'm working on, if you like?"

Sam smiles. "I'd love to hear it."

He follows me, and I want to hold his hand. He held my hand in the lift without any hesitation.

Sod it. I take his hand, and he makes a startled sound of surprise but then wraps his fingers around mine.

You know how some people hold your hand all limp? And others crush it? Sam's perfect and active, holding me right back but not overdoing it.

We walk into the great room, which is all glass facing out to the ocean. The furniture is low so it doesn't get in the way of the view.

My bedroom, the kitchen, and the great room are on the top level of my house, which is the entry level from the street—although to get to my house from Highway 1, you have to go down a private drive and through some gates. Down one floor, there are guest bedrooms, a bar area for entertaining, and a library-lounge area. On the bottom floor, besides my studio, are a game room, media room, and sauna.

He smiles at me. "Your place is fantastic. I like being this close to the water." He steps through the open doors to the balcony, tugging me with him.

"Me, too." The late afternoon sun gilds the ocean, making it sparkle.

We stand for a moment looking at the Pacific, and then I remember my manners. "Want a drink?"

"Water would be great." He lets go of my hand but follows me into the kitchen.

I tilt my head. "Do you not drink alcohol?"

"I do. But not when I'm working."

That disappoints me. Not that he doesn't want to drink alcohol right now—that, I don't care about. But that he thinks he's working. Still, I fetch him a glass of water.

Colin pads out, clad in jeans and looking like he's going to leave as I requested.

"Oh, Sam," I say. "This is my brother, Colin."

Sam holds out his hand. "Nice to meet you. I'm one of the lawyers representing Lighthouse Records."

Colin looks between us, interested. "A lawyer?"

"Yeah."

Colin opens his mouth to say more, but I butt in. "Colin's going to let us have the house tonight."

"Right, see you," Colin says. He grabs his keys and scurries out the door.

"Thank you," I call after him.

Even though I'm the one who asked Colin to go out for the night, whenever he leaves, my heart squeezes. I've been responsible for him for so long. And yet we both need to be on our own.

Sam follows me to the studio. As we walk down the stairs, he chatters, pointing out that he has the same couch I do, and we both have art by the same artist. He shrugs. "I like things sleek and contemporary, too."

I would've thought we'd have different tastes, given how we dress, but perhaps we're more alike than it seems.

There goes Sam Stone, warming my heart again.

We enter the soundproof room bunkered into the hill, and Sam takes in the banks of recording equipment and the instruments scattered about.

"Have a seat," I say.

He settles in, crossing one ankle on top of the other knee. "What would you like to show me?"

I pick up my guitar, feeling nervous all of a sudden.

I can do this. Letting out a breath, I say, "I've been writing an album about facing my fears. My particular and very specific fears. Ones about lifts breaking down and about not being good enough. Ones about never finding someone to love. I dunno, maybe I'll end up writing about how I'll never touch an octopus."

He grins. "You're scared of octopi?"

I shudder. "Yes. Very much. They're too smart."

"Aren't a lot of animals smart?"

"Not smart and squishy."

He presses his lips together, trying not to smile.

"Okay, maybe it's not the smart part that's entirely the issue. Once, in primary school, my class visited the London Aquarium, and I got separated from my group. The place was packed, and somehow I ended up pressed against a tank with a big octopus, and it decided to stick itself—with its suckers, or whatever they are—on the glass right by my face. It seemed like it was ten times my size. I think I screamed the place down."

Sam frowns. "I'm sorry that happened to you."

I shrug and set my instrument back down, open up the little fridge, and get a drink. "Funny how those childhood fears stick with you. They can be the starts of songs, though."

"Do you want to play me what you have?" he asks.

I nod, gulping, then pick up my guitar again and strum a chord. "I have a bunch roughed out, but I'm okay with playing you three of them. This first one is about the lift."

Sam closes his eyes, and I love that he does that, because it means he's listening—and he's also giving me space.

Taking a deep breath, I play the song about the walls closing in on me and a kind voice and blue eyes making the panic go away. When I get to the part about a man in a bow tie, I risk a look at Sam, who grins after he hears the lyrics.

When I'm done, he opens his eyes and claps. "I got chills. Look at my arms." He rolls up his sleeve, and I see this sexy, toned, veiny arm with goose bumps up and down it. "I love how you took something that happened to you and turned it into art."

"Thanks." My voice is husky. We look at each other, and after a moment I say, "Want to hear another?"

"Of course," he says quietly.

I play him the song about selling your soul to the machine and being scared you're turning into an automaton. This time he opens his eyes and watches me. I think he knows exactly what I'm talking about.

And while it's hard to feel his blue eyes on me, I make it through the song.

"Yeah," he says. "You're being vulnerable. That takes a lot of courage."

I give him this goofy grin. "Now I'm thinking about writing a song about that feeling when you're being vulnerable and showing someone the real you."

"Do it," he orders. "I'll wait."

So I pull out a scrap of paper and scribble down some lyrics.

Finally, I decide to get brave. "I have one more that's okay to play."

"Yes, please."

Haltingly, with a few messed-up lyrics and chords, I play a song about three dots that appear and disappear as I'm wondering what he's thinking. Wondering if he's ever going to say what I want him to say.

Sam watches me in wonder. If I share this song with the world, the pronoun will provoke questions I've spent years not answering.

The pronoun might scare away fans. The pronoun might bring me more hate than I already receive. Those possibilities make me anxious.

But I want to be strong enough to record it. I've been thinking about what Sam said about responsibility. And I might be ready to take a small step toward being a leader.

The song isn't complete yet, but when I get to the end of what I've written, Sam clears his throat, and then he's on his feet, running his hands through his hair. "That's. I'm. Julian. How do you come up with things like that?"

I shrug. He's so agitated I want to take him in my arms and kiss him.

Maybe I will. I set my guitar down and stand still, looking at him, trying to decide. But before I make a move, the gate buzzer rings. I answer the intercom.

"Dinner's here," I say. "Come with me?"

He nods and follows me up the stairs.

The arrival of the meal changes the mood, breaking the tension that had been building between us. The weather is lovely, so we set up outside on the balcony, the crashing waves and cries of gulls our background noise.

I open a bottle of white wine. "Still not drinking?"

He shakes his head. "I think I'm off duty now."

Grinning, I pour us each a glass. We settle into enjoying the gorgeous paella.

He doesn't mention the song I wrote that's clearly about him. *Songs.* I don't, either, but regardless, conversation is easy. He tells me about restaurants he likes around here and his family's political moves. I tell him about the tour and the places I've traveled.

"Emily is your biggest fan," he says.

"What about you?" The words are out before I can stop them. "I mean, do you like my music?"

Sam's looking at me, and his expression is hard to describe. It's like he's paying attention to everything I'm saying, but it's not hero worship. More like he thinks I'm important and interesting, and what I say matters to him.

I watch him bite his lip, and again I have this rash desire to kiss him. To find out what he tastes like.

"I do now," he finally says. "I used to tease Em about how much of a fan she was, so I intentionally wouldn't listen to you. But I looked up your songs after I met you and before I went to the concert." He reddens. "I mean, of course I'd heard your music before, but I hadn't actually *listened* to it, if that makes sense. But once I slowed down to pay attention? Yeah, I'm a fan." He smiles at me, and it makes me feel as if everything in the universe is going to be okay.

"Thank you. I appreciate you listening."

Pink splashes appear on his cheekbones, like he was painted with watercolor.

And I'm either going to launch myself across the table and kiss him or keep this PG. Against the urgings of my heart, I move to a safer topic and ask, "Do you play any instruments?"

"I do. I took piano lessons growing up."

"Then you should accompany me when we're done with dinner."

A laugh escapes him. "Uh, no."

"C'mon. I bet you're good."

"I can play a few classical pieces competently. Like, intermediate stuff. I can't create something original."

"I'll do the creating for us." I wink. "But I want to hear you."

"Sometime," he agrees. "I'll be embarrassed, but maybe it can spark something creative for you. I'm willing to do that."

I don't need Sam to spark any more creativity in me. He's already done that. I'm simply enjoying having him here with me. He's easy on the eyes and has elegant table manners and is so fun to talk to. It's like we've known each other for a very long time.

When we're done with dinner, we clear off the table but find ourselves back out on the balcony with fresh glasses of wine, watching the sunset. A breeze has picked up, and while it's not cold, it is cool enough to make me stand close to him. He nudges me with his shoulder, and I want to wrap my arm around him. I don't, but he doesn't move away.

I'm looking for any excuse to touch him. And with the way he's looking at me, I can sense that he's attracted, too.

I bet I could get him in my bed.

But I don't just want him in my bed. I want him in my life. We barely know each other, but he's already more supportive of me than almost anyone else I know. Obviously, he's working for the label, but he doesn't treat me that way. He treats me like … like I matter as a human being rather than just a singer.

That's heady stuff.

When the air turns chilly, we go inside and sit on the couch, still watching the waves.

"What comes next? How can I help keep you moving forward?" Sam asks, and I think he might be trying to make this evening go back to being about business. "I liked seeing you at the festival. And it sounds like you're making progress."

"Just keep checking up on me."

"I can do that." He looks around. "This has been interesting. Fun, too. I like watching the way your brain works. It's very cool."

His reticence is frustrating, because I thought we had something going. Am I wrong? Finally, I say, "Thanks. I'm not one to normally share this part of me, but something about you got my creative juices flowing."

"I'm glad." His eyes are bright. "Well, thanks for dinner and everything. I'd better get going."

"You sure?"

He bites his lip and nods, but he makes no move to stand.

I find myself scooting closer and closer to him.

Waves crash on the shore, over and over and over again, a slow, building inevitability.

I think he may want me as much as I want him.

Sam is right there. He's handsome, but I've met lots of handsome people. People aren't beautiful unless they're beautiful on the inside, though. And Sam is one of the most beautiful people I've ever met.

I want to make a move, but I'm wondering what to do. If Sam would say he's interested, I'd make a move.

I want him more than I've ever wanted anyone. My feelings for him are the kind that fill albums with passion.

And yet I don't want to make things awkward if I'm wrong. We still have to work together.

If I make the first move, am I being a complete fool?

Well, hell. I *am* a fool.

I reach over and grasp his cheeks. He has the beginning of rough stubble coming in.

At first, I can tell he's questioning what I'm doing, but then his eyes soften.

I *know* what desire looks like.

So.

Sod it.

I lean in and press my lips to his, and the whimper that comes out of him makes me absolutely wild. He parts his lips, and I climb into his lap, and he's holding me, and I'm holding him, and for the first time in my life, it feels like I might have met someone who sees the real me.

Sam

Julian Hill is straddling me, holding me in his arms, and my hands are squeezing his ass and all I can think about is how *right* this is, although something niggles at the back of my brain. A gut reaction that I'm not supposed to be doing this.

But my brain's turned off. I'm a *feeling* being, not a thinking one. There's only sensation rippling through my body.

"You're so beautiful," he whispers against my lips.

I shudder.

He pulls back and bites his plush lower lip, studying me. My body zings with his nearness as he stares at me for a long moment with those dark, soulful eyes, his thighs on either side of mine. He opens his mouth, but I lean into him and silence whatever he was going to say with a kiss, this one hard and fierce. I cup his butt, needing to touch him.

Our tongues enter each other's mouths like we're fucking. Jules tastes like the wine we've been drinking and salt and all the temptation I've ever known. A surge of need like I've never felt before—desire, true desire—washes over me as I pull his hips closer so he's grinding against me. I'm so aroused that I'm having trouble thinking of anything other than relief and release.

My body has taken over with single-minded determination to feel, feel, feel. In the back of my brain is a prickly idea that we can't do this, but as I kiss him again, I can't remember why that is.

I'm fantasizing about what his skin would feel like against mine. What his throat, his chest, his cock would taste like.

It's like we're in our own world, in this huge beachfront mansion with no one around us for miles. All the windows to the sea are open.

I want this.

I want *him*.

Jules keeps pace with me, matching my kisses and my movements, and we're fighting for dominance without moving our bodies. He's on top, but now I'm the one controlling the kiss, grasping his face and bringing it to mine. A moment later, he takes over, bearing down on me and making me groan. Then I wrest control back again.

Fuck. I love that we're so evenly matched.

And I realize it's been a long time since I've kissed anyone with this kind of enthusiasm. If I ever have.

We break apart, panting, and he trails a rough finger down my cheek as I gaze up at him. I take in his tanned arms, the tattoos and veins and lean muscles braced against me and holding me to him at the same time.

In this moment, I could surrender. To sex. Lust. Craving. Exploration. I could let him take me on a journey—it doesn't matter where—and I'd be lost in utter pleasure.

He makes a delicious moan in the back of his throat. "I'm so glad you got assigned to my case."

His words make me realize what the problem is. "Wait. I'm a lawyer."

"I'm not your client," he murmurs against my neck, sucking and tracing my skin with his tongue.

"But you're contractually obligated to my client. You're—*fuck, that feels good*—an adverse party."

"It's not illegal, is it?"

The word "illegal" jolts me, and I struggle back, trying to gather my wits, which have soared out the window on an ocean breeze. "Wait."

This time he pulls his hands up and scoots off me, then kneels at my feet, hands on my kneecaps. My face burns. His morphs into a concern that's almost too much to handle.

"Sam, I'm sorry. I'd never push you. I thought you were okay with this." One of his fingers taps my leg, like he can't stop touching me. Like he wants to move it higher, clasp me tighter, but he's keeping himself from doing it.

I take a big breath, finally forming words about why this isn't right. "I was okay. But now I'm not. Actually, that's not true. I'm way more than okay with this. With *you*. I want you badly, and I can't have you."

"Because you're a lawyer?"

"Yes. And no. But yes."

A big paw rubs his face in frustration, but his voice is calm and gentle. "My sweet Sam. Do lawyers not have sex?"

My cheeks burn. "Lawyers have sex."

"Then whatever the issue is, I assure you we can work through it. That is, if you want to."

"I do. But—" I open my mouth to say it, but no words come out. It's like if I admit them they'll be true, and I don't want them to be.

His voice drops to dangerously seductive levels. "Please tell me. What's the problem?"

"My client's adverse to you," I say. "I like you and am very much attracted to you. But there are lots of reasons why I can't get involved with you. At least not while my client has a potential claim against you."

He tilts his head, then nods solemnly, standing up. He dusts off his knees, then chooses a chair to my side, leaving me alone on his couch. "What you're telling me is that even if you wanted to, we couldn't get together."

I lean toward him, looking him in the eyes. "I'm telling you I *do* want to. But we *can't* get together."

I can't believe I didn't think of this before. Guess I never considered being involved with Julian was a real possibility.

Jules runs his hands through his hair again and then lifts his hips and adjusts his pants, his erection having not flagged at all. When he speaks, his voice cracks. "You're the first person in a long time—maybe ever—who has seen me for myself. Not as a singer. Not as a celebrity. Not as a product or someone rich. You want *me*."

My hands start shaking, because this feels like the most important conversation of my life. "I do, yeah."

"And I think you're the sexiest man I've ever seen." He sighs. "Something about you—your looks, your smell, your voice, what you say. How you dress and act. It's like you were created specifically for me. I find everything about you attractive."

"I'm flattered, but don't go thinking I'm perfect. Trust me. I have unattractive qualities. Many."

"We all do. All I'm saying is that I find you irresistible. I think if we got together, it would be explosive."

"I think so, too," I admit in a small voice. "Very much so. And I very much want that. And we very much can't do it. At least not now."

We look at each other, and he's the one who breaks our staring contest, turning to gaze out the open windows to the vast ocean beyond.

I don't know if it's seconds or minutes that pass. I should leave, but I don't want to. It feels like if I leave, everything will change. I'll have to admit that I can't have him.

It's better to stay in limbo.

"If the issue is an ethical one, what would happen if I finish the album?" Jules asks.

"Well …" I think on it. "If the label had no claim against you, I guess you wouldn't be adverse anymore."

"And in that case, you would be interested in … in pursuing whatever this is between us." He waves his hand.

"Yes." Now it's my turn for my voice to crack, and heat singes my cheeks.

A smile spreads across his face. "Done."

I rub my cheeks with my palms. "Oh, god. This is going to be awkward, isn't it?"

"No," he says. "This is going to be the fastest album ever written."

"And we can be friends," I blurt. "Right? I mean, while we're, you know, waiting for the ethical issues to be resolved?"

"I'd like that."

"Wonderful. We're friends." I stand up, my own erection tenting my pants. I palm my dick through the fabric, and Julian groans. He stands, too, but stays about six feet away from me. I give him a sheepish smile. "Sorry."

"Nothing to be sorry for." He looks down at his own erection. "I'm staying away, physically away, because otherwise, I'm afraid I'll maul you. I have self-control, but"—his voice drops to a whisper—"I've never wanted anyone the way I want you."

"Me neither." I look at my shoes. "But we're friends. Just friends. I'd better go. Thank you for dinner … and everything. I'll be checking in with you because, well, you know. It's my job. But as always, no pressure."

A crooked, cheeky smile stretches his lips. "Oh, I'll be feeling *plenty* of pressure." He leans forward and wraps me in a quick hug, and it feels so good to be touching him, I almost give in to starting something more. "Soon," he whispers in my ear and ruffles my hair.

We break apart, and I open the door and leave.

He stands in the doorway as I drive away.

Seventeen

Jules

In the darkened arena, I lean into the microphone stand, the world at my feet, the tight black leather of my pants creaking as I move. My torso's bare, but a peacock-blue feather boa hangs around my shoulders like a real boa constrictor. The wind machine makes the individual feathers wave.

And I'm very aroused, my cock pulsating with need.

Before me, a blond, bow-tied man kneels, which is my first indication that this is a dream.

It's a very, very good dream. I think I moan.

Another indication that this is a dream? If there's an audience around, it's silent. All my focus is on Sam.

He's looking up to me, reaching for me, but he's showing me his hands, which are tied with thick ropes.

Okay, dream. Thanks for the symbolism. Got it.

I feel this tremendous need to be with him. Holding him.

My impulse is to reach for him, but my hands don't move. And despite how I try, I can't seem to stop singing, like a force field is holding me to the microphone. To the performance.

Then the boa turns into chains that hold me in place.

Sam looks up, a tear streaking down his face, and I wake up on a gasp, to a knock on my bedroom door.

I'm utterly disoriented, because the dream felt real. I've been on stage so many times, and I think I've even worn that outfit.

Normally, when I sing, I feel like I'm winning. Right now, though, I feel like I lost something I maybe never had.

Bleary-eyed, I look up from where I'm sprawled on my stomach and see my brother in my doorway. Colin's dressed and ready to go somewhere. I'm not sure what time it is, so it must be later than I imagine.

Stretching, I gather the sheets and tug them up, then sit against my headboard.

I'm still lost in thoughts of Sam. In thoughts of his kiss.

Which I can't have again until I finish this album.

"Jules," Colin whispers, "I hate to bother you, but can I borrow some money? Nat's got control of the bank accounts, and she's taken me off."

I yawn. "Good morning to you, too, Colin."

"Yes, sorry. Morning. Sorry. I'm just panicked, because I have some bills to pay and I can't get to my money."

Like this is the first time he's asked me for a loan.

Loans he's never repaid.

But then I think about him with a dirty face and bare knees in that home in London. And I never want him to go without.

Will I miss the money if I give it to him? No. And what is family for, if not to help each other out?

Especially when we're the only ones left.

I take my phone and transfer what he asks for to his new account. "Done."

"Thanks. I owe you."

I shrug and turn over, wishing I could go back to my dream.

Just so I could see Sam again.

That evening, I take a wary step out of the town car and try not to cringe.

A loud scream rises, the screeches like those of birds. But they're here for me. The Hillions. I love them. I can't lose them.

I smile and am grateful for sunglasses to counteract the flashing lights. I raise my hand and wave to everyone, turning up the charm. My charm thermostat is normally set pretty high, but I can always give a little more.

The only person I feel like I'm myself around is Sam.

Christ. I have Sam on the brain.

This is a special meet-and-greet event for fans who've donated to a charity or won tickets. It's always a tough balance—I want to raise money for good causes, but I don't want to exclude my fans who aren't well-off. So I try to make sure there are at least some opportunities to get in without a lot of cash changing hands.

Loren hired me a bodyguard for tonight. I try to get around without one, but in crowds like this, there's no help for it.

But after the initial frenzy, this crowd seems patient enough to wait their turn. They know I'll stay until the last of them gets their photo or autograph or whatever. I sign phone cases and album covers and skin. I take photo after photo, shake hands, give hugs.

"The Hillions are the best," I muse to Loren as we wait for another person to come up.

"They are. And you treat them right." Loren steps back to get out of the photo.

"I hope so." I turn to a teenage girl, about fifteen or so? "Hey," I say. "I'm Jules."

"Stacy. Oh my god, I can't believe I'm getting to meet you." Her bright, glossy eyes watch me, rapt.

"Same for me," I say with sincere enthusiasm. "I'm well chuffed to be meeting all these fans. I hope you're having a good time?"

Her hands visibly shake, and she presses her palms to her cheeks. "Yes. This is a dream come true. Will you take a photo with me?"

"Of course."

Stacy releases an appreciative sigh. "Even my grandma is a fan of yours."

"That's wonderful! What's her name?"

"Vicky."

I scan the crowd. "Is she here with you?"

Her face drops. "No, she doesn't do well in crowds these days."

"Want to record a video for her?"

She lays a hand on her heart, and her voice squeaks. "You'd do that?"

Loren's expression says, *Oh god, Jules, there's a line*. "Yes, of course."

Stacy pulls out her camera and turns on the video. I smile and wave like a dork. "Hi, Vicky. Your granddaughter Stacy came to see me, and I wanted to say I'm sorry you couldn't make it today and hope all is well. Lots of love!" I press my hand to my heart and blow a kiss.

She hits the button to stop recording and looks at me in amazement. "Thank you," she whispers, her voice close to tears. "She's my relative I'm closest to. Do you think I should tell her I'm gay? I don't know what I'd do if she said she hated me."

I swallow hard, amazed at the confessions I receive on a regular basis. "That's a decision only you can make. But I always think you should embrace who you truly are."

"Yeah. I think I'll tell her." She grins at me. "If Julian Hill can wear skirts, I can tell my family I like girls."

I give Stacy a hug when she asks, then blink to refocus for the next fan, wishing I could really talk with her.

Loren comes up and murmurs in my ear, "At this rate we're going to be here all night."

I lift one eyebrow.

They put up their hands. "Okay, you wouldn't be you if you took less time with them. I get it."

"Precisely. Can you get her contact info? And send some merch or something?"

Loren's eyes narrow. "You can't give things away to every fan, Jules."

"She's dealing with a big decision. If I can give her something to smile about, shouldn't I?" I feel like that's something Sam would say. I smile at myself for taking his responsibility philosophy to heart. "Will you please find out the details?"

"Of course. I'm just registering my complaint that you don't need to swoop in like a fairy godfather all the time."

I roll my eyes and focus on the next fan in line.

Eighteen

Sam

"I'm by the fountain," I say into my phone, whirling around and searching for her. "The one in front of Coffee Bean."

"Oh," Emily says. "I'm at the wrong fountain. I'll be there in a jiffy. I'm almost—"

She hangs up, and a moment later, there's a tap on my shoulder, which makes me turn again, and I open my arms for a hug. "There you are."

"Sorry, I got lost," she says into my neck.

I set her down and shrug, happy to see her. "No biggie. Shall we?" She falls into step beside me as we head into the bistro for lunch.

I kissed Julian, I rehearse in my mind. Do I tell her now? Wait? Either way, I'm going to have to peel her off the ceiling.

The restaurant's got a library theme, with books on shelves at the end of each booth, on side tables where waiters perch trays of ale, and along the benches where people wait to get in. I made a reservation, so we don't have to wait an hour for a table.

When we sit down and each order an iced tea, Emily puts her hands on the table and stares at me expectantly. "Did the Jules Hill concert change your life?"

I snort. "Absolutely not."

Kissing him did.

She pouts. "You're no fun."

"I am, too." I know I sound like a child. Might as well get it over with. I pick up the menu and mutter into my drink, "So, I went to his place for dinner and to hear the songs he's been working on, and … we kissed." Then I flick my eyes up to catch hers.

Emily shoves her fist in her mouth and screams. The entire restaurant turns and looks at her. "You waited this long to tell me!" she gasps.

I lean forward and press my palms down in the air. "Keep it down! I'm scared I'm going to get disbarred."

That stops her, and she blinks, then crosses her arms and gazes at me. "Why?"

"Lawyers aren't supposed to have romantic relationships with the other side."

"You're not in a relationship with him." She looks up with a raised eyebrow. "Right?"

"Right. I'm not." I lick my lips.

She squints at me. "But you want to be. Oh my god, I'm so jealous."

"Yeah," I admit, my voice husky. "Who wouldn't want to be with him? But we decided to be friends."

Em sighs dreamily. "And you heard his new music before anyone else."

Our server comes, and we order our meals: soup for her and a chicken salad for me.

After he leaves, I say, "And maybe, if we clear this hurdle of him finishing the album …" I shrug.

She bites her lip. "Part of me is excited for you. The other part is worried. I mean, you're well-known in your own way—"

"Gee, thanks."

"You know what I mean. But J—" She stops herself from saying the name. "*He's* on a whole different level in terms of recognition. People who get together with celebrities get shit on by the public for not being the right ones for them. Are you prepared for that?"

I sigh. "I'm not even going there for now."

"Why?"

"It's all so … up in the air. I don't know if I'm some passing fancy and he'll forget about me by tomorrow, or if he was serious. We said we'd try when we're all clear. But right now, I have to act like nothing happened. We're just friends. I have a job that I worked for years to get. I don't want to get fired or brought before the state bar ethics committee."

"But you like JH."

"I do," I admit, my pulse hard in my throat as I think about him and the kisses we shared. "And he might like me."

"Squee!"

The waiter drops off a napkin-covered bread basket along with a ceramic pot of butter. Em and I each take a roll, and I rip into mine, a yeasty scent escaping along with some steam.

"Can I tell you something I'm scared of?"

"Of course."

"So, I don't need love."

"Agree to disagree. But go on."

"What if what I'm feeling is a fanboy crush?"

"No," Em says firmly. "I have the fangirl crush. You've never fanboyed over anyone in your life. He kissed you. Right?"

"Right. But what does a kiss mean, anyway?" I realize I'm staring off into space and focus back on Emily.

"A kiss can mean a lot. Especially when it's from him to you. Although that raises another question. He wanted to kiss you in private, but do you think he'd be willing to do it in public? That could drastically shift his image."

I wrinkle my nose. "With the way he dresses, a lot of people already think he's gay or pan."

"Confirming it is something different."

"I guess you have a point."

"I always have a point." She pauses. "Nothing's ever guaranteed, but I don't think you're a passing fancy. So I'm going to be excited for you and hope if I can't have JH, I can live vicariously through you. If this is something you really want, then I'm going to push you. Because you could be very happy with him. I hope he finishes his album fast so you can have his babies."

I laugh. Because it's either that or choke out a sob. "I don't want his babies. Or any babies. I'm trying to figure out how to make it to work tomorrow knowing that I kissed the talent."

"I think you mean a talented kisser."

"Ha ha. It's going to be awkward, because I can't lie for shit and I'm going to be all guilty-faced."

"Don't be. You're allowed to be attracted to someone."

"Not him."

"Why not him? I mean, yes, I know the ethical reasons, so okay, bide your time until he's done. But after—"

"Assuming no one finds out—"

"You're not going to get disbarred for one kiss. It's not like you're in a relationship with him." She eyes me. "Even if you wish you were. Hell, I'd say a million people wish they were in a relationship with JH, some of them lawyers, but they're not getting disbarred."

I snort. "My situation may be a wee bit different from theirs, and I don't want to go that close to the moral line. Kissing but no sex feels like I'm playing games. I devote so much of my professional life to dealing with technicalities. I don't want to justify my personal life with one."

Nineteen

Jules

Loren leaves me alone for a few days and then stops by. They commandeer the comfy armchair in the corner of my studio and survey my disheveled hair, ratty tracksuit bottoms, and three-day scruff. "Jules, how are you?"

Which means, "How are you coming along with the album?"

But I have a surprise. I grin. "About ready to call the band to work out arrangements."

They blink at me in surprise, taking in the stacks of notes on every flat surface—a pile for every song I've written so far. "Wow."

I hand them a bottle of water, sit down across from them, pull a guitar out, and strum a chord. "Yeah, well. Two-month deadline. Also, I've had this great streak of inspiration."

Loren shakes their head, smiling. "That attorney. You like him."

No sense in hiding it. "I do." As I pluck a tune, I think about Sam's bow tie, and my cheeks heat up. Not much need for secrets between me and Loren, is there? They're at least a couple of decades older than me but have always treated me as an equal, and I trust their judgment. While I pay them handsomely, I get the feeling they aren't my manager primarily for the money but because they want to see me do well. That's why I admit, "When I'm done with the record, I want to see if we can …"

"Be more?"

"*After* the record," they confirm. "I don't think you should go rubbing your body parts against a lawyer who's threatening to sue you."

I roll my eyes and strum a chord. "He said the same thing. And he's not going to sue me."

Loren leans forward. "How do you know?"

"Because I'm going to get the album done. Then we'll be free to do as we please."

They harrumph. "So let's say you get the album done—"

"*When* I get the album done—"

"Yes, I believe you and I believe *in* you. *When* it's done, if you spend any significant amount of time with him, someone will notice, and the press will start discussing your sexuality even more than they already do."

I can't say I haven't had the same concern. But I keep pushing it aside, because … *Sam.* Loren is a worrywart, I tell myself. "The press won't find out. Sam can keep a secret." *I think.* Something dawns on me as I study Loren. "But you'd like me to be out."

Loren and I have never talked about their opinion of my insistence on sexual privacy.

They shrug and, after a moment, nod. "You live your life, I live mine. I understand why you make the decisions you do. But it would mean a great deal to me—and a lot of other people—if you were more open about who you really are. I mean, you're vocally supportive of queer rights, there are plenty of rainbow flags at your concerts, and you donate generously to charities—and that's great. But I feel like you're doing it for me, not for yourself. And Jules, news flash: You're not straight."

I laugh to hide my flinch. "Never said I was."

"But you never publicly acknowledge it, either. I'm not telling you what to do," they add hastily. "It's your decision. I just kind of wish you would, as much as I hate to put pressure on you about the one thing you detest talking about. I know you're in a different position than most."

"You're the one who's usually telling me I do too much for the fans."

"In general, I don't think you should give as much of yourself as you do. But in this regard, I'd like to see you be a leader. You could inspire people even more than you already do."

I set down my guitar and study Loren's face. No trace of wrinkles; smooth skin and full lips. Eyes that have seen a lot. "You never said anything before," I mutter.

"Because it's none of my business."

"But now I feel like a wanker, thinking of every time you stopped someone from asking me questions about my sexuality when you wished I'd just answer and put them out of their misery—even if I didn't have a good answer. Thank you for doing your job and protecting me, even when you don't like it."

"I wouldn't say I don't like it. I respect your desire for privacy, and my opinion isn't relevant to your music. But your sexuality always comes up. It will only get worse if you start seeing your lawyer. Things will come to a head, and everyone will have a label for you."

"They already do."

They shrug in acknowledgment.

"I try to say I don't care about the speculation, but I do. I just want to be who I am and not to have to define myself for the press. Still, something about Sam …" Something about Sam is making me consider changing the way I present myself in public. Being more open couldn't hurt, could it? I think about the impact I might have on fans without even realizing it.

Loren isn't done, though. "Setting aside the fans and the press, I worry. Do you know anything about him? Sam."

I scowl, pursing my lips. "I know what he's told me. We talked when I got stuck in the lift with him. And a few other times."

Loren raises their eyebrows. "Have you even bothered to look him up? Basic due diligence?"

I blink at Loren, then sigh. I usually ignore the internet, because I don't want to be tempted to look up rubbish about myself. I barely manage my own social media. "I suppose you're right. Have you?"

"Actually, no. I wanted to give you some privacy."

"What privacy?" I can't help my laugh. "We just talked about my lack of it."

"Exactly." Loren smiles kindly.

My heart squeezes. "Thanks," I say quietly. "I appreciate that. I'll look him up before …" Before what, I don't know. "Do you think I'd lose fans if I make a statement?"

They nod. "Some. I hate to feed your nerves, but it's better to face the truth. People behave weirdly, and some won't like you in *any* relationship, same-sex or not. You could get a boost among the queer communities, but you'll likely lose some support elsewhere. And losing fans means—"

"Losing money," I finish. "Which means I'd better get cracking on this album. Well, I already have."

They settle in. "Enough with the lectures. Look up Sam when I leave. For now, play me something new."

So I do.

While we're discussing Loren's reactions to the new songs—and their unusual (for me) degree of intimacy, Stu calls. "Are we booking time in the studio?"

His question sends a bolt of anxiety to my gut. I want to get this album done to remove a barrier between me and Sam, but absent that motivation, I could put off writing it forever. Sharing ideas with the band is scary, because even though I know these guys, they might hate something I really love. The songs are new seedlings that could get stepped on, or freeze, or burn in harsh conditions. But the way to make those tender shoots hardy is to get the band involved and develop the arrangements. While I want to keep the songs—and by extension, Sam as my inspiration—to myself for longer, I need to be practical.

Rolling my shoulders, I take a deep breath and hold it in, then let it out. "Let's check schedules. I can't wait for you guys to hear what I've been working on."

I can hear a smile in his voice. "Cool, man. We'll set something up."

After Loren leaves, I take a break and type "Sam Stone" into the search bar on my phone.

I feel invasive doing this. People do it to me daily—hourly—*minute-ly*? So I know what it feels like to be on the other side of the equation. Still, I'm curious, and Loren is right. I don't know that much about Sam. This is basic due diligence.

Hundreds of photos show up, with him always smiling and gleaming and—

Crap.

—on the arm of a very handsome man. I wince, feeling sick.

They say curiosity killed the cat. What they don't say is that it also kills the burgeoning crush of a bloke who thought maybe he'd finally found someone special. I can't help a bitter smile as I wrap an arm around my belly.

No wonder he pulled away the other night.

But.

Maybe it's just a friend. Sam would've said if he had a boyfriend, I'm sure. I click on one of the articles.

Sam Stone and longtime partner Kurt Delmont attend a gala event supporting ...

My hand holding the phone shakes. He already has a boyfriend. Must have been that "friend" he texted before we danced.

Fucking hell. I wipe away a ridiculous fucking tear.

I wish he would've told me. Now I feel like he was leading me on.

But he wasn't. He's just doing his job, and I got distracted because he treats me differently than other people do. Kind, but not obsequious. Listening, but not passive. Polite, but real. At least I thought he was real.

My heart feels like something is squeezing it, and I rub my chest.

Shaking my head, I keep reading. Sam has a Wikipedia entry that talks about how he's a member of a political dynasty, the grandson of a current gubernatorial candidate, and an accomplished attorney in his own right. He has other living relatives, including his father, who are prominent politicians, as well as some ancestors. The extent to which his clan has affected American politics is significant.

Because I must have some latent masochistic tendencies, I click on photo after photo and find Sam all captivating smiles on the arm of his man, who's as polished as he is.

I shouldn't be so disappointed. We don't know each other. But Sam's the first person in a long while—perhaps ever—who I felt instantly at home with. I'm usually the one trying to make other people feel comfortable around me. With Sam, everything is different. Apart from me reassuring him that the Great Pants Catastrophe was no big deal, all the support and encouragement has been going in the other direction.

But.

It's good that I now know this can't go anywhere. That way I won't get my hopes up.

Too late, a small voice inside my head says.

I pout.

After sitting for a moment, I decide it's time to emulate Duke Ellington and take the energy it takes to pout and write some blues.

Switching to my notes app and pacing around my bedroom, I write fragments of a song about wanting someone and being let down by them.

Which brings up my deepest fear: that of never getting what I want. Sometimes I don't even try because I'm scared I'll be disappointed.

Crikey. Even when he's making me sad, Sam Stone is my muse.

When I run out of steam, I close the app and glance again at some of the online pictures of him.

Sodding hell. Looking at him with another man makes my heart hurt.

Still, while his smile is bright, something about it strikes me as odd. It's like he's posing, wishing he were elsewhere.

There I go, reading what I want to see into things.

I rub the back of my neck. That's just like me—and one of the reasons why I haven't dated recently. Because I don't seem to be able to interpret people's intentions. I don't know if they want me for me or if they want me because I'm *Julian Hill*.

I'd thought Sam was different. And maybe he is, but it still doesn't mean he wants me like that. He just got carried away in the moment.

But I can't deny that spending time with him has made me the most productive I've been in years. Even if I can't have him, I want to see him.

I pull out my phone.

> **Jules**: Do you want to go to lunch? I'm convinced you're my lucky charm for writing music

In no time at all, he responds.

> **Sam**: Do you think it would be okay?

I sigh. All too okay, given that he's dating someone else. This is just to keep up the way he inspires me.

This is because I want to see him, even if I can't touch.

> **Jules**: Just lunch, as friends

> **Sam**: Then, yes. When?

Yes!

I suggest a date.

A long pause. Is Sam checking his calendar? Is he canceling something? Is he trying to think of a way of letting me down easy?

> **Sam**: That sounds great. I'd love to see you. Please let me know where to meet you.

I do a very undignified fist pump.

Then I remember I can't have him, he doesn't want me the way I'd hoped he did, and all I've been doing is dickful thinking. I have to stop reading into what he says.

He isn't for me.

I throw myself face-first onto my couch, the churn of the waves outside the only noise.

Twenty

Jules

I GET TO THE WESTSIDE RESTAURANT EARLY. I'D RATHER BE here first than have him show up and wait for me. This place has a VIP room in the back, partially behind a curtain, so I won't get interrupted by fans.

Right on time, the hostess shows Sam to my table, and I wave and stand up to greet him. He glances around. While I'm sure he's had plenty of nice restaurant meals, he might not be used to ones where we're the only people in the room. There's no hustle of waiters going by, and the din of the main room is muffled. It gives us privacy and quiet.

Maybe too much privacy and quiet.

Sam clears his throat. "Hi, Jules."

"Sam!" I want to hug him but instead shake his hand, enjoying the feel of his slim, cool fingers in mine.

I gesture at his chair, and we both sit.

He looks amazing. He's wearing a suit for work, but he's taken off the jacket. I love his ties and braces—he pulls off the look, not like he's a little kid from the 1930s, but like it's meant for him.

I'm wearing a long, sheer black tank dress over jeans. I got a few looks from the staff, but I don't care. This is what I felt like wearing.

Seeing him in his bow tie makes me want to write a song about how we put on clothes to hide ourselves.

I smile at him.

He blinks rapidly and fumbles with his napkin. Then he blows out his cheeks and releases the air. "Okay. I made it here. Good to see you."

"It's good to see you, too."

Seemingly unable to meet my gaze, he picks up the printed sheet for today's menu. "How are things going?"

"We're about to start recording."

He sets the menu down, his eyes lighting up. "That's great!"

"With you as my inspiration, I've written a whole lot. I have to thank you." I smile. "You actually gave me an idea as you walked in right now. I'll have to remember it for later."

"Go ahead." He waves his hands. "Write it down. I don't want you to forget it."

I pull out my phone. After I've jotted down a few ideas, I say, "Thank you."

Sam's been watching me, elbows on the table, chin resting on his clasped hands. "It's fascinating to see you do that. Like catching lightning in a bottle."

"I see you, and all these ideas just come to me." I glance up at him, and the softness in his eyes makes me want to reach across the table for him. Then I remember that he's dating someone and stop.

Thankfully, we're interrupted by a server who takes Sam's drink order. After he leaves, we sit, toying with the spoons.

I want to ask him about the man he's dating and how serious it is. And whether our kiss meant anything. And if I have a chance with him even after I finish the album.

"What do you think of this china?" I blurt, pointing to the Versace bread plate.

Really? What the hell, Jules?

Sam blinks. "It's kind of wild, honestly." It is, with starbursts and cheetah spots and gold.

"Not something you'd put on your wedding present wish list, then?" *With your man?*

He gives me a weird look. "Uh, no. I'm not planning on getting married anytime soon. Or ever, probably. Don't think there's a need to pick out china. If you got married, would you want a design like this?"

I shrug. "I mean, it might be fun. But you've seen my house, so it might clash." I grimace. "Sorry. That was a strange thing to ask."

I was thinking about you and some chap you haven't told me about. I was wanting to give you a chance to tell me without me asking.

"You can ask me strange things." He grins. "I figure that's the creative process, right?"

"Yeah, it is."

"Have you written an octopus song yet?"

"No, but I've been writing about other fears. Disappointing my fans or my family. Hurting people or letting them down. Not living up to my potential."

Not having the person I want like me back. Always being alone. Not being worthy of someone sticking around.

He reaches across the table and taps the back of my hand. "Does this mean I have to take you to an aquarium? To face marine life?"

"Yes," I reply immediately. Because I want a date with Sam, even if we're not calling it a date. Even if it's research. Even if there can't be anything between us, because he's taken.

Except in my brain, it's totally a date, despite so many reasons why it can't be.

He nods and grins. "Great. Let's do it. Is there a special time when you want to go? Like when it's not so busy?"

"You're serious?" This seems way too easy, but I'm not going to argue. "My manager will call and make arrangements. After hours, if that's okay with you."

"Of course." He tilts his head. "Is it going to be okay with *you* to be mere feet away from eight-armed creatures with suction cups on their tentacles?"

"No," I admit. "It's not. But I'm hoping it will spark something to write about."

"Then it's a date," Sam says. And the tips of his ears turn pink.

I'm charmed, but then I hold my breath. Because he has a relationship he isn't telling me about. My jaw tightens.

Ask him.

But I can't. Because there's no right answer. If he has a boyfriend, then what the hell was he doing kissing me back?

I want to spend time with him, though, and not just because he helps me with songwriting. I like him—as a friend, if I can't have more than that.

He presses his lips together. "You look irritated."

"Sorry. I had an unpleasant thought. But it doesn't matter."

"You don't like to admit to being irritated."

I shake my head. "No."

"Hmm." He looks around the room, which is empty except for us. "It's okay to not be such a nice guy all the time. You can have opinions about things."

"I do."

"But you don't want to express them."

That brings a laugh out of me. "I express them."

"Even ones that cause friction? Where you disagree with someone? Name something you don't like but everyone else does."

"Pie," I answer immediately.

He tilts his head and wrinkles his nose. "Are you serious?"

"As a head-on collision. I don't like pie."

"Are you un-American?" he accuses, then chuckles. "I guess you are. Well, pretend I'm force-feeding you pie. What would you do?"

"I'd eat some, to be polite."

Sam scowls and massages his temples. "No!"

"Why not?"

He throws out his hands. "Because if you genuinely don't like something, you shouldn't have to eat it."

"Okay. Then I'd lie and tell you I was full."

Pursing his lips, he gives me a mock glare that makes me laugh. "Do you really think that's the right answer?"

Chuckling, I shake my head. "No. I'd just say no, thanks."

He slow claps. "Right. Was that so hard?"

"Kind of," I admit. "I don't want to disappoint you. I mean, the public. Anyone."

"Pretty sure that's unrealistic."

The waiter comes and puts our starters down. We pick up our forks, and Sam says, "Okay, you don't like pie. You might be the first person I've ever met who doesn't like pie. What else?"

"Pancakes and maple syrup."

His mouth drops open. "You are so different."

"I'll eat them if forced, but I'm choking them down. Or, I guess if I'm following your advice, I should politely decline instead."

"Wow. So, your tastes are not the same as mine." He shakes his head. "What's something not food-related that you don't like."

"I'm not a big fan of cynics or critics. Or when everyone else is drunk or stoned and I'm not."

"Okay, I agree with you about all that. What's something you like?"

I answer him, and we pass the time easily, enjoying our entrées and chatting. Until he looks at his watch.

"Sorry, Jules. I have to head back to the office. I can put this on the firm card."

Which reminds me that this is a professional lunch. And I remind myself that he's dating someone else.

"I've got it," I say. "I invited you."

"Then thank you." Sam's eyes are sincere, and they make my heart ache and confuse my brain. He stands up to go and then reaches down, squeezing my shoulder. "This was nice."

"Yeah, it was." I look up at him and manage a smile.

If only he would admit he's taken.

If only I could ask.

He leaves, and I watch him go, then take out my phone and start typing into my notes app.

There. That's a much healthier way of coping with disappointment.

My phone buzzes.

> **Sam**: Jules, you should know. There's paparazzi outside. You may want to be careful when you leave.
>
> **Jules**: Thanks

But why didn't he warn me about himself?

Sam

"Breathe in," the instructor says in her new age hippie voice.

I do.

"Breathe out."

I do.

I look around the warm, clean, dimly lit studio filled with yoga equipment, with cheerful paintings on the walls. This is my favorite extracurricular activity that I get to engage in on any kind of regular basis. I'm right next to Em, as usual. It's late, almost time for bed, but she and I go to these evening sessions to help us sleep.

Her eyes are closed. I know this because mine are open and I feel like a cheater. I'm restless, though, and ready for the class to be over so I can go home and stew.

Because there was something off about Julian this afternoon. I can't stop thinking about it. *Him.*

Was it something I did? Or is he just being good and not getting too close, respecting my ethical requirements?

I concentrate on my breath.

My job pays for yoga as a benefit, along with childcare, lunches, parking, and vacation days no one ever uses. Yoga helps me align my body and maintain flexibility.

But the whole chill-out vibe isn't working one bit tonight, because my mind is racing.

Em must sense me shifting around, because she opens an eye and glares at me. "What is up with you?" she hisses. "You're supposed to be om-ing."

"I am om," I insist in a whisper. "I'm all about the om."

"You're not at all om."

No, I'm not.

Thankfully, the hour is up. Our teacher quietly dismisses us, and we all namaste our way out, rolling up our mats and putting away our foam blocks.

When we get to my car, I open the door for Em, and she asks, "Are you going to tell me why you're so distracted? You're worse than a cat with a laser."

"It's Julian."

She sighs and gets this dreamy look in her eyes as she settles into the passenger seat. "JH. Have you figured out how you're going to fall in love with him yet?"

"No. I keep telling you I don't need to be in love."

"You keep telling *yourself* that."

"And I don't have time for it."

"That may be true. You need a job that's less stress, more fun."

I shrug. "Yeah, but not too many law firms offer the same type of pro bono opportunities."

"Yeah, I know." She gives me a small smile. "You care so much about others. When do you start caring about yourself?"

"I do," I insist, although it's not wholly accurate. "When I'm not in the office, I take good care of myself. I exercise, I eat right."

"There's my boring old Sam." She pats my leg. "But that's not what I'm talking about. Don't you want to live a little more?"

"I live plenty. I'm out all the time."

"At what? Political events? Those don't count. You can't live without love, Sam."

"We're back to this, are we?"

"I know Asa fucked you up."

"Don't remind me of the bastard," I mutter.

My ex wanted a film career, and when his agent told him to break up with me so his fans would see him as single—and therefore more attainable and desirable—he did.

"You can't use him as an excuse to never fall in love again. He was ambitious and using your political connections to get noticed by Hollywood's elite at those parties you always go to. JH is already there. He doesn't need to use you, and I don't think he would anyway. I think he likes being around you. Because you're someone who is nice to be around." She pokes my shoulder playfully.

"But being with him—it would just create problems. With his fans. With my grandfather's campaign. With my job."

"Answer me this: How much of what you do, do you do because you think you have to? Because someone else told you to do it? Because of a path you decided on when you were nineteen? It's okay to change what you want." She looks at me earnestly, and I take an eye off the road for a second, then return to driving. "You only get one life, at least as far as we know. You might as well spend it the way you want to."

I nod.

"Try this, lawyer. Construct an argument as to why you *can* have what you want."

"I can't," I mutter. "Because the truth is, I want *him*. But I don't need him, and he doesn't need me. We could go on about our lives and never cross paths again, and it would be perfectly fine."

"That's a lie, and you know it."

"Do you really think *Julian Hill* and I are a good idea? On any level? Because this is big. He's *international rock star* big."

"He's just a man. And yes, I think based on how you're talking about him, it could be a good idea." She grins. "Ooh! Then I'll get to have the talk with him, the one where I threaten him if he hurts you. Oh, that is going to be an all-time high point."

"I'm beginning to think you just want me to be with him so you can hang with him."

"I want you to be happy. And if that happens to result in me spending more time with the love of my life—"

"You mean me."

She snorts. "Yes. You. Julian's a bonus."

I pull up in front of her house. She leans over and kisses my cheek. "Think about being happy, Sam. You can. It's okay."

"Okay," I say. And watch her walk up to her door, yoga mat under her arm.

Twenty-Two

Jules

You'd think a Malibu mansion would have enough space for two people.

You'd be wrong—at least if one of those two is my brother.

As I exit my bedroom, I hear him banging around downstairs, so I traipse down to see what he's doing and find him in the library. I have a collection of art books on subjects including music and fashion, as well as novels and biographies.

Apparently none of my books are good enough for him, though, because he's sitting at a table, flipping through the pages of a large coffee table book on film noir so violently I fear he may rip them out.

"What's going on?" I ask, coming into the room.

He turns, startled, and looks at me, his eyes red from crying. "Sorry."

"Hey," I say gently, putting an arm around his shoulders. "Must you assault my literature?"

"Just looking for … for something to read."

"And nothing here suits?" I ask lightly, stepping back and indicating the shelves full of what I think are interesting reads.

He closes the book currently in his hands and rubs his face. "You're right. I'm upset and taking it out on inanimate objects."

"Better those than sentient ones." I sit on a couch. "I get it. You're stressed. How can I help?"

Colin presses his lips together. This doesn't surprise me. He's never been one to share personal issues.

"What happened between you and Natalie?"

"Nothing I can't fix."

I raise an eyebrow. "Really?"

He begins to nod, then shakes his head. "Actually, I think this time she may have kicked me out for good."

Natalie's an Australian model who wants to be a supermodel. How she ended up with my prat of a brother, I have no idea.

We stare at each other until I ask, "What's really going on?"

He heaves himself into a chair across from me and puts his head in his hands. "I lost my job, okay? Natalie found out and said I was a worthless muppet and she never wanted to see me again. She gave me a few minutes to pack me bags and sent me off."

"That's rough." I tilt my head. "What happened at work?"

Colin's been trying to be an actor. I'd thought he'd found a good project.

"They sacked me because I was late a few times."

Translation: He was late every day.

"I was supposed to be the star, so they should've started when I got there."

Translation: He had a bit part for probably a few days, and since he didn't show up, they found someone else.

I sigh loudly. "Why do you do this to yourself, Col?"

"Do what?"

"Sabotage everything."

"I don't."

He does. And he expects me to bail him out.

And I promised our mum that I always would.

"Anyway," he says, "it's not like you do what you're told. It's not fair. No one says boo to you."

"That's not true. I could get sued if I don't finish this new record."

Colin waves me off. "Yeah, like they'd do that. And besides, you'll get it done."

"I still have to show up and do the work."

"Well, you putting off doing that album is no different than me showing up a little late to work."

"I didn't put it off intentionally."

"And I wasn't late intentionally."

"What were you doing that made you late?" I ask, a hand on my hip.

He gives me a slick smile. "A friend had a party on one of those megayachts. I had to go."

"And that made you late?"

"Well, I stayed up and partied pretty hard. It made it difficult to get up for their ridiculous call time. They should have been grateful I was getting them publicity. Photos from that party were all over social media."

"I wouldn't know," I say. "I barely ever check it."

"It was major," he insists.

"I know this isn't what you want to hear, but I'm going to say it anyway. Why don't you go back to university? You quit to be an actor, but it doesn't seem to be working very well."

"Not all of us can have success fall into our laps, Julian."

"I didn't have—" I start, but he's already standing.

"Look. I'm grateful for you giving me a place to crash. And for spotting me some cash. But you don't have to rub your success in my face."

I stare at him as he leaves.

Bloody hell.

My phone vibrates with a text from Sam.

> **Sam**: Hi. Has your manager picked a date to go to the aquarium?

It says something that I'd rather go see my least favorite creature with a man I can't have than figure out how to fix my brother.

> **Jules**: We must face our fears, no?
>
> **Jules**: Or rather, my fears
>
> **Sam**: I'm happy to help you do that, and if you happen to get an album out of it, all the better.

Business. This is business, Jules.

Jules: Hold, please

I hastily text Loren and explain what I want done. Because they're a miracle worker, it doesn't take very long before they come back with a time and date that aquarium management is willing to grant us access, and I send the information to Sam.

Jules: Will that work?

Sam: Sure.

Jules: Loren will send you the details

Sam: I look forward to it.

Jules: See you soon <Winky face emoji>

It's early evening, right as the aquarium is closing. I'm sitting in a dark car with tinted windows, waiting for Sam Stone to start our *date that's not a date and don't even think that way, Jules.*

Yes, this is going swimmingly. Why do you ask?

I'm more jittery than before a performance, and that's saying something. I don't know if it's because we're facing those suction-cupped creatures—*shiver*—or because Sam will be so close and yet so far.

My car brings me around the back of the building to a staff entrance, where I wait for him.

Not a date, Julian. This is not a date.

This is an excursion with a friend. A creative baby-minding trip by a lawyer. A …

Whatever it is, it can't be a date, because he has a boyfriend. If anyone asks, this visit is inspiration for my album.

Which is true, even if it's not the whole truth.

His red Audi pulls up, and my heart bangs against my rib cage like a dog at the rescue shelter struggling to get out of its plexiglass prison. I can't keep my fingers from trembling. Still, I manage to exit my car and walk over to him.

Sam Stone looks glorious, all polished and shiny, but I know that his glossy, magazine-perfect smile and conservative suit are covering a passionate heart. I repeat all the reasons why I can't have him, and yet when I look at him, I think, *Mine*.

Irrationally. Hopelessly. Selfishly.

I don't want him because he's my muse. I want him because he cares enough to do this, and he's doing it for me, not for him. He's doing it to help me get over my fears, not to blast on social media that he hung out with me.

That's revolutionary.

"Hello!" I say and give him a hearty handshake.

I want to hug him.

He shakes my hand warmly and smiles at me. I like how direct his gaze is. I take off my sunglasses so I can fully appreciate his beautiful blue eyes.

"Hey, Jules. Nice to see you."

I don't want to let go of his hand. "Sam. I'm …" *I'm embarrassed that words are failing me.* "Scared."

"We don't have to do this," he says quietly.

"No. I want to." I let go of his hand, and we walk to the back door, where we're greeted by the program director.

"So nice to have you visit, Mr. Hill."

"Jules, please. And this is Sam Stone."

She shakes both of our hands. "You're interested in seeing our octopus exhibit?"

We nod.

"Follow me."

It's quiet, and while there are workers around washing windows and cleaning glass surfaces, we otherwise have the place to ourselves. We stop at the entrance to "Creatures of the Pacific."

"Here's a map," the director says. Sam takes it, folds it neatly, and sticks it in his pocket. "Your manager told me you wanted to visit for artistic inspiration?"

"I do."

"In that case, while I'd be happy to accompany you, I expect you'd rather look around with minimal distractions. The exhibit is set up as a self-guided tour, so there's plenty of information provided along the way. Take your time, and Winston at the security desk can let you out when you're ready. If you have questions, please ask him or one of the crew to find me. Thanks for visiting, and enjoy."

She leaves us, and I stand at the entrance to the exhibit, not making a move to go in. It's like my feet are encased in concrete.

"Hey," Sam says quietly. "Are you okay?"

"No," I admit, looking at the creepy aquatic environment. "All this water. What if the glass just, you know, gives way?"

"It's not going to give way." He gives me a reassuring pat. "Want me to hold your hand?"

"Yes," I croak. My feet start working again.

He tugs me down a corridor to a dark room featuring tanks of octopi, and I almost die.

I spin around, tugging his hand. "Fuck, no. I can't be in here."

"We can leave if you like." His kind eyes are on me. "But I thought this was about facing your fears, and you wanted to tap into that for the album."

I take a deep breath. I can do this. I drop his hand.

"You're not afraid to feel emotions, Julian."

I'm not.

"Okay." I take a step closer to the nearest tank that has an octopus in it. This small, swirling, tentacled thing with suction cups. It's sitting in a corner. Well, I suppose it's not sitting since it doesn't have an arse, but it's certainly parked there, and it seems to know that it's the king.

Queen?

Nonbinary royalty?

Fuck, I know nothing about them except that they scare me.

Illogically. The way some people are scared of spiders.

"What's going on with you right now?" Sam asks.

"I'm petrified. I'm reminded of my school trip."

To his credit, he doesn't roll his eyes. "Okay. I want to try something." He looks over my shoulder and swivels his head. Then his voice lowers. "It's just you and me here. No one else." He takes my hand again. "Look at the octopus, take a deep breath, focus on your actual, physical body right now, and tell me what you're feeling. Not what your brain is telling you to think you're feeling. Understand the difference?"

I nod a few times, close my eyes, then open them again.

"I notice my hand in yours, and that feels safe." He squeezes it but doesn't say anything. "This room is cool and feels strange because of all the water. Like the water isn't supposed to be here." I think a moment. "I have this weight in my stomach. No, it's higher than that. Lower than that. Actually, I'm chasing it around. This turbulent, heavy feeling." I focus on the creature in the water in front of me, one of its tentacles waving lazily, like some current is rocking it. "Tightness in my chest. I can breathe, but it's not easy. I don't know how to explain it. I'm not asthmatic. It's more that I have to remind myself to breathe."

"Okay."

"And I'm noticing this squishy creature seems to have these eyes that are … *there*." A shudder racks me. "And tentacles."

"Stay in *your* body."

"Okay, right. My body. My body is …" I start internally scanning my body, starting at my toes. "My feet are fine, and my legs are fine." I close my eyes and grin. "My nether bits and bobs are perked up because you're around," I admit. He squeezes my hand one more time and knocks me playfully with his shoulder but doesn't say anything. "My arms are fine. Hand feels secure. Head?" I pause. "Hmm."

"Hmm?"

"I'm beginning to think the fear isn't in my head but in my torso somewhere."

"In your gut?"

"Yes. But it moves."

"To quote my yoga teacher, what happens if you accept that feeling? Because all feelings want is to be acknowledged. What happens if you let in that tightness in your chest and the roiling in your stomach. Just … let it exist. Don't fight it."

"Don't fight it," I whisper. "That's a good song theme."

"Excellent. I'll remind you of that. But what happens if you truly allow those feelings in?"

"I normally allow in all feelings, love. I'm an artist. I feel things strongly." I hesitate. "But I've been scared of being scared."

His voice is quiet. "We're getting somewhere. Being scared of being scared is a secondary fear. Focus on the first fear. The fear of this octopus."

"Well, he's not really that big. I mean, I've seen larger rats."

"If you had to box him, I think you could win."

"But I don't want to hurt him. Or her. Or it." A wave of understanding washes over me. "I'm so big, and it's so sensitive. I don't want to hurt anyone, and I'm scared of doing precisely that."

Again, Sam doesn't say anything. He just lets me process.

This man.

I close my eyes and focus on my body and realize, "I feel a lightness inside. I never thought I could feel this way. Not here, I mean."

"Good!"

"I feel clean. Like the fears just, I don't know, dissolved."

"Are they still in there somewhere? Is there any part of you that's still afraid?"

"I don't want to touch the octopus."

"Then don't. I wouldn't recommend it. But you can be in the same room?"

"Apparently. More importantly, I can have it in my thoughts. Before, I was scared of *thinking* about an octopus. Is that silly?"

"It's not silly at all. Most fear is in your mind. Unless you're on some adventure and, like, facing a real situation, there are only imaginary octopi. The closest you're getting to one in reality is here, behind a pane of glass. You're safe."

I close my eyes again and nod, feeling bouncy.

I'm also feeling like I want to kiss Sam.

"You make me feel amazing," I admit. "I'm giddy. I walked in here with these irrational fears, and they're just … gone."

"I'm glad. And can you do something with that for a song?"

"Octopi in the mind?"

He nods.

"Absolutely." I drop his hand and pull out my phone, hurrying to take notes. When I'm done, I glance over at Sam, who's waiting patiently for me.

I end up holding his hand as we walk through other exhibits—fish and seahorses and jellyfish and all kinds of sea creatures.

"I don't think I'm ever going to be someone who falls in love with fish," I say. "But I'm okay with being here. Progress."

"Good."

When it's time to leave, we find the security desk, and Sam lets go of my hand. "Back to reality," I murmur. Then I give him a huge smile. I want to hug him tight and kiss him and kiss him and kiss him, and I wish he were available and I could do that. But he isn't, so I can't, even if there were no chance of being caught by security cameras or passersby.

The stab to my chest is physical, and unlike the feelings I just experienced, I don't want to welcome it in.

Once security has let us out and we're on our own again, I look at him. "Thank you. I feel like I treated a wound with peroxide. It still hurts to think about my fears, but I can face them. You did that, Sam Stone. You."

"You're the one who was brave enough to face them," he insists. "How many people will go in a room with spiders or snakes or whatever they're scared of? Not many. I just walked you through it. Now, go see if it encourages you to write anything else for the new album."

"I will. Will you come over again?"

"Sure."

We make arrangements, and with a last look, we separate. He walks to his car. I stride over to my own and get in, fighting an urge to follow him. To call after him, because I want him to be mine.

Maybe that's the fear I should face.

The one of never getting who I really want.

Twenty-Three

Sam

ANOTHER EVENING, ANOTHER POLITICAL EVENT. ANOTHER night of holding Kurt's hand and smiling for the cameras. Another group of rich people, celebrities, and politicos laughing loudly and vying for my grandfather's attention.

Meanwhile, I'm trying to be photographable but not noticeable. That's a weird balance.

I lean over and whisper into Kurt's ear, "How many of these are we expected to go to before the election?" I notice his tie is crooked, so I fix it, and he slips an arm around my waist.

He yawns and then morphs it into a laugh. "All of them. It's not like we have lives."

"No kidding. I have so much to do at work that these extra events mean sleep is a distant memory."

Kurt groans. "Sleep. What's that?"

"Let's go outside for a minute and see if it's quieter," I say, having had enough people walk up to us and say hi. They know us from the ads, but we don't know them. Still, they shake our hands, smile, take selfies.

We keep holding hands as we move and receive a few curious looks.

"What is so interesting about us," he mutters.

"Two men displaying mild affection. Must be something to look at."

"To be fair, I think a lot of het couples aren't affectionate, at least not after the first little while. So anyone showing love is, you know, sweet. Revolutionary."

"If only we were in love."

He shakes his head. "It would make things easier. Too bad it's never happening."

"Nope," I say, popping the P.

As we laugh, my father comes up, drink in hand, gesturing between us. "Keep this up, you two. Dad's polling strongly with the LGBT demographic."

"Yay," I say, trying to make it sound sincere.

Kurt's more enthusiastic. "Mom's leading in the polls. This is so cool."

"Do you have any plans to run for office?" I ask him. He's mentioned it in the past as a concept, but we haven't discussed it recently.

He shrugs. "Yeah. I mean, I've always been interested in politics."

"You think you can handle even more rubber-chicken dinners?"

"We've certainly had plenty of practice, haven't we?"

A major donor comes over, interrupting us. I want to ask Kurt what he would think about us breaking up—er, fake breaking up. But making any changes this early in the election cycle is a bad idea. I have to be perfect. Someone voters can point at and go, "See, gay men aren't scary." As much as I hate that concept.

Besides, it's not like anything is happening with Julian. And nothing *can* happen until he gets the album done.

Best to let sleeping fake relationships lie, so to speak.

I smile and get my picture taken one more time.

The following evening, I recline on a low couch in Jules's studio, watching him close his eyes and belt out a new song. Earlier, I tried accompanying him on the piano but gave that up fast. Now I'm just enjoying the performance. He's giving it his all, like he has a full audience.

But his audience consists of one person: me.

I must be the luckiest man in the world, to receive a private concert by one of the best singers on the planet.

Have you ever sat close to a singer and watched them let loose? His voice makes my arms and spine tingle and my eyes tear up. It's got a depth and resonance, like complex wine or epic poetry, and like anything beautiful, it forces you to *experience* it. Knowing his eyes are closed, I quickly swipe at mine with the backs of my hands.

As I listen, I'm trying not to read too much into the lyrics, because it's a love song … and if I'm his muse, what does it mean?

Something *unnerving*. Something that makes me simultaneously excited and panicked.

And maybe like I've finally found what I've been looking for my entire life: meaning. Julian makes me slow down and pay attention to things I usually gloss over. Life seems richer when he's around, like there's more to it than work and yoga.

Like there's a reason for the things we do and relationships we have.

Emily would tease me if she knew, since I've been such a cynic about love since Asa. While I'm not ready to go draw hearts on the margins of my school papers, I dunno. I feel it. I *feel* what Jules is trying to convey.

Maybe emotions matter more than I've let them.

He runs a hand through his dark hair, and his throat strains as he closes his eyes and hits a high note. It makes me shiver even more, and I'm having trouble keeping it together.

When he finishes, I clap, and he gives me a sheepish grin. "That's beautiful," I say, after gulping and taking a deep breath. "I think you've really got something there." My words feel insufficient to express the feeling of utter love he conveyed—and I experienced—as he sang.

"Thanks." His eyes cut to the side, and my dopamine evaporates.

I feel … alone again.

Maybe emotional manipulation is the name of the game with music. After three minutes of him embodying and projecting deep feelings, once the song is done, we go back to our lives, unaffected until we listen to it again.

But I don't think that's it. Things feel off tonight. Instead of talking with me, Julian steps back, setting his guitar down and reaching for a bottle of water from his little refrigerator.

I can't pinpoint why he's acting this way.

"I'm going to have to give you writing credit," he says amiably after he takes a swig of water.

That makes me smile. "No, you aren't. I haven't written a thing. I'm just sitting here looking pretty."

Now his grin matches mine. "You very much are looking pretty."

Then he frowns, leaving a weird pit in my stomach again.

To move past his mood swings—he's been like this all evening—I note, "It seems like you've made major progress. I'll be sure to keep Lighthouse informed. Got anything else?"

"A few ideas, yeah." A brief smile, and then his face shutters. Once more he's thrown a blanket over himself, dampening the emotions he just expressed so beautifully. Two steps forward and one step back. Or maybe it's one step forward and two steps back.

Worse, he picks up his cell and starts scrolling, dicking around on it, which is something he's *never* done around me. Normally, his phone is barely in sight when we're together, unless he's showing me an article or video or jotting down song ideas. Maybe I'm spoiled, but I've liked the attention he showers on me.

Am I just a brat, or is something going on?

I have to know. I scrub my hand over my face, my emotions all jangly from his song and watching him come forward and retreat, again and again.

"Why are you acting this way?" I blurt, with zero finesse.

"What way?" His careful tone indicates he knows what I mean.

"Cagey. You've never been that way with me. In fact, that's one of the things I like best about you. While you hide your secrets from the world, it's never felt like you hid them when it was just the two of us."

He sets his phone beside him and takes a deep breath, then leans forward, his elbows on his knees. "I guess it's because you're hiding one from me."

I furrow my brows and draw my head back. "What on earth are you talking about?"

His lip curls. "What does your *boyfriend* think about you spending time with me?"

Oh. I don't miss his pained look or the grimace he makes after he says the words.

I scoot closer, grateful he doesn't shy away, and focus wholly on him so he can see my sincerity. His deep brown eyes are as expressive as his voice, and right now they're full of hurt. "Julian. I don't have a boyfriend."

"Then all those articles"—he picks up his phone again and shakes it—"are lying? The ones that show pictures of Sam Stone *with his boyfriend?*"

Of course he's upset. I don't know why I didn't think to tell him about this sooner. I guess at first I didn't think Julian Hill, rock god, would really be interested in me, much less be jealous.

Except this isn't Julian Hill, rock god. This is Jules, who worries about not being enough, not being loved. I close my eyes for a second, realizing I've truly hurt him. I didn't even fathom the need to bring it up, because I know there's nothing between me and Kurt. "I'm sorry, Jules. I should have explained. Kurt Delmont is my *fake* boyfriend. We've been 'dating' for PR purposes for years. We're just friends. I swear it. I'm not— I wouldn't have kissed you if I were with someone else."

Jules blinks at me, and I practically see the wheels turning inside his head, as if at first he doesn't believe me. Then, after a moment, he mutters, "Christ. You're telling me the grandson of the future governor of California has a faux relationship so Fred Stone can parade it in front of the cameras."

I sag back in my chair, nodding. "Our families decided the fiction that we were together was the right narrative, and Kurt and I have gone along with it. But we're not together."

Julian shakes his head. "You're going to have to give me a minute to process this." He chuckles softly. "I guess … now you know how insecure I can be."

I squeeze his hand apologetically, wishing I could kiss him or at least hold him, but knowing I shouldn't. Instead, I give him an arch look. "Julian Hill," I say. "You of all people should know you can't believe everything you read. I mean, if I judged you by your online presence …" I let out a breath like "phew" and fan myself. "Em's mentioned fan fiction about you. I bet that's, um, *different*."

"It can be strange, yes." He scratches at his cheek. "I'm still stuck on the fake boyfriend thing. I'm surprised you'd go along with a scheme like that."

Pressing my lips together in a mirthless smile, I raise my eyebrows and say, "Family."

Jules lifts his chin and studies me, his eyes narrowing. "I understand. I'm just …" He sighs, rubbing his palms over his eyes. "It's hard for me to trust people."

"Yeah," I say quietly. "I bet."

"How long do you have to keep up the charade?"

"Not sure. I haven't raised the issue of breaking up. I mean, I have a life and can do what I want. I agreed to this to help my granddad, but they can't keep me trapped in it forever. Still, I don't want to disrupt anything right now."

Jules cringes.

"Sorry," I say. "That sounds bad." I glance at him. "Once the album is done, if we still want to, you know, move things forward, I'll talk to the campaign about how we can spin a breakup."

He gathers me in his arms, smelling like his rum-vanilla scent plus some kind of pheromone, and kisses the top of my head. "Yes, please."

"Good." I sit back and shake out my shoulders. "I need to change the subject, or my ethical rules are going to be in big trouble. What's a safe topic? Um, what's the most ridiculous fan fiction you've read about yourself?"

He chuckles. "To me it's all ridiculous, but I'm biased. Do a search. You'll find something."

"This should be interesting." I type "Julian Hill fanfic" into my phone.

A long list of results pops up. I choose one and start reading out loud. "Hashtag Julian Hill slays dragons, hashtag ass for days, hashtag shifter …" I scan the notes. "Where's the actual story? Oh." I clear my throat. "'Jules walks through the castle, a devastatingly intense expression on his completely gorgeous and perfect face. He turns around, and we can see his assless chaps. "Come here, dragon. I'm waiting for you," he growls.'" I snort. "Oh my Gaga."

Julian nudges me with his shoulder. "Right?"

"And aren't all chaps assless?"

"As far as I know."

Clicking out of that page, I follow the hashtags and am staggered by the number of stories. "You seem so chill about all of this. Has it ever been an issue for someone you were dating?"

"No, because I don't date."

I set my phone down and stare at him. "You don't?"

"Nope."

"Why not?"

He reddens. It might be the first time I've ever seen him blush. "A few reasons. There's always the issue of why someone wants to be with me: is it because they really care about me, or do they want the money or the publicity or whatever. On the flip side of that, it's hard to date me, because whoever it is will be in the public eye and picked apart by fans and the media. Even if I thought my partner was the best thing that ever happened to me, someone out there would express the opinion that they weren't, which can be hurtful. Add in the fact that I want to keep matters of the heart just for me—to keep some things private—and …" He shrugs. "Plus, I'm busy. Touring and appearances take a lot out of me. Either I'm gone or I'm tired, and there's nothing of me left for someone else." Then his voice lowers, and it makes *me* blush. "Most importantly, I'd never found anyone I wanted badly enough to make it worth the trouble. Someone I wanted to spend the whole day with and then all night and then repeat it the next day. Someone like you."

"Oh," I say, breathless. "I'm amazed that you feel that way about me."

He reaches out and traces my jaw. "I do. We could consider what we're doing dating, if you wanted. Just with no, you know, shagging until the album's done."

"Pretty sure dating's against the rules."

"Pretty sure we're pushing the rules."

"Yeah," I say quietly. "We are."

He squeezes my shoulder. "Look, if what we're saying or doing is getting too close to that limit for you, we can take a step back."

"I know. I appreciate that." I stare down at my feet, then look back at him. "I don't want to stay away from you."

"Me neither."

We pause, gazing at each other. My knee rubs against his. He takes my hand, and we sit quietly for a moment.

Finally, I speak up. "Part of me thinks this ethical rule sucks and we're being tortured for no reason. First, I'm a professional and would never hurt my client. If I thought being with you wasn't in their best interest, I wouldn't be here. In fact, I think our ... friendship, relationship, whatever you want to call it helps them—or, at least, thinking that helps me soothe the ethics beast. But second, perspective: we're very lucky to have found each other. And this gives us a trial dating period without the pressure of going out."

"You're aware we've been out in public multiple times."

"You know what I mean."

He gives me one of his private smiles. It's smaller than the one he flashes for the cameras, but no less sincere, and it makes a rare dimple appear.

"I'd love to get to know you better," I say. "But I feel foolish. Everything I want to ask I could probably find out in a deep Google search."

"No." He shakes his head. "Not true. I hold things back."

"I also don't want to be all, 'Jules, what's your favorite color?'"

"Turquoise." Again, that secret smile.

"I could have figured that out by googling, though, right?"

"No. I usually say black. Because I like it, too." He gestures down at his black T-shirt and black jeans. "It's easier to have a pat answer that's true, even if it's only part of the story, than to give a long explanation of what I feel deep down."

"That's interesting."

"My current favorite color is actually—and forgive me—the color of your eyes."

I blush again. "Um."

"Sorry," he says. "Didn't mean to embarrass you. What's *your* favorite color?"

"Orange," I say, flopping back in my seat. "I know a lot of people don't like it. But I like a burnt orange. Like sunsets and goldfish and California poppies."

"Sam likes orange. I wouldn't have guessed. Can I ask more questions?"

I make a "Go ahead" gesture.

He gets a mischievous look in his eyes and raises one eyebrow. "When's the first time you kissed a boy?"

My heart rate kicks up. "So we're going there? Okay." I tap my finger on my knee. "In college." *Asa.* "I knew I was gay before that, but I didn't have the opportunity. The only gay guys at my school weren't into me, nor I into them. I ended up dating him, and then no one really until Kurt. Can I ask you the same question?"

He nods. "I kissed a boy behind the caf in secondary school."

"And he hasn't sold his story?"

"He's my best mate. He'll never tell."

"Do I need to watch out for this 'best mate'?" I do air quotes.

"No," he says with a stroke of his finger on my thigh. "James is like your Kurt. No chemistry but lots of friendship."

Chemistry. That's what I feel with Jules. Like he and I react to form something new and better and different. Something *more*.

"Be good," I say, putting a hand over his and stilling it. "Otherwise this isn't going to work." I'm noticing how close we are. How our legs are touching and I could be in his lap in one move.

His voice gets husky. "I want us to work."

And he's just so … *here*. Sexy-haired and rich-voiced. Sweet and kind and giving me a chance to explain. Seeing the best parts of me.

He wakes me up and makes me want things I've never had.

I stare at his lips.

"I want to kiss you," I murmur, not wanting to pull away and not letting myself move forward. "Even though we shouldn't. For so many reasons."

Jules's expression goes mischievous, and he strokes his chin with one hand as if he's got a real beard rather than stubble. "While we can think of all the reasons why we should *not*, it's a lot more fun to think of the reasons *to*."

"To kiss?"

"Yes." His eyes are intent on mine.

"And those are?"

He swivels his chest so he's facing me fully and centers himself, his face serious. Then he takes a deep breath. "Because you're so sexy I feel like I'm going to explode when I'm around you. Because I'm so fucking attracted to you that nothing else makes sense except to kiss you. And because I like the way you smell and taste and feel."

Whatever blush I had going on is now increased in density and volume. Just like my dick.

"We need to stop," I say, starting to move away. "Because I agree, but that doesn't change the ethical issues. You need to finish the album."

"Right."

I look at my hands.

He lifts my chin up with a knuckle. "Sam. This whole album is foreplay."

Bless us, Baby Spice, it so *is.* "Am I going to have this reaction every time I hear it?" I gesture to my lap.

The smirk returns. "Hopefully?"

Fuck it.

We've done this before. What's once more?

I lean in and kiss him. It's more than a peck, but we're not tangling tongues. It's just … a real kiss. A kiss that says *Thank you* and *You're amazing* and …

He kisses back. Holds me behind my neck and pulls me to him, then breaks away and groans. Against my lips, he says, "I absolutely love kissing you."

"I'm forgetting all the reasons why we shouldn't do this," I admit. "It feels right."

"When I finish this album," he murmurs, "we're going to continue this."

"That's all I want," I say. He reaches over and kisses me again, and it's a dangerous kiss, full of promises and still not enough.

Twenty-Four

Jules

The next morning, I lie in bed humming. After Sam left, I jotted down another song. Before I can go down to my studio to flesh it out, my phone buzzes with a text from James.

> **Winterthorn**: How goes the celestial life, star?
>
> **Jules**: Hi, nice to hear from you James
>
> **Jules**: Can I call you?
>
> **Winterthorn**: Like, on the phone?
>
> **Jules**: Yes, an actual telephone call
>
> **Winterthorn**: Are you secretly 96 years old?
>
> **Jules**: <bald old man emoji>
>
> **Winterthorn**: Oh all right

I hit the button, and he answers immediately, his accent sounding like home. "Have they figured you out yet?"

Typical. James always launches immediately into whatever it is he's thinking about. Sometimes it takes a moment to catch up.

The sun streams into the room, and I yawn. "Figured out what?"

"That you're actually lip-synching, and your drummer is the real talent."

I laugh and roll over on my bed, noticing how empty it is, so I get up and start pacing. "How are you, Jamie?"

He lets out a loud, put-upon sigh. "So many signs. So little time."

"Nothing's changed, then?"

"Only the venue."

"Good to know."

I went to comprehensive school with James, so he knew me before everything. When I became famous, people either dropped me, assuming I was too busy to see them—often I was—or tried to get close in a way that felt fake. Jamie's never been like that.

He's also a delinquent inspired by Banksy. I think he's made it his mission to leave no sign in the world without his Felix the Cat stencil.

Yes, my best friend's a street artist. A tagger.

While I know him from the UK, he now lives about a half-day drive up the California coast. Some distant relative left him a mechanic's shop, and he spends his days fixing cars and his nights tagging redwoods or tall bushes or something. I don't know what's up there for him to spray-paint. But he keeps me grounded and reminds me where I'm from.

He was also that first kiss I told Sam about.

"What's on your mind, oh famous one?" he asks. "Why did you want to chat so early in the morning?"

I pause and run my fingers over my bare belly. "I think I met someone."

He immediately perks up. "Did you really? This is news. Tell Uncle Jamie everything."

Plopping down on a chair and looking out at the beach, I contemplate how to tell him about Sam. "Where to start?"

"Boy or girl? A bit of both?" Jamie's the only one who knows my preferences.

I grin. "Boy."

"Go on."

"I like him," I admit.

"Does he like you?"

I watch the waves crash outside, the Pacific Ocean immense and blue and fathomless. "I think, yes."

"Then, no problem. Next topic."

He makes me laugh. "You know things are never that easy."

"A man can hope. What's up?"

"This man is really kind to me. He's also somewhat familiar with being in the spotlight, and he doesn't seem to give a flying fuck about my fame or money."

"All promising."

"But I can't date him because his law firm represents Lighthouse Records. And they're a wee bit peeved with me because I've taken so long to write the new album."

"How peeved?"

"I'm on a short leash now. Naught but bread and water for forty days."

"Ah, you'll get it done, drama queen. You always do." James snorts. "I can't get over the name of your label. You should come up here and see my friend's lighthouse."

"Is that some sort of euphemism?"

"No. I mean a literal lighthouse." He makes an interested humming noise. "So you've got a thing for a man with a briefcase. Never knew that was your type."

"Bow ties, actually. Although, come to think of it, he probably has a briefcase, too."

"Bow ties, plural, *and* a briefcase. Sounds deadly dull. Are you sure this fellow has any passion in him?"

"If the way he kisses means anything—"

James screeches. "Hold the phone. You kissed the lawyer for your label? You rock and roll bad boy, you."

"Piss off," I mutter.

"You know I won't tell your sordid tales." He pauses, and his tone gets serious. "But it's not like you to date. You must really like him."

"I do."

"And there's another problem," I say. "Or complication, anyhow."

"And that is?"

"He's sort of dating someone else."

"Jules! Are you the cheating bastard in this scenario, or is he? Because neither looks or sounds good."

I clear my throat. "Neither one of us is cheating. We're not actually dating, and he's only fake dating."

"That's perfectly clear. Thanks for the explanation."

James makes me chuckle. "His position is such that it helps his family with the press if he's seen being photographed with another bloke. So they've pretended to be a couple for years. But apparently they really are not."

The sharpness in James's voice surprises me. "Fucking hell, Julie. I can't believe you bought that line."

"I don't think it's a line. I trust him."

"Why?"

That gives me pause. "I guess … because I do."

"Ah. Sound logic. But can you really?"

I sigh. "How do I know if I can trust anyone? I can't. He gives me a good feeling, though." And I have to start somewhere. Might as well be with Sam, who has given me every indication it's okay to do so.

It's like James's shrug is audible. "Whatever you say. If you think this isn't a recipe for disaster, then I'll support you. But I may say 'I told you so' if you end up all angry and hurt because it was you he was faking out and not the general public. So. What are you going to do?"

"Finish the album and then pounce."

"Are you sure you'll be ready for a public relationship, even if the album's done?"

I sigh. Here's where it gets tricky. "I don't know. I hate to live my life for the fans, but I'm kidding myself if I say I'm not considering their reaction."

"There's only, what, eleventy billion or so that follow you on TikTok." His tone gets thoughtful. "That's a lot for you to handle. And what about him? You say he's familiar with publicity?"

"Yeah, he's from a political family."

"That's not the same thing as your fame."

"It's not, but it is in some ways. He knows what it's like to face the press and answer questions. I think he could handle it. But what if we get together and they tear him apart?"

"Isn't that a decision for him to make, not you? It's not like you hide your fame. If he can't figure out that being with you will make him a hashtag, then he's not the right one."

"He's smart enough to predict what will happen. It's more that I don't know how he'll handle it when it actually does happen."

"There's only one way to find out."

"And if it's a disaster?"

"Then it's a disaster," James says. "But it sounds like you kind of want him anyway."

"More than kind of."

"Then suit yourself. Finish your album, then go snog your briefcase man." James pauses, concern in his voice. "He's not using you, though, is he?"

What if Sam is part of some diabolical plan by Lighthouse to make me … make me … write an album? No. That doesn't make any sense. I believe in his sincerity. "If he had pic after pic on social media of himself on different people's yachts"—like Colin—"then I'd be worried. But he doesn't self-promote." His family does that for him. "He doesn't even have social media. At least none that I could find."

Not that I searched that hard. Social media makes me ill.

"Good." I can hear James's smile. "You sound happy. I'm pleased for you. I hope things work out."

"Me, too, James. Me, too."

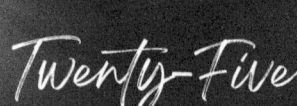

Jules

"Jules," Stu says, flipping through the sheet music and printouts of lyrics, "this is incredible."

I cock my head and scrunch my nose. "Not sure about that."

Despite my blasé words, his positive reaction is a huge relief. I get really vulnerable with these guys when I start new material, and I know they'll be supportive but honest.

We're in the fishbowl of one of Lighthouse Records' recording studios to work on the album. I look around, thinking about the countless famous musicians who have recorded here. A huge mixing board dominates the next room.

It's midafternoon, and we'll probably be here all night. Right now we're still fresh and enthusiastic. I played them what I've written, and now I'm receiving judgment.

Stu picks a bass line and grins. "No, it's incredible. I don't want to fight you about it, but I will if necessary."

That makes me smile. "Thanks, mate."

I'm perched on a stool behind a microphone, but I'm eyeing an ugly couch off to the side. I'm going to be spending most of my time for the foreseeable future in this place, so I might as well get comfortable. I wander over and flump down to watch my band tinker with arrangements.

Mitch peers at me from behind the drums. "Where did you come up with all this? You've tapped into something deep."

"I've got a new muse," I say, crossing one boot on top of the other. Again, I'm more pleased than I want to show.

"A new muse? Who?" Lizzie asks.

"A man," I say vaguely.

No one raises an eyebrow. They know that I've gotten together with guys before, and they can be trusted to keep their mouths shut. I have to be able to trust them; they're some of the people with the most access to me.

"Sounds pretty serious if you're willing to talk about him," Mitch notes, then hits the cymbals. Perfect timing.

I gulp and nod. "He is. I like him more than I like most people. And I tend to like people a lot."

They all laugh, and the producer gives us a signal that they're ready to begin rehearsals.

"Shall we start on 'Three Dots'?" I ask.

Everyone nods, and I pick up the guitar and start strumming. Mitch taps out the beat on the drums. I'm getting an excited, anticipatory feeling about this project.

It might actually work.

"What if we add in a riff like this, here?" Stu says and plays a few catchy chords.

"Yes!" I say. "Let's go with that."

Lizzie and Janice harmonize with me on the refrain, and it sounds so awesome, I might weep.

We spend the next several weeks in the studio, messing around, recording and rerecording lyrics, working on arrangements. The musicians and mixers and techs and producers are all magnificent, talented folks, and some of them come up with new melodies on the fly. With each song we get down, with each layered track, with each lyric, I get closer and closer to my goals.

Getting the stress of the contract off my back.

Feeling accomplished and creative.

And maybe, just maybe, being able to have someone in my life just for me.

Soon, I'll be well and truly done with this album.

That gives me a pang in my chest, because now that I'm into it, I remember that I like the process of writing and recording.

But I think I like the possibility of being with Sam Stone more.

Twenty-Six

Sam

Jules saunters toward me, a huge smile on his face. He's wearing a white dress shirt that has only one button done up—wait, that's my shirt—and little white shorts with blue octopi on them.

How did I not know he has sexy knees? He has the sexiest knees. His legs are lean and perfectly proportioned.

"Sam?" Jules says, and my heart rate increases, all these feelings coming to me. Not because of his knees, but because he's so lovely.

"Sam!"

I jerk to attention.

Terrill is standing in the doorway of my office, folding his arms over his chest. I'm embarrassed at being caught daydreaming, particularly because I can tell this isn't a friendly chat. He wants something.

I blink, trying to clear my head.

"So, what's he like?" he asks.

I furrow my brows. "What is who like?"

"Jules Hill."

I bite the inside of my cheek to keep from reacting visibly. He doesn't know what I've been imagining. Or doing. "You met him."

"I met him in a controlled environment. You're getting a better feel for him." He's right about that. "Do you think he's bullshitting us about getting the album done?"

"No. He's working."

"He came to visit you a while back."

"Yeah," I say. "He wanted to check in and show me the progress," I lie. Because saying he wanted to give me back my pocket square seems weird.

"Why couldn't he just text?"

Not showing you those. "Maybe he doesn't trust the internet. Maybe he was in the neighborhood. Maybe he thought a face-to-face meeting would be more effective. I don't know. I didn't ask."

Terrill looks thoughtful. "Has he come here again?"

"No. But I've met him at his house and a few places for, um, work."

His expression turns mean. "Uh-huh. He's like you, right? He's gay?"

I bristle. "I have no idea." *More like, it's none of your business.*

"So why does he wear women's clothes? Lace and shit."

"They're not women's clothes. They're Jules's clothes. He's very fashionable."

He rolls his eyes. "Uh-huh."

What's with the casual bigotry? "It's not like what he wears reflects on you."

"It's just weird."

I'm one joke short of getting sexually harassed. Terrill never quite crosses that line, because he knows as well as I do what is legal and what is not. But it's clear he doesn't like me and that my sexuality threatens him.

Tool.

"Whatever," Terrill says. "Just make sure we get an album out of him."

"I will." I get up from my desk. "I'm going to grab a bite."

A short elevator ride later, I'm standing in line at Southwinds Coffee, which has a branch in my building's underground mall. The shop was founded by some surfer, and he's opened up a bunch of them. Their drinks beat any other brew I've found.

As I wait my turn, I try not to be frustrated at the time I'm not billing. But I suppose if I work on emails while I'm in line, then I can bill.

I pull out my phone.

Two guys get in line behind me. One is tall, confident, and Latino, with a sharp fade haircut and a square jaw. Totally handsome. The other's shorter, more delicate, and White, with blond hair and a face kind of like Colin Jost's.

"I can't believe Anderson ruled against us!" the taller guy says.

"I know," the shorter one groans. "I mean, we can appeal—Velvet has deep enough pockets. But I really thought Anderson was our best chance."

I subtly turn to get a closer look at the guys and realize I know who they are: August Ramirez and Noah Weston, the founders of a well-known local firm that specializes in LGBTQIA+ causes.

And they represent Velvet? As in my favorite porn star?

Cool.

"Anderson's known for making some wild-ass rulings these days," I volunteer.

They turn to me. "You've appeared before him?"

"Yeah. I filled in for a partner recently and watched his whole morning calendar. I don't think many people left his courtroom happy. Others in my firm had similar experiences."

"Pretty hard to piss off both sides in a lawsuit," August says.

"I know, right?"

I turn back to the counter because it's my turn to order, but I really want to ask him and Noah if they're hiring. I didn't know they were in this building. But, in a building this big, I don't know all the firms—just the major ones. Noah and August's firm is a boutique.

I make a note to myself to start scouring their website for their hiring partner.

Jules

AFTER A PARTICULARLY LONG DAY OF RECORDING—following several days of marathon sessions—I'm knackered. I stumble into my house, grungy and worn out. My vocal cords need a break, and my brain is tired from working relentlessly on lyrics. I dunno where my brother is, but I'm glad the house seems empty.

Checking my phone, I see that both James and Sam texted me earlier. I check James's first because I want to savor Sam's.

Winterthorn: What's going on with the album?

Jules: Almost done

Winterthorn: When can I hear it?

Jules: Buy a copy like everyone else

Winterthorn: Pouts

I grin and rub my face, then yawn, turning to Sam's text.

Sam: I hope recording is still going well.

Jules: The shape of it, yeah. It's not complete rubbish. And it feels good to be singing something new

Sam: Does it frighten you to write and sing songs about your fears? Or does it feel like you're letting the fears go?

Jules: Both

> **Jules**: Nervous energy that I transform into music and it makes me feel better

What I don't text is that it also makes me horny. I don't know why that is, except that I'm expressing so much emotion, maybe I need a different kind of release.

This is why groupies exist. Because there's a high from performing, which translates to the need to keep it going.

Except that I don't want to go find *someone*. I want one man. Him.

My phone buzzes.

> **Sam**: I'm so glad! Not just that you're getting work done on the album, but that you're transforming your vision into something that we can all experience.

Holding my phone, I look at his name and the contact photo I snapped of him, all sweet with his bow tie and golden hair.

I want to experience *him*.

But that's not possible ... yet.

So it's me and my hand. I'm so tempted to text him something sexy.

Walking into the bathroom, I take off my clothes and turn on the shower. As I wait for the water to warm up, I take a photo of me making a face. Only I'm standing in front of the mirror, so you can see the back of my head, tilted up, my entire bare back, and my arse.

I shouldn't send this. I should not. I never sext, because it can end up in the wrong hands.

But Sam feels like the right hands. Because he's soon to be mine, once we work through all the shite in our way.

Also, I'm seeing space on my back that needs a tattoo.

Sod it.

> **Jules**: Thanks for all your help. Gotta get cleaned up now
>
> **Jules**: Found a spot for a new tattoo. See attached photo
>
> **Jules**: <picture>

Three dots appear after the read receipt, and I hold my breath. Then they disappear. Then they appear again.

I start humming the song I wrote about those dots, because bloody hell, what's he thinking? Did I just make a colossal mistake?

Finally, his text comes through before I go around the bend.

> **Sam**: David Bowie in heaven, that is the sexiest picture I've ever seen.
>
> **Jules**: Even with my tongue sticking out?
>
> **Sam**:
>
> **Sam**: Sorry, I hit send by accident. I don't know what else to say but: can you please finish the album very fast? I want
>
> **Sam**: AGAIN, I hit send too fast.
>
> **Sam**: I want you.
>
> **Jules**: You have me

I toss the phone on the counter and step into the shower. Hot water cascades over my head and my shoulders, my cock already hard from thinking about Sam and his gorgeous, peach-like arse that he showcases in perfectly tailored trousers. And his kind smile. I would like to do a lot of things with and to that smile.

I like his elegant fingers and efficient movements. I like the way he bites his lower lip when he thinks. And when he tries not to smile or show his emotions. And even more when he ends up showing them to me anyway.

I spread a dab of shower gel in my hands and start shuttling up and down my hard cock, enjoying the slick lather and scent.

Fuck, that feels good. It makes my abs tighten and my arse clench.

Will I ever be able to enjoy a shower with him?

Will Sam ever send me a sexy pic? Or video call?

That makes me harder, thinking of Sam jostling the phone, slowly letting it pan down, down, down his body until I get to see his hard dick.

I want that.

Even though it's dangerous, because someone could hack my photos.

Sometimes I just want a normal life. Is that too much to ask for?

At the Fly by Night show, I got dizzy seeing him shirtless, his shorts low on his narrow hips. He says he does yoga, and you can tell—his body is toned and lean.

Does that mean he's flexible?

I grimace from pleasure.

The waterfall shower casts a wide spray over my body. It's an extravagance in drought-ridden California, so I installed a rainwater recapture system along with the solar panels. That makes me feel better about taking my time in here, but I'm still lonely. I want someone next to me. I want to live my life with the kind of passion Sam ignites in me.

My hand moves faster. With the one that was propping me up against the wall, I start fondling my balls, then press a finger under my taint.

Sodding hell.

I come, fast, whispering "Sam" into the shower's spray.

After a few pulsing pumps of release, I'm quivering but relaxed.

What we're doing is all normal.

I can handle it.

I hope I'm telling the truth.

Twenty-Eight

Sam

MY HEART IS BEATING FAST—IN A BAD WAY.

I'm reading an email from an attorney representing the other side of a transaction, and it's like he goes through life trying to be a professional pain in the ass instead of solving problems.

When I get shit like this, I have to process. If I snap back with my emotions, it will escalate, and I prefer to solve problems, not cause them.

I need a distraction.

As always, Julian pops into my head. My favorite distraction.

I can't pull up his text from last night while I'm at work, though. Holy shit, there's no way his tattoo status—or gorgeous ass—is ending up in a progress report. So I end up typing his name into a browser search bar. Recent articles pop up talking about his appearance at Fly by Night, rumors of him recording, an appearance at some function or other, and how "Hill Frolics in the Sand" outside his house—complete with photos of Jules in a bathing suit.

He really has no privacy.

I scrutinize the beach pic, feeling only a tiny bit guilty. Hundreds of thousands of other people have looked at it, after all. He was wearing yellow shorts and a floppy hat, but there's no hiding that it's him. Not with all those tattoos. You can tell it's him from just a thumbnail.

And oh, that photo is number four trending on Twitter.

Now begin the memes and the comments.

WHEN WILL HE MARRY ME?

OMG JULES PLEASE

No wonder he wants to keep some things to himself if his fans scrutinize his every outfit, expression, word. If they take his actions and make them into videos—with commentary.

As if he heard me thinking about him, my cell phone rings, and my pulse speeds up even more.

"Jules?"

"Sam. Hey." I want to bathe in his luxurious accent.

"Can I help you?"

A pause. "No, you can't help me. I was just thinking about you."

One of the most famous men in the world is thinking about me.

"That makes me smile," I say. "And it definitely improves my day."

"Oh? What's wrong with your day?"

I mutter, "You don't want to hear about it."

"Now, there's where you're wrong. I do."

"Really?" I can't help the wistful tone in my voice. I click out of the photos and clear my browser history.

"Really. If you need me, I want to be there for you."

"God, you're sweet. I'm frustrated at work. I don't understand why people have to be assholes. It doesn't achieve anything. It doesn't make me want to help them more or let them get their way. It's just a way to have power or to ruin someone's day."

Jules doesn't say anything for a moment. Then he clears his throat. "I'm listening, Sam."

"I worked so hard for so many years to become a lawyer, and a good one. I got into great schools and passed the bar, and now I'm at this firm … and it's not what I thought it would be like."

"How so?"

"I thought I'd be doing things that were more intellectually challenging. Or more based on the actual law. Instead, I'm having to manage people."

"Like me."

"Not like you, Jules. Like opposing counsel. Some of my coworkers. And my boss."

"Well, he's an arsehole. Even I can see that."

I chuckle, and his simple empathy loosens a fist that's been constricting around my chest.

Jules continues, "I know it's been a decade since I've had a real job—thank you, Tesco—but I understand what it's like to have to please other people. And also how getting to the top doesn't feel quite like what you thought it would feel like when you were on the way up."

"That's exactly it," I say quietly. "It's bait and switch. I expected to wear a suit and participate in reasoned debate and intellectual conversations on cutting-edge subjects. Instead, I spend my days listening to my boss swear about how our clients aren't paying him enough. Even though we just jacked up our rates. Again." I rub my hand over my face. "Sorry. I don't mean to complain."

"Sam." His voice gets this sexy sternness to it. "If we're going to have a relationship, I want to know everything. You can complain. Let me know how you truly feel. I'll try to help if that's what you want, and I'll listen if that's what you want."

"You're so nice."

"It's my pleasure." A pause. "Is there something you want me to do about your job?"

"Just distract me from it."

"I can do that."

I shift in my chair, my voice dropping. "You are *very* good at that."

"So, perhaps, let's go do something. Like, um, mini golf."

I snort. "What?"

"There's a course and arcade a ways up from my house. Let's go."

"You want to play miniature golf." I shake my head.

"Yes."

How can one word sound so alluring?

"With me?" I ask.

"Yes."

I look around to see if I'm being pranked, but Jules's voice is so sincere, I know I'm not. "Do you have a fear of golfing?"

"Uh, no."

"How does this fit on your 'facing your fears' album?"

"It doesn't." His smooth, confident voice makes me feel all kinds of anticipation. "But I could make it relate. Maybe I want to scope out locations for a video."

He's asking me out on a date. With no pretense of it being related to the album.

"Okay," I say. Because there's nothing else I can say.

A laugh bubbles out of him and across the phone speaker. "You will?" Then he coughs. "Excellent."

"Will it be a time when it's closed, again?" I click on my calendar.

"Yes. A weeknight. Will that be okay for you?"

If I have to miss yoga, I will. "I'll make it work."

"Wonderful. See you then."

"Oh, and Jules?"

"Yes?"

"How's the album coming?" I should ask, for work. And I *want* to know, for … not work.

"We have ten tracks down and being mixed. We might record another song or two, but it's getting close to done."

And then the fun begins. In the meanwhile, I have a résumé to polish and a cover letter to draft.

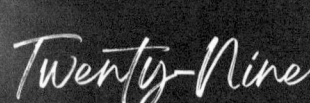

Sam

Emily flops down on my couch and toys with my remote as the first scene of *Dunkirk* begins. She knows I line everything up on the coffee table at right angles, so she's doing it to mess with me.

I'm not compulsive about neatness. It just soothes me to have things be in order. I shake my head, because what are friends for except to mess with you when you need to be messed with?

She narrows her eyes at me. "You've been MIA."

"No. I've been out with Julian when I'm not at work," I admit. "To lunch. To an aquarium. To his house."

"You're dating him." It's a gentle accusation.

"I can't be dating him. This is all related to getting his album done. It's my job to help him make that happen."

Emily crosses her arms. "Have you slept with him?"

"*No*," I say, matching her crossed arms.

She gets a knowing look in her eyes and raises an eyebrow. "Have you kissed him again?"

I sigh and pick up the remote.

"I knew it," she crows and claps her hands.

I turn the TV off. We've seen this movie a dozen times anyway.

"I knew it!" she repeats.

"You know nothing."

"I knew you were looking for love. I knew you *needed* love. All your bullshit about it not solving problems was just your fear." She leans back on the cushions, her fingers forming a steeple.

I smooth my hands down my thighs. "Yes, Em, you said that, and yes, I have feelings for him that frankly frighten me, because I can't sort them out. We're not even really together. Am I just bowled over by his charisma, like millions of his fans? Or do we genuinely like each other?"

"I think it's real," she assures me, tapping my leg. "It might be the only real thing you've ever done."

"What's that supposed to mean?"

"Your whole life, you've lived to be respectable and accepted by other people, but you haven't ever once stopped to consider how you feel. Take dating. You and Kurt like each other just fine, so it hasn't been a hardship. But it's fake, and if you don't try to make things work with Julian, you'll be cheating yourself from what could be the most fulfilling relationship of your life."

I throw up my hands. "Or it could be nothing. Julian could be using me for my ... muse-iness."

"That's not a word."

"Well, what do you call being his muse? And if that's all I am, then when the album is done, or when he stops getting ideas from me, he'll want to move on." I bite my lip. "He'll want to find new inspiration."

Emily squeezes my knee. "Is that really what you think he's going to do? Because if it is, you should stop now."

"No," I admit, standing up, then sitting back down again. "It isn't. I think we're enormously attracted to each other, and I can barely explain it except that it's real, I feel it, and I want more of it *all the time*."

"See? Then this is all good."

"If you say so." I stare down at my feet.

"Why did you just get all sad panda there?"

"Thinking about my job being an obstacle to us getting together reminds me of all the other things I don't like about it. I think I need to find another one."

"Excellent. Your boss is a blowhard; I never understood why

you put up with him to begin with. Let me know if you want me to proofread your résumé."

"I did see some attorneys in my building from a firm I'm interested in, so that's something. I hate leaving, though. I don't want to abandon Jules to someone else at the firm. They're assholes." I groan and scrub my face. "God, saying that is disloyal to them, and I have a duty of loyalty to my firm and my clients. I'm gonna get fired."

"You're not getting fired. Don't forget, your client is getting a better product from Julian if he's inspired to write."

"I guess."

"You're just in this weird phase where you're getting to know one another, but you can't actually see if you're physically or romantically compatible because that would be a violation of a bunch of lawyer crap."

"Thanks," I say. "Lawyer crap. Way to minimize my existence down to two words."

She shrugs. "I'm simplifying. After he turns in his album and you're free to move about the cabin, then you can go on to the next phase: getting to know if all these feelings and impulses you have toward each other actually are something or just the thrill of the forbidden."

"I don't think it's that last one. I didn't think he was forbidden when he kissed me the first time. It totally slipped my mind. So I wasn't like, oh, I'm not supposed to do this, let me do it anyway. It more just … *happened*."

Her face slackens as she tries to picture it. Then she blinks and shakes herself. "Fuck, that's hot."

I grin. "I didn't mention it before, but you may have noticed. Julian Hill is really, really attractive."

She shoves me gently. "No kidding. I saw him first. I listened to him first."

"And there's gonna be more music. Any day now, he's going to finish the new album and turn it in. Then we're going to be able to figure out who we are to each other when we don't have to hold back."

Emily closes her eyes and sighs. "That's so exciting. I want to watch."

"No fucking way."

"Yeah, that sentence sounded way less pervy in my head." She snickers. "I didn't mean it like that. I want you to have your privacy. I'm just so happy that you seem to be finding a real love life instead of this fiction that you've perpetrated for years."

"It's not fiction. It's just … what we did."

"You need to break up with Kurt."

"I will." I sigh. "I have to find a way to broach it to him and the campaign."

"No one except you and your partner should have that much input into your love life," she insists.

"Yeah, I know. But it's just political positioning. It has nothing to do with my real feelings."

"And you're finding out that you can't actually live without love."

My gaze flicks upward. "Plenty of people do."

"But is that how you, Sam, want to live?"

It isn't. After meeting Julian, I'm realizing that not every entertainer is like Asa. Julian surprises me at every turn with the way he isn't into traditional rock star activities like partying and drugs. I like the way I am with him and the way he makes me feel. And he tells me the feeling's mutual.

I shake my head. "I want to try and see what it's like. The possibility of love."

Glancing from side to side, I note the world does not appear to have ended.

She gasps and holds her fist to her mouth, her eyes shining, then fans her cheeks with her hands. "I never thought I'd see the day."

"Me, either."

I don't know whether I'm scared or hopeful. Or both.

Thirty

Jules

I walk next to Sam at the arcade while the manager points out the Skee-Ball machines. We're visiting under the ruse that I might film a music video here, so we nod politely as if we couldn't see the games just as well on our own. I'm not-so-surreptitiously taking video of Sam as we walk around.

This place, with an ancient arcade, a miniature golf course, and dodgem cars, smells like spilled beer, buttered popcorn, and candy floss. It's dingy and grimy and run-down.

I love it.

It's past sunset, and most of the property's lights are off, although we can see the grounds. Loren paid for us to have the whole place for the evening, so there's a skeleton crew but no other patrons.

"We can arrange for tickets to come out," the manager says, "if you want a practical effect. Or I suppose you can do it digitally."

"I'll check with tech," I say. "Do you mind if we play a round of golf? Since we're here?"

"We're actually doing this?" Sam asks.

"Would you like me to get putters and balls?" the manager asks.

"Absolutely."

He trots off.

"It's good to see you," I say, leaning over to whisper in Sam's ear.

"You, too."

"Even if this is not the way I want you to see my balls." I rub my hand over my face, hiding my grin.

"Ha ha. Yes. Me, too. I can't believe you went there." In the dim light, I can't tell if he's blushing. I think he is. "But there's truth in it."

The manager returns and hands us the equipment, then shows us to the first hole. "Do you want me to turn on the rest of the lighting?"

I shake my head. "We can make out the course. Better to not draw attention to ourselves."

"Whatever you like," he says. "Take your time. Just let me know when you're done." He turns and heads back to the office.

I smile. "Shall we begin?"

"Hit the ball through the windmill. Then it will roll down the hill and right into the little cup." Sam gestures helpfully at the large windmill that is part of this challenging hole.

"Like that's easy," I mutter.

"Just don't pound it," he warns. "You have to use some finesse."

Steadying the putter between my hands, I line up like I'm some famous golfer and attempt to hit the thing straight. To my surprise, it misses the windmill blades, passes under the fake building, and goes where it's supposed to go.

Sam grins and gives me a high five. "You're a natural."

"Pretty sure I'm not."

"I'm not, either." Sam lines up and swings. The ball bounces, hits the windmill with a *donk*, and ricochets back to us, and I snicker.

"It's not as easy as you made it seem," he grumbles, picking up his ball and repositioning it on the mat at the start of the hole.

"Let me show you, love." I come up behind him, and he feels so snuggly, I can't help grinding against him before I reach my arms around his hips and guide his movements.

Sam shudders, and I lean into him.

He hits the ball again, and this time it goes into the shrubbery.

I try not to react, but then we look at each other and start laughing so hard we both double over.

My phone chimes with a familiar ringtone, and my face drops.

"What's wrong?"

"It's my brother." I don't answer the call. "I'll talk to him later."

Sam opens his mouth to ask, I'm sure, and then closes it.

Giving me privacy.

And for that, I want to tell him every single thing about me.

"Since Colin moved in, he's been a problem. He's asked me for money. He doesn't seem to be trying to find a job. He's estranged from his wife." I rub my face. "I worry about him."

"What's he calling you for now?"

"No clue. But it's never to ask about me. Not really."

"I'm sorry."

I glance at him. "Colin's been jealous of me ever since we both tried out for that talent show. I got on, and it launched my career—and he didn't make the cut. Not many people know that."

"I can see how that would be hard. For both of you."

"Do you ever get frustrated with your family? Feel that they've just asked for one too many things?"

"All the time."

"Yeah," I say. "You go to so many events for them. What would happen if you declined to go to one?"

Sam blanches. "I mean, I could." He looks at me, and I can't read his expression. It's not exactly shame, but … it's nothing good. "I've spent my whole life trying to go along with what everyone else told me to be and work really hard at a respectable job, because I have this basic defect in my character."

"What defect?"

"That I like men."

That makes my heart hurt. "You know that's internalized homophobia."

"I do," he says sadly.

"Might be internalized capitalism, too."

Sam presses his lips together. "That's a new one for me."

"The idea that we must always be working? I think you Americans have it more. Europeans are better at taking time off. Although some are still workaholics and sacrifice fun for money. But to what end?"

"To what end is right." Sam sighs. "Hanging out with you is making me realize there's more to life than keeping my house pristine."

"You can do whatever you want with your life."

He nods.

"Pristine house, eh?"

"Speaking of which," he says. "I've been to your house, but you haven't been to mine." He pauses, looking thoughtful. "It has an underground parking area, which you could use so you don't get photographed. I could give you the code. I have an extra parking space."

"I'd like to see your meticulously organized home."

"I'm not sure it's meticulous— Okay, yeah, it is." He gets this adorable sheepish expression on his face. "My pantry is labeled perfectly. What can I say? I like being able to find things."

"Yeah, labels have their utility. But I find them stifling."

"I can't picture you being stifled in any way. It seems like you're always going to be a free spirit."

I nod. "In school I had to wear a uniform. But I still managed to tweak it sometimes—coloring my shoes or growing my hair long. My mum never used to mind. She liked me expressing myself." I gulp. She's been gone for a very long time.

Sam tilts his head. I think he's going to inquire about my mum, but instead, he asks, "Do people's comments about you ever bother you?"

"Of course. I'm human. That's why I don't go online, try to stay away from what the fans and the media are saying."

"I can understand that. It must be overwhelming. But at the same time … you're in this position of power. You could effect so much change. And you don't do it." He holds up his hands, then picks up his club again. "Sorry. I don't know why I'm being like this."

"I'd rather you tell me what's bothering you than keep it inside."

"I guess I'd like to see you live your life so that some kid out there could say, 'If Julian Hill can do it, so can I.' Or at least, 'If Julian Hill is that way, it's okay for me to be that way, even if other people tell me otherwise.'"

"Don't I already do that?"

Sam shrugs. "Yes, as far as your fashion. But not as far as your sexuality."

I press my lips together. "Loren said something similar. But my sexuality isn't anyone else's business."

"And see, that's where you're wrong. Or, not wrong, but … You could do so much good. If you said, 'I'm pan,' or 'I'm gay,' or 'I'm demi,'—or even, hell, just that you're queer—someone out there would think, Jules is brave enough to say it." He holds up his hands. "I know, you want privacy. And I do understand that. But you're squandering this opportunity to be a leader."

I nod. "I get what you're saying. I'll think more about it. I'm not actually in the closet, but perhaps I can be more open." Perhaps I need to be, if I want him in my life. But I can't make any decisions about that tonight. "We should finish up here. I need to get back to the studio in the morning to finish the album."

Thirty-One

Jules

Jules: What does a lawyer like yourself get up to on a Saturday night?

Sam: What does a rock star like yourself get up to on a Saturday night?

Jules: Funnily enough, when said rock star has a deadline and is listening over and over again to the masters of his new album, he doesn't go out partying

Jules: Not that I do too much of that anyway

Sam: I'm pretty sure you're not a saint.

Jules: I'm pretty sure you're right

Jules: But you didn't answer my question

Sam: I'll show you.

Sam: <Photo image attached>

Sam: I'm sorting my junk drawer. See? Everything has a label for where it goes.

Jules: <3

Jules: <smiley emoji>

Jules: That might be the most adorable thing I've ever seen

Sam: Thanks. It makes me feel good to have it all orderly. Only, I have to make some decisions.

Sam: Should I store scissors here or in the desk?

Jules: While I should let you ponder the mysteries of the junk drawer, my vote is for your desk

Sam: Mine, too.

Sam: I can't believe I just bothered you about cleaning out my junk drawer.

Jules: I like everything about you, Sam. Down to your junk <devil emoji>

Sam: That's

Sam: Jules!!

Sam: Grrr I keep hitting send too fast.

Sam: What I mean to say is, thanks. I like everything about you, too.

Jules: <Kissy face emoji>

Two days later, I message Sam.

Jules: I'm done

Sam: Are you serious?

Jules: Deadly. Weeks in the studio with almost no sunshine, but we did it. Album complete

Sam: Are you happy with it?

Jules: All I want is to see you

Sam: Okay, but you didn't answer my question.

Jules: Yes, I am so happy with it. When can you come over?

Sam: Hold, please.

Sam: I just sent an email to Terrill saying I need to recuse myself for ethical reasons, and that I want to talk with him to explain.

Sam: You may need to hold me.

Jules: I can do that

Sam: Thanks. I'm checking his calendar, and his next available meeting time is tomorrow. I sent him a meeting invite.

Jules: But you're in the clear now?

Sam: I am.

Jules: Do you need to say anything to Kurt?

Sam: We've always been free to hook up with others.

Sam: Not that I consider this a hookup.

Sam: Shit. I'll tell him.

Sam: Done.

Sam: And I'm on my way.

"Hey," I say softly when Sam appears on my doorstep, as rumpled as he gets—which is to say, not very. He's in shirtsleeves with no tie, and his hair looks like he's run his fingers through it repeatedly.

He smells good. He gleams in the sun. His shy smile tugs at me, and I can't help my stare.

Or the surge of desire.

Finally I can touch him.

I hope.

"Hey," he responds. He kicks at the ground and shakes out his hands, then puts them deep in his pockets.

"Come in." I step back and let him inside, closing the door behind him. He glances around as if he's never seen my house before.

It's a beautiful, sunny afternoon, and I've got the windows open to let in the ocean breeze.

We're luckily all alone. Colin said he'd be out until late evening.

"I wanted to thank you," I say, not sure why I'm stalling, except that I don't want to just maul him.

Sam tilts up his chin and takes a step closer to me. "For what?"

"For being my muse."

He makes a derisive sound.

"Being a muse is everything," I insist. "You kick-started the process. You got me over the creative humps. I'm truly grateful."

"Well, then, I'm glad to have been of service."

"That's not what I mean," I whisper. "I've waited for you. Now that I have a chance with you, I want you. I *want* you."

Sam's eyes widen, and his breath hitches. I can see him get aroused—feel it on his skin and in his energy. Feel the way he comes alive.

"Is anything keeping me from kissing you now?" I ask, my voice low and my body close to his.

He looks at me with those turquoise eyes. And smiles. "No."

The word is barely out, and our lips meet.

I have him in my arms, and he feels so fucking good.

Sam Stone in my arms is perfection.

This kiss lacks any semblance of restraint or tinge of we-shouldn't-be-doing-this. Because now, we most definitely *should*.

Our tongues stroke each other, and the kiss gets deeper, sexier, stronger.

We're making up for lost time.

I'm surprised but not surprised that he's the one who moves next. His hands lower, and he cups my bum cheeks in his palms, squeezing and bringing my hips tighter against his.

His hardness rubs against mine.

"Fuck," I groan, my lips on his. "I've wanted you so much."

"Me, too."

I reach between us and grip his hard dick. "Yes, please. Yes, yes, yes," he chants, and he slumps against me, shuddering at my touch.

I've had sex where the other person was beyond excited to be with me. But it's rare I return the passion.

With Sam, though, it's unleashed, out to rule the world. I can't get enough of him.

Because of that intensity and meaning, this is the hottest sexual experience of my life. And we haven't even taken our clothes off yet.

With one last kiss, I'm on my knees before him in my entryway. He's panting, eyes hot.

"Is this okay?" I whisper, tilting my head up to gaze at him through my lashes.

"Y-yes." He strokes a gentle hand across my cheek.

I bury my nose in the fabric covering his crotch, enjoying his scent and the scrape against my skin.

"Julian," he says. His voice has gone husky, and Sam—*my* Sam—looks like he's about to explode.

Together, with fumbling hands, we get his pants undone, divvying up the work. He takes the belt portion while I take care of his button and zipper. I slide his trousers down, along with his boxers.

Finally, I'm face-to-face with his hard dick, which stands straight up. I take a moment to admire it, because he's a very handsome boy. I grin.

"What?" he asks, seemingly self-conscious. He tilts his head and takes a step backward, but I catch him and look up.

"You are so fucking, *fucking* gorgeous."

Before he can respond, my mouth is on him, because I know this will make him feel incredible. I can't swallow him whole, but I can get a ways down and then give him a good suck, the way I like it. Wet and no teeth and lots of, well, sucking. Repeatedly. Getting into this rhythm where I take short pulls over and over and over again, lapping up his precome.

He gasps. "Holy shit, Julian."

I grin around his cock and keep going.

He slumps against the wall as I use one hand to massage his balls.

I *love* doing this. I love taking care of him.

He puts one hand gently in my hair and caresses my cheek with the other.

"Don't wanna come in your mouth," he warns.

I pop off. "It's okay. I've been tested, and I'm negative. You?"

"Negative." He laughs. "I haven't had sex in a long time, except with my hand. Too busy."

"I shall make it my personal responsibility to rectify that."

Before he can say anything else, I suck him down again, one hand firmly holding the base of his cock, the other pressing behind his balls. Sam makes these sexy noises in the back of his throat, whimpering when I won't let up until he's pumping into my mouth, the salty warm release validating me in some way I didn't know I needed.

Like, *fuck yes*, I made him come.

When he's done shivering and groaning, he eyes me, his expression glassy and satiated, and then tackles me to the floor.

I start laughing, but I stop when I feel how thoroughly he's kissing me. How he's rushing to get my trousers and boxers off. How when he does, getting his soft, wet dick next to my hard one feels so good.

It makes me moan, *loud*.

I'm rubbing against him, and he scoots down, tucking himself in hastily and tugging my shirt toward my chin. He kisses the length of my torso, lingering on a few tattoos and gripping my cock.

With a delicious wink, he admires me for a moment, then licks me all the way from my balls to my tip, slowly, while maintaining eye contact.

He's savoring doing this to me. Most people I've been with were in some sort of race to get me off as fast as they could, so him taking his time is a revelation.

It feels like affection. Hot, dirty affection.

But I won't last long, even though he's lingering, because I'm so turned on. In a matter of moments, I let myself go, emptying into his warm, wet mouth.

Then he grins at me, I tug him up for a kiss, and we lazily make out on the floor.

"We didn't even make it to the bed." I laugh. "We barely made it inside my house."

"That can be round two."

Thirty-Two

Sam

Okay, having my mouth all over Julian—and then having his mouth all over me—was all I've ever really wanted.

I've had sex before, of course. I've even had what I thought was good sex. But I've never had anyone be so *passionate* with me.

"Want to join me in the shower?" he murmurs, still stroking my hair.

An excuse to see him naked? "Sure."

He pulls me up from where we're sprawled in the entryway, and before we go anywhere, we shed our clothes, which we'd barely dislodged earlier. When he's standing next to me without a stitch, he's so beautiful I forget everything else but him.

"Your tattoos," I say, reaching out one hand, then pulling it back.

Jules smiles. "You can touch."

I put a hand on a drawing on his chest, and he holds it in place, his fingers atop mine. I follow his arm up, then notice that he's moved his gaze from our joined hands to my body. His eyes sparkle.

"You're gorgeous," he says, then pulls me into him. "I'm so lucky."

I stand naked in Julian Hill's beachfront mansion, chest to his chest, hips to his hips, while he kisses me. His hands move to my ass, and he squeezes.

I kiss him back, tasting him, enjoying the feel of him next to me. My dick, nowhere near satisfied, wakes up and twitches. And in response, those famous hips undulate against mine, a slow, sexy beginning of a dance.

"Fuck," I say as we break apart, panting. "We'll never make it to the shower."

He presses his lips together and tilts his head from side to side. "Not sure that would be a bad thing, but I want to see you all wet and slippery." He takes my hand and pulls me down the hall to a bathroom the size of a boutique. He turns on the water, tests it, and we step in together.

This is a porn fantasy brought to life. Wet, warm, naked Julian Hill in my arms. The shower sluices down his back and torso, making him glisten in the late afternoon sunshine that pours through the large windows.

He holds me low on the waist and starts dancing as he croons in my ear.

I dissolve in happiness.

We soap each other up, and soon we're both hard, I smell like him—or he smells like me—and we're both clean.

I tug on his cock. "I want this in me."

"Then you may have it. Now?"

"We might need a condom and lube."

"Fair point." He grins wickedly. "But there's nothing stopping us from doing this."

With some conditioner in his hand, he holds both of our cocks, stroking us up and down together.

Warm water.

Firm pressure.

Slick fingers.

Sexy Julian.

Even though I came a few minutes ago, I'm going to do it again.

His breathing gets shorter and shorter, and mine is coming out in pants. My hands are holding him to me, listening to the little noises he makes as he brings us both closer and closer to orgasm.

I have never been more aroused. That interlude in the hallway just whetted my appetite.

And I can't help the way my hips thrust into his hands or the way I tingle all over. With a few more strong strokes, I come, spurting into his hand.

That seems to trigger him, as he comes immediately thereafter.

And then we collapse into each other, breathing hard.

I search for his face with my hands and kiss him, certain that this is going to be the best day of my life.

Later, as afternoon turns to dusk, I've borrowed a pair of Julian's black Balenciaga sweatpants and am lounging on his couch, snuggled up beside him, a movie playing on the TV. He's wearing a similar pair in navy blue. His hand cradles the top of my head, and I have my ear pressed to his bare chest, feeling it rise and fall.

After we loosened the valve—twice—on the sexual tension that had been building between us, while I'm nowhere near sated, at least I'm calm. I also don't think I've ever wanted anyone as much as I want Jules. I crave him the way I imagine performers crave an audience.

"Want me to have Paolo make us dinner?" Before I can ask him who Paolo is, he adds, "Personal chef. He comes a few times a week."

"Sure. That would be nice."

Nice isn't the right word. *Decadent.*

He reaches for his phone and does something—presumably texting Paolo. Meanwhile, I bask in the newfound comfort of being in his arms.

"I don't want to move. Do you?" he murmurs.

"No." The room darkens as the sun sets into the Pacific. Neither of us is paying attention to the movie. I'm just enjoying being near him. I turn so I can wrap an arm around his waist, lying half on him and half on the couch.

Jules lifts my chin with his knuckle.

There's something about him doing that. Like he wants to admire me from afar or check to make sure I'm still here.

It makes me feel precious.

Then he leans in, and his soft lips ghost against mine. Barely a kiss, but it makes me shiver. He smiles against my lips, and I can't help smiling back. I love this intimacy. I love his touch on my skin.

I love the way he feels this close to me.

He wraps his arms around my waist and tugs me closer until I'm straddling him.

And oh, Nelly, what a view.

His hair's a mess. Not the stylish mess it normally is, but rousingly sexy bedhead, real and touchable and evidence of how much I've been playing with it.

His relaxed eyes hold a tinge of fire, like he's storing up energy to explode again. I'm into it.

"I'm getting used to being able to touch you," I say, as I run my hands down his bare chest. His soft, warm skin jumps at my touch, and his nipples pebble. His dick jerks under me where I'm sitting on him, making mine do the same.

His hands roam, too, fingers splaying over my thighs, dancing over my ass and up my back, until he weaves them behind my neck and pulls me down on top of him. "You feel so utterly perfect," he murmurs, squeezing my ass between kisses. Then he sighs.

"What?"

He tugs me back far enough that we can look at each other and eyes me seriously. "If we do this for real—and it's not a secret—if someone writes a biography about me someday, you'll be in it."

"I understand." I'll always be that guy who dated Jules Hill.

Hopefully not in the past tense.

Jules's phone buzzes on the coffee table. "That should be Paolo." He picks it up and frowns.

I wrinkle my nose. "What's wrong?"

"Colin says he's on his way back."

I scramble off the couch and start to look for my clothes and phone.

Julian stands. "Where are you going?"

"Do you want him to know we're … like this?"

He gives me a firm stare. "I do. You're becoming important to me.

I may not be ready to be out in public, but I'm not hiding in my own home." He taps his index finger against his lip. "Unless, of course, *you* don't want him to know. I realize it's early days."

I clear my throat. "No, it's fine. I just didn't want to assume—"

"You're not assuming a thing." He gives me a once-over. "He'll figure out what's going on right away, since he knows what's in my wardrobe—and he's had his eye on those tracksuit bottoms. But he can deal with that."

We've barely had time to pull on T-shirts—doubtless designer quality, too—before there's a knock on the door. We eye each other, but it turns out to be Paolo. Julian introduces us, and Paolo sets about preparing dinner for three.

Ten minutes later, Colin drives up. Jules opens the door and greets him.

Colin's a watered-down version of Julian. Smaller, with a pinched face and a sleeker hairstyle. Jules gives him a hug and gestures toward me. "You remember Sam."

"Nice to see you again," I say.

Colin cocks his head. "You two are together? I thought you were a lawyer." His accent is similar to Julian's, but he has a higher-pitched voice.

We both nod.

"Well, good for you." He looks between us. "Sorry, I didn't know you'd have someone over."

"That's perfectly fine. Join us for dinner?" Jules asks.

"I'd love to."

We all sit at the table, and Paolo serves us a delicate salad with white wine. While Jules eats carefully, Colin scarfs it up like he hasn't eaten in a week. I'm not sure he actually tastes anything.

"This is delicious," I say.

"Well done, Paolo," Jules says when his chef returns to take our plates and bring in the next course—an Italian dish with fish and vegetables and pasta.

"Nothing like the boys' home," Colin mutters.

Jules pales.

"What boys' home?" I ask before I can stop myself.

A look passes between Jules and Colin, and then Jules says, "It's not public knowledge, but our mum died of cancer when I was thirteen and Col was eleven."

My face falls. "I'm so sorry." I realize I know little about Jules's background, though he's mentioned his mother in passing. His wiki page just said he was born in London and came to fame by being on a televised talent show where the host put him together with other boys to form a band.

"Thank you," Jules says. "Our dad was never in the picture, and we didn't have any other family. So we were in what you would call a group home until I got on the show and started making money."

"He got on. I didn't." Colin's sour expression tells me his light words are a front covering deep hurt.

I look at him in sympathy. "I'm so sorry." I'm not sure whether he'd want Jules to have told me, so I leave it at that.

He snorts. "Julian isn't the only Hill with talent. They don't report the people who try out and don't make it."

I'm a bit surprised the show didn't want them as a package deal. Singing brothers seems like a good marketing angle. But I don't want to push such a sticky subject. So after taking a few more bites, I switch the conversation to safer topics like the balmy Southern California weather compared to London. I talk about turning on the air-conditioning on Christmas Eve at my grandparents' house every year when I was a child, so we could have a fire, and seeing all the sweaters in the stores and knowing they'll mostly go to waste.

Colin seems particularly interested in me—and who my grandfather is.

Something about him makes me not trust him entirely. I'm not sure what it is.

After we eat, we go outside to watch the sunset. Jules stands close to me, his hand low on my back, almost inside the waistband of the pants I'm wearing.

Colin follows us out, holding his phone. "You two make a cute couple. How long have you been dating?"

Jules and I grin at each other. "Since today."

"No shit?"

"No shit," Jules says. "We had reasons not to, but those have gone away." Jules puts an arm over my shoulder. "Sam had work reasons for us not to be together, but they're all resolved now." He boops my nose. "And in the category of good things we do that no one ever sees, we didn't get together until today. We were perfectly ethical. Mostly."

"Mostly," I agree.

"What does that mean?" Colin asks.

"We waited until I turned in my album to …" Jules rubs his face.

Colin chuckles, but it's interrupted by a yawn.

"I've been linked with someone else," I say. "But that was just for the cameras. So, if you see something online that says I have a boyfriend, I don't. It's just Jules."

Colin nods. "Interesting. Why did you do that?"

"My grandfather's campaign. You can't believe everything you read."

"Don't I know it," he says. He glances at his phone. "I'd best be headed to bed. Talk to you later."

After he leaves, I find myself yawning, too. "Sorry."

"Don't be sorry," Julian says. "It's late. Want to sleep here?" He leans in, biting his lip.

It makes me smile. "I can't. I need to get to work early tomorrow."

"Okay," he says, and kisses my forehead lightly. "You can wear that home if you want."

I look at him. "How often is your brother here?"

"All the time, for now." He sighs. "But he's my responsibility." I want to ask what he means, but he keeps going. "We've been lucky that we've had some privacy. I don't feel like I get much of that these days. It's my most precious commodity."

"Even at home."

"Even at home."

"Do you want to get away for a bit? We can go up to my family cabin in the woods. There's no one around, it's on a dirt road, and there's no way paparazzi could find you." I grin. "And since you finished the album, you deserve to celebrate with a couple of days off."

"Let's do that. It sounds amazing."

"I'll set it up," I say and give him a kiss. "I just have to explain myself at work first."

Jules's expression turns worried. "I wish there were something I could do to help."

"Thanks." Even though there's a leaden lump in the pit of my stomach, I also feel like I'm doing the right thing, both for myself and for my work. While I'm sure there's going to be fallout, I know my time at this office is short-lived.

And I think I'm okay with that.

Thirty-Three

Sam

"What's this about you recusing yourself? What ethical issue?" Terrill demands, storming into my office ten minutes before we're supposed to meet.

It's the morning after sexy time with Julian Hill. A morning of cold, hard reality after a night of my dreams.

I'd been staring out the window. From my vantage point thirty stories up, I'd seen a helicopter land on a rooftop below me. I'd wondered if it could take me away when it leaves.

"It's exactly what I said in my message. Going forward, I can't work on any Lighthouse Records matters involving Julian Hill, because I've developed a conflict of interest."

Terrill's eyes narrow. "How so?"

"It's confidential."

He rolls his eyes. "I understand confidentiality. Unlike you, apparently."

"Hey," I protest. "I understand the rules. That's why I'm recusing myself."

"What's the conflict?"

I bite my lip. "Confidentially."

He raises his hands in the air. "Confidentially."

Swallowing thickly, I square my shoulders and look at him. "Julian Hill is my boyfriend. I'm in a relationship with him."

To my surprise, Terrill seems unconcerned. "The album's delivered, right? Where's the issue?"

"If the label has some other concern with him in the future, I can't work on it."

"Fair enough." Terrill's expression turns approving, though in a way that turns my stomach. "I never knew you had it in you," he says in admiration. "Sleeping with someone to get them to cooperate. I've underestimated you."

"No!" My outburst surprises even me. "It wasn't like that. Not at all. We waited until he had turned in the album," I trail off, realizing that making excuses sounds bad. As if I could prove it, anyway.

Terrill holds up his hands. "I don't care what happened, and I certainly don't want any details. We'll block you electronically from any files relating to Julian Hill, and I'll let the client rep know another attorney will be taking over for you." He scrubs his face. "I'm not sure if I should say 'What the hell' or 'Good job,' Sam. I guess I can't argue with results. You got him to finish the album, which is what the client wanted."

I nod, wanting him to leave.

I've got another thing to fix, and I'd rather do it in person, so I text Kurt to meet at his house—he works from home—on my lunch hour.

Taking a deep breath, I knock on Kurt's door. I've been here a few times, but not regularly. It's a tiny bungalow in a nice part of town.

He answers the door wearing jeans and a T-shirt and beckons me in.

"So you got lucky?" he asks. "Who's the guy?"

I trust him, because we've been in this together for years. He knows how to keep a secret.

"Well, it's complicated. You know many of the firm's clients are musicians?"

He nods. "Sure."

"I got assigned to browbeat one. Only problem is, I like him. And we, um, got together."

A huge grin stretches Kurt's mouth. "Are you serious?"

"Yeah. I wanted you to know. I haven't told anyone else yet, though. Well, other than Em."

"Holy shit. A clandestine affair."

"It's not like that. But he's famous. Like, really famous."

Kurt raises his eyebrows. "Will you tell me who?"

There's no reason to keep it from him, I suppose. "Julian Hill."

His mouth drops open—legit drops open. "Really?"

I nod. "But you can't tell anyone."

"Honey, if I haven't told anyone the thing you and I have had for years is just for optics, I'm not telling them this."

Squeezing his hand, I lean in. "I know. I trust you."

A concerned look passes over Kurt's face.

"What?" I ask.

"Just be careful, okay? A lot of shit can go bad when you get involved with a celebrity. And I'm not even talking about the Stone-Delmont campaign. It's more … I don't know if he's good enough for you."

I burst out laughing. "He's a wonderful man."

"Eh. He's famous and probably full of himself. I don't want you getting hurt."

"I appreciate your concern, but I got this."

"If you say so." He thinks for a moment. "Are you going to bring this up to our families?"

I nod. "I think it's serious enough that I need to."

"Is it serious enough that we need to 'break up'?" He uses air quotes. "Because I get as much out of our deal as you do, since my mom can hardly pester me to get into a real relationship as long as I'm appearing with you at her campaign events. If I'm suddenly 'single,' I know it'll be mere moments before she starts setting me up with other guys. What if we just leave things as they are?"

I nibble on my lower lip. "What about when we get found out?

Because I'm kidding myself if I think that won't happen. I mean, if I'm dating a rock star."

"Then we put out a press release that you and I have been broken up for a while but we kept it to ourselves."

I shake my head. "No, I don't think so. We should do it now."

"And have the poster couple split before the election? Give the pundits something to talk about?"

"I don't want that, but it's going to come out. Better sooner than later, give it time to settle down."

"Then let's talk to the PR team and let them decide what the best strategy is. Until then, we should keep things as is."

"I don't want you to have issues with your parents—and I don't want to hurt the campaign. And actually, there's something to be said for giving Jules a certain amount of plausible deniability until he's ready to make a public statement. But I really feel it's a question of when, not if, the news gets out. If we haven't managed the story beforehand, people will think I'm cheating on you. Or Jules."

"Well, you aren't."

"But it's hard to change public opinion once it sours."

He pauses. "I think if anything happens, we can deal with it."

I shake my head. "It seems like a recipe for disaster, honestly. If the public found out we've been making this up all along, that could blow up into a PR nightmare the campaign might never recover from."

"No one wants that." He shakes his head. "That's all the more reason we should talk to the professionals before we do anything. I can call Mom's PR lead and try to set up a call. But until then, I say we keep things as they are."

"One photo of me and Jules, and it will be all over."

"You can say you're friends."

"It depends on the type of photo," I say wryly. "Some things don't look like 'friends.'"

He bursts out laughing, then gets serious again. "In any case, you don't need my permission to go get laid. We can figure the rest of this out later."

"Okay," I say, and give him a hug goodbye.

I'm going to kick ass all week at work and then take Jules up to the woods. Everything else can wait until we get back.

Thirty-Four

Sam

Julian pulls his car up under a pine tree, and we open the doors, get out, and stretch. At this altitude, the air smells cleaner and fresher. The place feels secret and quiet, our steps muffled by the needle-covered ground.

He swivels his head, taking in the mountain vistas. Then he gets a good look at the cabin and blinks. "This place is yours?"

I grin. "Yup. My family's, but I'm the one who uses it most."

"It looks like a fairy tale."

My family has owned the 1930s-style storybook cabin, nestled in the Angeles National Forest, since it was built. "It does. You kind of expect Hansel and Gretel to come out with a big bad wolf."

"I think those are two different stories." Jules purses his lips and rubs his chin like he's stroking a beard.

I shove him. "It's also very, very secluded. We can be outside and not worry about it."

We walk up the cobblestone path to the arched door and open it. When we go inside, dust motes dance in the sunlight.

But the place looks good. Jules turns to me and smiles, shutting the door behind him. "This place is utterly perfect. It's—"

I cut him off by kissing him hard. While I know we should be responsible and bring in the food, all I really want is to pull Jules into the bedroom. When we're both breathless, I rest my forehead against his. "I wanted to take you somewhere special to me. And this is as private as it gets. We can do whatever we want."

Jules spins me around so my belly is pressed to the front door.

I moan, because fuck, that's hot.

He crowds up behind me, his dick notching in the crease of my ass, teasing me through our clothes, and I shove back into him, wanting more contact.

It's his turn to groan. He wraps an arm around my chest, his lips against my ear, and he murmurs in that delicious voice, "Is this okay, Sam?"

I nod vigorously.

"Tell me."

"Yes," I gasp. "More than okay."

"Anything that isn't?"

"No." My voice is hoarse. His hand reaches down and cups my hard cock.

I suppress a whine. Because I want him to move—or I want to move—but I'm trapped by the delicious torture of his lips kissing the sensitive spot behind my ear, nibbling on the outside shell, sucking on the lobe.

He rams me harder against the door, manhandling me and positioning me where he wants me. My face is pressed against the wood, cool under my cheek. With my eyes closed, I writhe against him as his hand expertly undoes my pants and frees my erection.

His calloused fingers on my skin make me shiver. I want more of his touch, of his exploration.

Cool air hits the back of my neck, and I realize he's stepped back so he can push my slacks down. Underwear, too. And one of those talented fingers—*literally* talented fingers—slides down my crease. With the other hand, he tugs up my shirt, and suddenly I have a beautiful man kneeling behind me, kissing the dimples above my ass, palming it, and oh god, he's going to—

He licks down my crease, spreading my ass cheeks as he goes, and it feels so fucking good I slump into the door.

I'm also very happy I made sure I was super clean before we left.

Jules chuckles against my skin. "You're ready for this."

I nod into the door. "Oh god," I whimper. "That feels so—"

But I don't finish my sentence, because he's licking my hole, and the nerves there are intensely happy. As he explores me with his tongue, I'm reduced to a sobbing mess. It's sensory overload. It's too much. And it's bliss.

"You. Need to stop," I finally moan, looking over my shoulder at him. "Or I'm coming right now."

He grins up at me. "I'm not opposed to that." He tilts his head. "But what's this you say about yoga? How flexible are you really?"

"*Quite* flexible," I say. "Wanna see?" He steps back and lets me move away from the door.

He nods, his face serious.

"Okay. Um, well. This is downward dog." I keep my feet and heels flat on the floor and fold in half, placing my palms in front of me. I feel goofy having my ass out with my pants around my ankles, but Jules places a hand on my thigh, then caresses upward, squeezing my ass when he gets there.

"Interesting position."

"There's also this," I say. I get on my back and push up into bridge position. My hands press flat on the floor, my feet shoulder-width apart, as I hold my torso steady.

"What do we do with this?" he asks, amused, trailing his hand around my cock. "We could get creative."

"Or this," I say, and get into a modified warrior pose with my hand on the floor, my legs not separated entirely. "You can just come up behind me—"

"No more talking," Jules growls. I can see the thick ridge in his own tight jeans. "We shall be trying all of those."

"You're wearing too many clothes," I point out.

"Let's fix that." He falls backward on the floor, and I kind of collapse onto him, scrambling to take his clothes off. I'm still mostly dressed, but he helps me get his jeans unbuttoned and shoved down, and now I'm looking at his perfect dick—hard and long, with a dark vein on the underside.

I can't resist. I lick a stripe from balls to tip, then swirl my tongue around the crown.

And I start sucking.

Now it's his turn to writhe, helpless, as I straddle his knees to suck him off.

Using a hand to stroke him while I suck, I take my other finger and press behind his balls, messing with his taint, trying to see what he likes. I know what I like—which is a lot of hard suction—and I go with that.

"Fucking hell, Sam."

I keep going. "That okay?" I whisper between sucks.

"Yes, absolutely. Please."

I love it when his British politeness comes out. I can tell by the way he's straining that he's close to coming, and I keep up the rhythm, wanting him to release, wanting him to let it all out.

But I also really want him to fuck me. "Where's a condom?" I ask.

"In the car."

"Fuck. That's where the ones I brought are, too."

"I can't wait," Jules says. "I'll fuck you later."

I nod over and over. "Do whatever you want."

Pulling back from my caresses, he glances over at the kitchen and points to a bottle of olive oil on the counter. "I love what we're doing, but I really want to try something. Can we use that?"

"Yes."

With his pants half down, he gets up and hops over to grab it, then comes back, pulling me up to my feet. He kisses me deeply, then pushes me back around so I'm facing the door again.

"Dunno what this is called," he says, "but until we get a condom, I'll fuck your thighs."

"Yes," I hiss.

Looking over my shoulder, I watch as he pours oil on his hands and then rubs his cock. With both of our pants around our feet, he slides his dick between my legs and then uses his slick fingers to stroke my cock.

As he thrusts faster and faster, jerking me off in time, I'm lost in pleasure, Play-Doh in his hands. He groans, getting the friction he needs, and between his intensity and my need for him, I release so hard I hit my own face, tasting the salty-sweet fluid. He keeps pumping, coming hard, then collapses onto me.

He holds me to him as we catch our breath. Then I look around and burst out laughing.

"What?" he asks.

"Look where we are. Again, we didn't even make it two feet into the place."

There's that wicked grin. I'm coming to love that expression on him. "That just leaves us more to explore later." He stands back and pulls me with him, shoving my pants the rest of the way off. I toe out of my shoes and shuck off my shirt. He does the same and then grabs me for a hug.

"Come get cleaned up," I tell him. "I'll feed you. Then let's see what happens."

"Deal."

After showering and bringing in the groceries, I pour us each a glass of water and ask, "What would you like to eat?"

Jules has been busy opening up every cabinet and drawer, inspecting the contents left by years and years of use of a family cabin. He's currently looking at the bookshelves, which feature a few decades' worth of bestsellers, mysteries, thrillers, and romance novels. With a hum, he pulls one out and inspects it. "Well, Mr. Stone, can you cook?"

"Yes. Can you?"

He shrugs and wanders to a cabinet that's nothing but board games. Clue. Life. Monopoly. Scrabble. "Eh. I can do some things. Like toast and tea."

I smirk. "Let me show you how it's done."

Julian Hill, barefoot, wearing only a pair of sweatpants, joins me in the redone but still vintage kitchen. His pants are so low I see his hip bones, and all his ink is on display. His hair is chaotic, and his lips are kiss-stung. He looks thoroughly debauched, which is appropriate, because I know what we've just done. But he also has this feline grace. The same way he is on stage, able to always land on his feet with everything going the right way, weaving through the equipment and other musicians without ever tripping.

Even here, in an unfamiliar place, it's as if he's always lived here. As if this were his home. As if a mountain cabin is a normal place for a rock star to be.

Or maybe that's just how I feel. Like he's always been here, even though he hasn't.

Given Emily's years-long fan obsession, he's been a familiar backdrop for some time. In person, though, he's different. He's a real being with blood running through his veins. With so much life and vigor.

And he's *mine*. At least for now.

"What are you thinking, Sam-I-Am?"

I grin. "I've never had anyone call me Sam-I-Am before."

"Whaaaa? Isn't that an American classic?" He reaches behind me and refills his glass from the tap.

"True. But I've always wondered, shouldn't other people have called him *Sam-You-Are?*"

"I believe you're deflecting from my original question. Which was, what are you thinking, Sam-You-Are?"

I swallow, watching him drink the water, his Adam's apple moving. "I'm thinking you are the sexiest being I have ever met in my entire life, and I can't believe I get to touch you."

Julian steps forward, setting the glass down on the counter. Leaning in, he brushes the lightest whisper of a kiss over my lips, which makes me close my eyes and swoon all Disney-style. "I feel the same way," he murmurs. "And it's not just sex appeal. It's *you*. I like everything about you."

"Even the part of me that argues with you?"

"Especially that part. Because it means you have your own mind and you're not about to let me or anyone else walk over *our* rights."

I smile at him. "Are you accepting a label, Julian Hill? Should I call *People* magazine? Or *Tatler?*"

"Don't you dare."

"I certainly would *not* dare. Your trust is too precious, and I accept it as the gift it is. Would saying you're something make you feel more like you belong, though?"

He wraps his arms around me. "I don't know. I certainly am not what other people would consider to be straight. And maybe it's time to stop keeping that to myself."

His statement is a big deal. Maybe he's willing to be in a relationship with me, in public.

Because that's what I want. An out-in-the-open relationship with Jules.

We smile goofily at each other. And this time it's my turn to lean in and kiss him, only I don't do it gently. I tug the back of his neck and make his lips part and taste his tongue on mine.

My tired dick even twitches as if it thinks, *This could be interesting*.

But Jules wraps his arms around my waist, then squeezes my butt. "What was that about you making dinner? It seems like you're slacking."

"Only because you're right here."

"Should I move somewhere else?" He steps between my legs so he's bracing me against the counter.

"No," I whisper. "I don't want you to go anywhere."

"Same."

Jules reaches for his phone and navigates to a music app, putting on a slow pop song. "Before we cook, then, will you dance with me?"

I nod and move into his arms, and we dance, smiling and kissing. Unlike before when we danced a box step, this is chest to chest, hands on each other's asses, with no one around to break us apart.

I'm about to pull away to start cooking when the next song cues up. And it's one of his.

I chuckle and open my mouth to say something about it, when he starts singing in my ear. Quietly, but harmonizing with himself. It gives me goose bumps. It makes my mouth water. It makes me *want him* more than anything.

I'm lost, listening to him murmur in my ear. The ground has

dropped out, and the ceiling is limitless. And all that exists is Julian and me.

When the song is over, Julian kisses the bolt of my jaw, his mouth soft against my stubble. "I've always wanted someone to sing that song to."

Our eyes lock, and I'm speechless. I swallow hard and kiss him.

And eventually we make dinner.

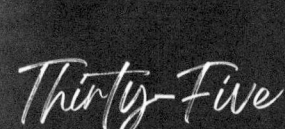

Jules

It's late, and the room is lit by candles burning on the dresser as I push Sam's naked body into the clouds of the bed.

I lean down to kiss him, my legs settling between his. I'm torn—skin to skin doesn't seem close enough, but I also want to watch him. Watch the way he wiggles and shimmies. Watch how he handles me touching him—his breath coming sharp and fast, his pupils dilating, his thighs quivering. Watch his pleasure.

We kiss leisurely and sensuously, and it builds until we're both breathless. I roll off to one side, my head propped on my hand, and trace my fingertips along his body. I like his pale, uninked skin, although I can't help but think he'd look good with a few tattoos. He'd look good in anything.

He's shivering, but it's not from cold. Seeing him respond makes my body roar to life. The earlier orgasms didn't even take the edge off. If anything, they made me hungry for so much more.

"Want you," he murmurs, one of his hands skipping along my side. "Inside me."

"Fuck yes, please, yes." One more kiss, and then I help him flip to his stomach.

It's deeply satisfying, seeing him like this, his bubble arse popping up and his shoulders defined and beautiful.

Moreover, the way he's offering himself to me—trusting me with his body and, I think, with his heart—makes me want to do anything and everything for him.

I'm going to take care of him.

Lightly, I rub his back and pepper him with kisses. My cock bumps into his leg and then his bum cheek as I reposition myself to touch all of him.

I take out a bottle of lube and squidge some on my fingers. Then I trace along his crack until I get to his hole and breach him. "You good?" I whisper, my hair touching his ear.

He nods and moans.

I take my time with the prep, not wanting this to be too much for him. Because it kind of already is too much for me—too many emotions. All this nakedness. All this skin. All these feelings, both physical and in my heart and, hell, my soul.

But when he's loose and ready and squirming for me, I move so I can see his eyes. He closes them and nods, then looks at me fiercely over his shoulder. "Please," is all he says. "Please fuck me now."

"Okay, love," I whisper. I get a condom on and line up. Pressing into him, mounting him, I feel how tight and hot he is around me, and I can't deal with all the sensations happening at once. I need a moment—and likely he does, too. I wait for him to adjust to me, disregarding how much I'm shaking.

Usually sex is just a way to get off. Usually it's down and dirty and done.

But I don't ever want this to end.

I barely want it to begin. Because things that begin usually end, so in the past I've protected myself from getting in too deep.

With Sam, though, I'm already in. Not just inside his body—watching him breathe heavily to let me fit—but also in deep with my heart.

And I don't want to think about potential consequences. I want to let myself be here, present, now.

"Oh god," I groan. "This. I. You." My body curls over his. I bite the meat of his shoulder, then haul him up on all fours so I can reach his cock.

"Fuck me," he begs. "Please."

I nod. And I start to thrust: in, out. In, out. I hold his hips and carefully begin to fuck him, my movements at first slow and long, then getting faster and more shallow, losing the rhythm and the plot and the beat.

For a musician, it feels bad to lose the beat, but it's also freeing. Like a drummer who's lost a stick, I'm off, but it feels more real. Like it's us. Something I can take with me for the rest of my life: what it feels like to fuck Sam Stone.

He's into it, too, making a stream of sexy noises, and I can tell when I hit his prostate because his tone shifts to one of utter need.

I need to see him. I pull out and tap the side of his hip. "This way."

He nods and turns over, lifting his legs. I slide back in and growl at the feeling. It's not about owning him or possessing him. He's giving me this gift of intimacy. Of letting me see him so exposed.

His eyes are on mine, and something shifts deep inside me. Maybe something that was already there. But this man's *it* for me.

I don't know how I know that so fast—except that it isn't so fast. I've met a lot of people. And none of them created the reactions in me that he does.

I want to stay in this moment forever, but my body doesn't agree. "I'm about to come," I whisper.

"Me, too." Sam gasps, reaching down to bring himself off, but I bat his hand away. He nods and does this sexy grimace-smile at the pleasure of me handling his cock. "Okay."

I try to find my rhythm again, timing my strokes on his dick with those inside his ass. And now I feel like I'm taking over his body—and he's letting me.

It might be the best feeling in the universe. Better than the feeling before I get on stage. Better than having a song come to me.

This, right here. This connection with a man I really care for. This might top everything.

"Jules," he murmurs, and I can tell by the desperation of his movements and the hardness of his dick that he's going to come. So I keep up the pace, and he rewards me with bursts of warm spunk trickling down my fist.

Fuck, yes. I watch him tense with pleasure and release, falling apart on my knob. Then I let myself go and fall into him, kissing him as I come. I grunt loud enough that someone could hear me in a packed stadium, without a microphone.

I fall onto him after, trying not to squish him and failing miserably.

"That was sexy," Sam says. "Oh my god."

I grin against his ear, then pant, "So sexy." Holding the condom carefully, I pull out, and I can see the moment that he winces. "Are you okay?"

"Yeah."

I kiss him lightly. "One sec." I climb down off the bed and pad into the bathroom to toss the condom and clean off my hands and belly, then come back with a warm washcloth for Sam.

After we're sorted, I tuck in behind him and gather him up in my arms.

In the morning, there's a sleeping blond man in bed with me, and I pause to look at him.

My heartbeat quickens and my nerve endings tingle. I close my eyes to savor this moment and then open them again.

A tendril of his hair has flopped onto his forehead, and his cheeks look full, like a child's. He's rounder, softer when he's asleep, not all square jaw and broad cheekbones.

Seeing him this relaxed makes me realize that he probably works a lot and doesn't get a lot of rest. It also makes me want to care for him the way I'd want to be taken care of.

He's all man, don't get me wrong. He just looks less like a lawyer and more like a human. Not that lawyers aren't humans. Well, some of them, anyway.

He simply seems like my Sam.

I'm not sure when he went from "this bloke I met" to "my Sam," but it's happened. I want to know more about him and give him everything he deserves.

That makes me frown. Does he deserve what being with me might do to his life?

What if I take Sam out in public and he gets eviscerated by my fans? That would be awful for him. Moreover, what if my fans turn on me? That's been my biggest fear since I became dependent on them for my livelihood.

But I don't owe them anything beyond what I sell and they pay for: my music. They support me, and I love them, but they don't get a say in who I love. Anyhow, most Hillions seem to support me no matter what I say and defend me vehemently against the trolls.

Of course, there's also the issue that he still has this other guy he's attached to, at least on paper. Well, I suppose it's not technically "on paper," but it's not real.

Sam is real, though. Very real. And maybe nothing matters except him in my arms.

He yawns, waking up, and I snuggle close to him. "What do you want to do today?" I ask.

"Be with you."

"That sounds good to me." I kiss him.

"Let me feed you," he says.

I kiss him again.

After a leisurely breakfast, Sam lies on the couch with his head in my lap while I toy with his thick, soft hair. It's wavy and lovely. And I like the weight of his head in my lap.

This isn't sexual. It's just ... comfortable.

Nice.

I hate that word, but I don't know what else to call this. I basically went through puberty in the public eye, so I've never had a normal relationship, and this feels refreshingly normal.

"Sam?"

"Hmm?"

"What happened with your other boyfriend? The one before Kurt."

He stiffens and furrows his eyebrows before sighing. "We were young and in love, or so I thought. I was going to be a lawyer, and he was going to be an actor, and we'd live happily ever after. But while I was in class, he was meeting with an agent who persuaded him he should break up with me so he'd be seen as available." He grimaces. "After that, I decided romance wasn't for me. Because if Asa could fall out of love with me so quickly—just, 'Oh, let me go get famous'—then I didn't want anything to do with it."

"That makes me sad," I say. "Love is everything."

He shrugs. "Emily has been on me about that for years." He reddens, and the corner of his mouth curves in a small smile. "I'm starting to change my opinion about all that romantic shit."

"But he wasn't ever out about being with you?"

"No. That's part of why Kurt and I are so vocal about who we are. It's not just the two of us in the relationship. It's us and the whole world."

That makes my stomach drop. "And what about you and me? What do we do when this becomes more than the two of us?"

"You planning on making us polyamorous?"

I shove him lightly. "I mean when more people know about us than Colin, Loren, Emily, and Kurt. And our workmates."

"Then more people know." He sighs. "I do worry about my grandfather's campaign. I need to talk with the PR team."

"You dating me will have fallout even beyond the campaign. Whenever any celebrity does anything, people feel entitled to make comments. Are you truly prepared to be by my side?"

He sits up, an earnest expression on his face. "That question is really for you. Are you prepared for the public to know you like men?"

"I've never thought that was something to be ashamed of. Just none of anyone else's business."

"And are people going to see the subtlety in your reasoning?"

"The only person who matters is you. Do you understand my logic?"

"Yeah," Sam says quietly. "I do."

I sigh. "I want to keep you for myself right now. Because once I share you, I'm going to be sharing you for …" I trail off. Forever? For as long as we're together? "Is that all right with you? You get a say in this."

"Of course it's all right." He snuggles into me, and I hug him back.

"You know how I hate labels?"

"Yeah."

"There is one label I'd like," I say, my heart pounding. "That is, one that I'd like to use between us."

"What is it?"

"Boyfriends. Would you like it if we called ourselves that?"

Sam relaxes against me. "I'd like that very much."

Thirty-Six

Jules

WE SPEND THE REST OF THE WEEKEND DOING MORE OF the same. In between time spent naked in bed or in the shower or (ahem) on the floor (again), we cook and tidy up and go for treks out in the fresh air.

There's no one else around.

It's glorious.

All too soon it's Sunday night and time to go back to the real world. I drop Sam off at his house and then return to mine, where I find Loren pacing in my living room. They have a key, and I guess they decided a personal visit was necessary since I ignored my phone all weekend long.

"You still haven't received approval from Lighthouse?" they ask after I drop my overnight bag at the door and we exchange hellos.

"No."

They rub their chin. "That's surprising."

Their usual black talons, erm, nails, are now dark gray—a different shade on every finger—and they're wearing dark gray jeans and a black T-shirt from my latest tour.

I stare at the shirt, wondering what the artwork for the new album will be like. Part of me wants to put Sam's face on it, with an arrow that says "hot man muse."

Part of me wants to keep him for myself.

And all of me is concerned about the lack of response from the label. "Right? The engineers seemed to like it, but I don't know what the executives will say. Maybe they're paying me back for taking so long to write the flipping thing."

"Hmm. That is strange. I'll follow up." They shrug. "We shouldn't go directly to worst-case scenarios. Maybe the muckety-mucks are busy."

"Maybe." I tug my guitar into my lap and play with my fingering, then strum a few chords. "I actually wrote another song this week. Want to hear it? Maybe I'll do another album."

At the lack of response, I glance up and see Loren's sassy smirk and raised eyebrow.

"What?" I ask.

"Did Sam inspire this new song?"

"He did."

"And are you guys together now?"

I nod.

"Are you worried about anything?"

"The usual. But I have to manage the anxiety. I do everything because of my fans. For once, I want to do something for me." I scrub my face. "I believe in our relationship, and it's what I think that matters."

"I'm there for you." They catch my eyes. "You know that."

I nod.

"Did he ever break up with that boyfriend of his? Or do I need to prepare for a PR disaster far worse than 'OMG, Jules Hill is queer'?"

"He's going to talk with the campaign about it and work something out." I grind my teeth and crack my knuckles.

"You can't be seen as a cheater, Jules. That would undermine your whole persona."

Grimacing, I nod. "I know. I'm not one. And I'll … discuss it with him."

"On to another happy topic: is Colin still staying here?"

"Yeah."

"Is he doing anything at all to get back on his feet, or is he just lounging around, enjoying your beach access and eating your food? Oh, wait, that's not really a question." They give me a long look. "I know he's your brother, but even so ... I don't understand why you keep someone around who uses you as much as he does."

"I promised my mum," I blurt. I don't know why I'm telling Loren this now. Maybe talking with Sam is making me more ... open? Something like that.

"Promised her what?"

"That I would take care of him. No matter what."

"Oh, Julian. That's a tough promise to keep when he's such a slacker."

"What else am I supposed to do? I got the job he wanted, the exposure he wanted, the money he wanted. I get all the attention. He's forever standing in the wings, waiting for his chance. I can't say no to him. If he needs something, I'll give it to him."

"Do you feel guilty that you got picked and he didn't?"

"Yes."

"Don't. You have a better work ethic than him. You give it all to your fans. I think the producers could sense that about you, even back when you were first auditioning. Colin's only out for himself."

"That may be, but I'm the only family he has. And I can't let him down."

Sam

A FEW NIGHTS LATER, I make my way to Julian's house again. After another gourmet dinner, we sit outside on the beach-level patio, our bare feet up on a coffee table, drinking Bordeaux and watching the sky go inky purple. It's dark, but you can still see the water, gunmetal in the creamy moonlight. Paolo's in the kitchen cleaning up, which is why Jules and I are still clothed.

Well, that, and his brother coming in and out.

"I'm worried," Jules says into the nighttime quiet.

"Why?"

"I haven't heard from the label with the final approval on the album."

"Is that unusual?"

"Not necessarily, but I don't know. It feels weird. Loren said they'd follow up, but no word yet."

I lean over and kiss him. "I'm sure it'll be fine. It's a great album. They'll love it."

Seagulls caw in the distance, and a cool breeze ruffles our hair. Jules is wearing a silver lamé tank top and loose black shorts. I'm in a short-sleeved shirt and twill shorts, having changed when I got here. Not for the first time, I think we're an odd couple.

It doesn't feel odd, though, with his arm over my shoulders. The heat of the day has evaporated, but I'm warmed by being at his side.

I trace the tattoos on Julian's fingers, then slide off one of his silver skull rings and try it on. It fits.

"Keep it," he says.

I shake my head. "I can't wear one of your rings."

"Why not?"

A laugh comes out of me, and I gesture down at myself. "Skulls and preppy don't mix."

"I think they do." He leans forward. "Keep it."

The warmth of the heavy ring on my forefinger reminds me of him. "Okay," I say. Then I rub the design it had covered on his hand.

With his head cocked, he asks, "Would you ever get a tattoo?"

"No."

He raises an eyebrow. "You say that so fast."

"There's nothing I want permanently drawn on me. Have you ever wanted to get any of yours removed? Do you regret any of them?"

"Not a one. Even the ones that symbolize things long past. They're my history. Life is so digital, and digital can easily be erased after a few automated 'Are you sure?' messages. I like having the scars. I like having a record of things that happened. There are probably hundreds of thousands of photos of me out there, and I have heaps of memories, but if an event or thought or symbol made it onto my body, I know it's important." He sets his drink down. "What would you get? I mean, if you had to."

I pause, thinking about it. "I don't know. Obviously something meaningful."

"That's what I'm asking. What means something to you? A symbol of an event or something you love?"

"My P-touch."

"Your what?"

"My label maker."

He laughs. "That is a *whole* lot less interesting than what I thought a 'p-touch' would be." Then he sobers, taking in the look on my face. "You're serious, aren't you?"

I shrug. "What can I say? I told you I like things to be organized. Which reminds me, you still haven't seen my condo. I mean, not that it can compete with this place," I say, taking a sip of my wine. It's delicious and layered and smells almost chocolaty. "And besides, you can't go out in public without a plan. Does that bother you, or are you used to it by now?"

"I'm used to it. It's been a while since I've been able to pop into a shop without people taking my picture." He sighs. "No McDonald's for me." He leans forward to give me a knowing look. "With the way your grandfather's ad campaign's going, you'd get noticed there, too."

"I might get asked for an autograph. Like, *one* autograph. By someone my mom paid to ask me. If you picked up a chocolate shake, you'd cause a traffic jam for blocks."

Jules hides a grin and lifts one shoulder. "Perhaps."

"Do you ever feel trapped here?"

He shakes his head. "No. It's not a cage. I wanted to make certain of that. That's why I bought this heap and the surrounding land. Paps get a few photos, by hiking in or with a telephoto lens from a boat, but they have to really want them. For the most part, I can do whatever I want here. Especially in the dark."

"Whatever you want?"

"Pretty much, yes."

"Then we should take advantage of your good planning." I finish off my glass, put it on the table, and stand. "Come on."

He sets down his drink, and I grab his hand, then tug him with me out the gate. He laughs at my enthusiasm but follows me readily. "Um, Sam. Where are we going?"

I don't answer.

Jules lets me drag him toward the dunes at the north end where there are no houses for miles and miles. It takes intrepid souls to get to this part of the public beach.

When we're well away from the lights of his house and any other signs of civilization, I say, "We're going for a romantic walk in the moonlight."

He dips in to give me a light kiss. "Romantic walk, is it?"

I nod, very seriously, holding back from grabbing his neck and kissing the dickens out of him. "I want to try it. I've always told Em how I'm not romantic at all."

Julian squeezes my hand. "Rubbish."

Our bare toes squish the cold sand, and the waves sound on the shore, threatening to come up high enough to get our feet wet. The atmosphere has turned gray black blue purple—both the sky and the ocean—except the sea has bits of white foam, and it smells like salt and seaweed and fish and more salt.

And I feel this sense of joy. Tremendous joy.

It makes me take off running, pulling him with me.

We're holding hands, laughing, running as fast as we can. Thankfully, this part of the beach has little debris, just soft sand. We leap and whoop and *run run run* until we're panting and out of breath.

"Shit," Julian gasps, when we stop behind some dunes.

I tug him close so we bump into each other—chest to chest, pelvis to pelvis—and I take his other hand. Our skin is hot from exertion. I embrace him, holding both his hands behind his back, and kiss his neck. He tenses at first, then relaxes against me. "There's no one around," I tell him. "No one for miles that way." It's hard to indicate west over the ocean with my eyes while I'm sucking on his skin, but I think he gets the point … if his moan is any indication. "Even if someone is around, they can't see us, because it's so dark."

"No one to see me do this," he mutters against my ear. In an instant, I'm lowered to my back in the cool sand, his elbows on either side of my head. Jules hovers over me, his thighs between my legs and his lips on mine.

I groan. It's *so good*.

That kiss is the moment a match strikes. When it pauses and you wonder if it's going to catch. The split second before the flame gets going, burning bright.

The kiss starts tame but ignites my body in a flash. It's a deep, salty, hot kiss. A kiss with tongue. A kiss with heart.

I push him over and straddle him, my knees digging into the sand. "We're going to get messy, and I don't care. I just want you."

He holds me to him, then whispers in my ear, "You're getting in my bloodstream, Sam."

"And you're in mine," I whisper back.

Julian kisses me so hard we're panting, then leans back so I can see his dark eyes studying me in the moonlight. "I'm so fucking enamored with you, I don't know what to do with myself."

His words hit me in the soul and make me tingle in ways that have nothing to do with his kissing and his touch.

His next words are quiet. "The strength of my feelings scares me."

"I feel the same way," I admit, my fingers tangled in his hair, my cock straining at my zipper.

His hands knead my ass. "Yeah? You do?"

"I do."

"Christ. What am I going to do with you?"

"When you use that tone of voice, you always make me hard." I angle my hips to rub his cock with mine. "Correction. Hard*er*."

"Do I really?" His tone isn't mocking, but it isn't light either. More … curious. "You always make me hard. From the moment we met."

I bury my face in his neck. "Sorry again about that."

"No more apologies. I enjoyed your office hand job. It got us here."

He lifts up and cradles my chin.

Our next deep kiss burns that match to the end and sets the world on fire.

And then we can't get our hands on each other fast enough. I'm scrambling, shoving his shirt up, throwing mine off, so that we're skin to skin, both kneeling now. I rub his cock through his shorts.

He groans and unbuttons mine.

I grab his waistband and shove his shorts down. If we were

rolling around in the sand, this could get gritty, but up on our knees, we manage to avoid the worst of it.

Both of us are leaking precome, and I use that as lube to jack us together.

"Oh, fuck. Bloody fucking hell," he moans as I stroke him.

"Shh," I whisper, and take his tongue with my own.

This feels exposed and yet somehow safe. In the dark, in nature, with no one else around.

I'm about to lean down and suck him off when he makes a low noise in the back of his throat and starts coming in my hand, his hot release coating my palm and fingers.

He sags back on his heels, his pants still around his thighs as I finish myself. He watches me with wide eyes. "Hell," he whispers.

Between how turned on he makes me, the warm spunk in my hands, and the friction, I come quickly, seeing stars and nebulae that aren't visible to the naked eye.

Then I collapse back on my heels, panting, not totally sure what just happened.

"Come on," he says, and drags me up by my sticky hand. We both tug our pants up, and I grab my shirt. Then we head into the water, getting our ankles wet and bending to wash off our hands.

"This might be the freest I've ever felt in my life," he says, once we're both dressed and sort of cleaned off, our hands dripping with salt water.

"Agreed."

He kisses me lightly. I notice he doesn't even look around before he does it.

"A lot of the time, I feel like I'm in a cage," I continue. "But not when I'm with you."

"Maybe that's why we're so good together," he muses.

"It feels like a dream sometimes."

"No," he says. "It's better than that. It's real."

The tide's risen, so we walk back to his house, away from the water.

I feel safe. I feel free.

I feel cared for.
I feel hopeful.

Back inside, Jules and I shower together, washing off the sand and salt for real. When we get out, I follow him to his closet wearing a towel—and whistle at the sight.

Imagine a showroom for rock 'n' roll clothes, but add a few tuxes and lots of jeans. It's gorgeously lit, with ottomans to sit on and large mirrors.

"Being able to share clothes is a side benefit of having a partner close to your size," he says.

Partner. I like that word. It feels like a step up from boyfriend.

"Double bonus if he's sponsored by designers, like you. Too bad I'm not so fashion-forward."

Jules tilts his head. "Would you ever wear a frock?"

"Me?" I say, trying not to laugh. "I, uh." I rub my face, standing in his closet with a towel around my hips. "I don't know. I suppose … maybe? I never really thought about it."

"I love your bow ties, and I think they suit you. But I'd like to see how you'd look in something more avant-garde."

Swallowing, I make a decision. "Then dress me. However you like."

His face lights up, and he claps his hands. "Really?"

I nod. "Really. I mean, I'm not promising to wear whatever you pick out to work or anything, but I think here, with you, I can broaden my horizons a bit."

He holds my hand as we walk around his closet—which is as big as my bedroom—and he starts shifting hangers, searching through the T-shirts and leather and sparkle and lace and fabric.

Julian pulls out a see-through aqua blouse. "This might look good with your coloring." He already has a pair of slim black leather pants draped over his arm.

I stare at the garments dubiously.

"Fine," I say. "I don't know why I feel nervous. It's just clothes." He hands me the shirt, and I slip it on, then tug on the leather pants, freeballing it. It takes some effort to get them up, but thankfully it's not too embarrassing.

Running my hands through my hair so it stands on end, I examine myself in the mirror, not recognizing the reflection. "I look like one of the glam rock guys from the '70s."

Julian doesn't say anything. He stands behind me, looking at me in the mirror, then moving his gaze down my back.

"What?" I ask, crossing my arms over my chest and hugging myself.

"Your arse in those trousers would be illegal in several countries."

I burst out laughing. "Hardly."

"Very much so." He tilts his head. "You look wonderful. It makes me want to keep you all to myself a while longer."

"I don't mind being discreet for a while. But when whatever this is inevitably *does* get out in the open ..."

"Yeah." He sighs.

"Julian, I understand. You're not hiding. Though I suppose you are literally in a closet right now." I chuckle. "But I'm enjoying some quiet time with you, too. And we're not going to get much of that once we go public." I turn around and wrap my arms around his neck.

"Speaking of which, what about you?"

I furrow my brow. "What about me?"

"Are you going to break up with Kurt Delmont? Publicly, that is?"

"Oh, crap," I say. "I told the PR team, but they haven't gotten back to me. I didn't mean to hurt you with that or make you worry." I make sure to look Jules in the eye. "I'll get it done," I promise.

Even if staying here, in our own private cocoon, is awfully appealing at the moment.

Thirty-Eight

Jules

One of the first things I see the following morning is an email from Lighthouse Records asking me to give one of their vice presidents a call. Robin Jackson. I know him. I've worked with him before.

Still, it's never comforting to get a message like that. Heart in my throat, I dial.

After the usual pleasantries, he says, "Julian, we take it that a lot of songs on your record are written from a bisexual point of view."

"Hmm." I look out at the Pacific Ocean shining bright and scratch my belly.

"You're a man, and you are singing songs about a man. Love songs. But you've dated women. Does this mean you're coming out as bisexual?"

"I don't identify as bisexual," I say automatically, stopping my pacing. "And you're focusing on things that don't matter. There are songs on the album that are to men and songs that are to women. There's also a song about an octopus. It has nothing to do with—"

"So you're gay, then."

I pinch the bridge of my nose. "I don't identify as gay. I don't know what I identify as, nor do I feel like adopting a term because it will make someone else feel better. I can't call myself something that doesn't feel right to me. That's no judgment on anyone else," I add. "I think those terms are great for all kinds of reasons, not the least of which is building community. They're just not for me."

The last thing I'd want to do is alienate my boyfriend, who I'm proud of. Sam's got me to open up to the idea of labels and to the benefits of defining my sexuality in some way because it could help other people.

But that doesn't mean I'm going to call myself something that isn't me. Nor do I want to invite the world into our relationship yet. I'm already vulnerable enough in the lyrics of the songs. I don't need to have them speculate more about me. Or, at least, I don't need to confirm it and give them more to talk about.

"The label would like to identify this album as an 'own voices' production, but we can't do that without your approval."

I close my eyes. "Own voices projects matter very much, but again, don't force me into claiming a banner that's inaccurate. There are so many artists who authentically want to express their own voices. Please, please, please sign them. I get enough attention."

"So how do we describe you?"

"Just Jules. The content is the only thing that matters. Not my sexuality."

He huffs. "It's not as marketable to not have a label. We're asking these questions for your benefit."

"Are you sure about that?" I ask. "Because it doesn't seem that way."

He's quiet for a long moment. Finally, he sighs. "Look. With each album, you've evolved. We'd like to see you evolve to owning up to a LGBTQIA+ label." He lets out a not-humorous laugh. "It's hard enough to figure out what genre to place your work in."

"It's not up to me to categorize it. That's your job."

For the first time since I turned in this album, I question it. All this time, I've thought it was one of my best. One where the emotions came through. One where I bared my fears and vulnerabilities.

But apparently it's not enough if it doesn't fit neatly into a box to tick.

"The album is what it is," I say. "It's good. Release it."

"Thank you, Mr. Hill. The album is still in review. I'll report to marketing that we will need to come at this from a different angle."

If that isn't a mood killer, I don't know what is.

He hangs up, and my first thought is that I want to call Sam and tell him what he said, but I'm pretty sure that would fall squarely in the area of conflicts of interest.

If Lighthouse doesn't accept the album, are we back where we started? With a potential lawsuit?

Fuck, I thought we'd got past this.

All I know is that I need Sam. And I think I'm willing to take the next step to show that I'm not ashamed of what we are to each other, even as I reject other people's need to slap an identity on me.

I call him. When he answers, I say, "It feels like my life is out of control right now."

"With what?"

"The album. I'm still waiting for approval."

He's silent for a moment, and it reminds me of that long pause in my conversation with Robin. Which isn't ideal. "I'm sorry it's taking so long," he says. "I wish I could—"

"There's nothing you can do about it," I say. "I know. I'm just venting. I need a distraction. What do you think about going out on a date?"

"Generally, I'm in favor."

"Very clever. I mean, with me. Do you want to go on a date with me?" I pace, rubbing the back of my neck.

"In public?"

I pause, and my voice gets quiet. "Yes. Will you be okay with that? Your privacy's going to go out the window."

"Okay," he says, breathless. "I mean, I want to. I super-duper want to. I need to take care of the Kurt situation beforehand, though, to avoid blowing up Pop-Pop's campaign."

"Okay? You said that fast. Think about it. You won't be a private person for much longer. The media will find out who you are and where you live, and then news vans will camp out to learn every little detail they can."

Sam chuckles. "So I'll move."

"It's not that easy."

"Julian, it *is* that easy. I understand what will happen. I'm willing to deal with it. I want to be with you. We can work out any logistics. We don't have to plan everything."

His tone makes me laugh. "Wow. The organized one isn't planning."

"The orderly one wants to go with the flow and find out where this goes. Together."

I gulp. "I can live with that."

"Just … let me break up with Kurt first. Get that cleared away." He sighs. "I'll let you know what the PR folks say. You and I might need to wait a few weeks before being seen together, so it doesn't look bad."

"If that's what you need, you got it."

Even if I don't like it. And even if I'm worried about what the future holds for my album.

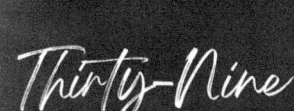

Thirty-Nine

Sam

A FEW DAYS LATER, I'M ATTENDING YET ANOTHER EVENT for my family, standing with Kurt, with whom I've been whispering furtively.

"We need to break up," I say. Between work and being with Julian, and PR apparently being busy with other things, I haven't had that planning meeting yet, and I'm getting antsy.

"Not now."

"Kurt, I don't want to wait any longer. I don't want to do this to Julian. And we're—your mom, my granddad—doing well in the polls. I would hope some little newsbite about us wouldn't matter too much." With time has come perspective. And with Julian being mine, I've become impatient.

The party is in full swing. This one's at a house in Montecito, with valet parking and more celebrities than ever. Guess that's what happens when your guests include European royalty and entertainment titans.

With all the bustle and noise, I hadn't noticed that my mother is now standing next to us. Her nails dig into my bicep, but her voice is pitched low and her smile doesn't waver. "Sam," she says, "what on earth is the matter? You and Kurt look like you're arguing."

"We kind of are," I admit.

For a second, she can't help looking shocked. "Why?"

"Because I have a real boyfriend."

Mom blinks, and the public mask is back. "Kurt is your boyfriend."

I snort. "He is not. You know this is just for the press."

"I thought over the years it had grown into something real."

Kurt's face is impassive.

My mom shakes herself almost imperceptibly. "Well, you can't break up now. Not during the campaign."

"Why?" I don't mean to sound like a whining child, but family sometimes reduces me to that.

"Think about what this campaign means, not only to your grandfather, but to all the people who are counting on him. All the gay, lesbian, and transgender people in this state. Do you want that"—she shivers—"monster to win?"

Now there's a scary thought. The leading candidate running against my grandfather has threatened to roll back all social progress we've made in the last forty years. I've seen legislation introduced seeking to prohibit trans people from playing sports or getting health care—but that's in other states. California's been leading, at least in some areas. I want to have faith that a simple change in power couldn't undo all that, but the prospect scares me.

"No," I mutter. "Pop-Pop is a much better choice. Still, what does it matter who I date?"

She pinches the bridge of her nose. "Like it or not, showing gay men in a lasting and stable relationship helps counter all kinds of negative perceptions."

"At what cost, Mom? At the cost of my heart?"

"Look, honey. I want you to be happy. But this is the greater good. I'm sure your new man—whoever he is—will be happy to support you. Ask him. He'll understand."

I sigh. "I promised him I'd make it clear I was single."

"Your mom's right," Kurt says. "You know I don't care if you're with your new man, but don't be seen in public with him. Just hold off a little longer."

I can't handle talking with either of them anymore. I turn and walk away, headed to my car, hoping no one can see my face.

Because I'm sure it's thunderous.

"It was bad, Jules," I say. "They want me to keep appearing with Kurt until Election Day."

I'm curled up next to him on his couch. He sighs. "I'm used to being the nice guy. The one who says, yeah, no problem, that's fine."

My eyes widen, and I reach out a hand to touch his thigh.

"But I really don't want you dating him anymore. I've never been jealous in my life, yet it's making me jealous to think that you're in his arms—even if it's only for the cameras. That he has his hands on you. That he's kissing you."

"I can refuse," I say. "But I'm scared."

He furrows his brow. "Of disappointing your family?"

"Well, that's unpleasant, too, but ... of the other side winning. The field is wide open, and any little misstep could cost the whole thing. And I don't want to turn California back to the Dark Ages."

"No one wants that, love," he says. "But do you really think who you are dating is important enough to swing the election?"

I give him a look.

"Okay, yeah," he concedes. "No one is expecting you to go and date, uh, me." He's silent for a moment, looking thoughtful. Then he says, "Can I at least meet your family?"

"Of course." I pull out my phone. "I'll tell them to expect my boyfriend for dinner."

"What should I wear?"

"That jersey dress that you wore to the Grammys." I'm irritated enough with my family's demands that I mostly mean it. He looked fucking hot in a sleek black tank dress that accentuated his lean frame and his toned arms.

"Pretty sure a dress, particularly one that's tailored to showcase a designer jock strap, isn't the thing to wear to meet the parents, even liberal ones."

"I'd be fine with you wearing it," I insist.

"Yeah, but I don't need to be in their face about my fashion choices. Besides, I have a new jacket I'm dying to wear."

I kiss him. "Sounds good."

Forty

Sam

"Are you ready for this?" I ask, as Jules and I walk up to my grandfather's midcentury modern showcase home, which isn't all that far from Jules's house. "Because we don't have to go in." I stop on the walkway. "If you want to leave, we can. We don't have to do this."

Jules stops me, turning to face me and put two hands on my shoulders. "I'm ready. They're your family. Of course I want to meet them. I only wish I had family to share with you. I mean, apart from Colin."

I stare at Julian and relax at the gentle look in his eyes. Then I brace myself. "It might take them a while to come around, since for years I've only been with Kurt. And also, well …"

"They may have heard of me before," Jules supplies.

"Right."

I bite my lip. Jules is wearing a tailored sapphire blue velvet jacket, dark gray striped trousers, and pointy shoes. And piles of diamonds—two dragonfly diamond brooches on his lapel, several rings, and an inch of bracelets on his wrist.

Fuck, he looks sexy in a luxe-louche way.

"Are you going to be okay, Sam?"

"Yeah. It's just that you mean something to me. And I don't want them treating you like this is a passing fancy."

He studies my expression and smiles, then leans in and gives me the lightest brush of a kiss. "Likewise. And since you're not a passing fancy, I think we'll be all right."

We walk up to the glass doorway, and I knock and open the door, our usual protocol.

Everyone's gathered in the living room, chatting and drinking wine.

"Mom, Dad, Pop-Pop, Grandma?" I say, as we walk in holding hands, "This is my new boyfriend, Julian."

Their jaws drop. They look like fish. Or some big-eyed creature from *Star Wars*.

My mom recovers fast, setting down her wine, standing up, and straightening her skirt. She walks over to us and gives me a quick hug, then holds out her hand to shake Julian's. Her head turns to me. "When you said you were dating someone, you should have told me who it was. Julian, so nice to meet you. I love your music."

And, oh god, now I remember that she does.

So now I have to share Julian with the whole world and also my mother.

That feels like just a bit too much.

My dad and grandfather come over, and we exchange introductions and get drinks before dinner is served.

I can see my grandfather react to Julian, but he recovers quickly, smiling and shaking his hand. I can see the calculations going on in his head. Will Julian Hill win him more votes or take them away?

He pulls me to the side and gestures between Jules and me, dropping his voice to a murmur. "I'm going to assume this relationship will hold off on coming to light until after the first Tuesday in November?"

"Well, that's something I want to discuss with you," I say. "I really don't want to wait that long. It feels like I'm cheating on Jules when I'm still with Kurt for the cameras, and I don't want to hurt either of their reputations."

My grandfather makes a dismissive gesture. "As long as you stay out of the limelight, it will be fine." His look hardens. "You will do that for me, right?"

I sigh. "Let's talk about it later, okay?"

He nods as if he thinks he's won, as usual.

But I meant it about talking later.

Julian, for his part, is utterly adorable, shaking hands and smiling. He takes selfies with my mom and grandmother and appears completely at ease, as usual. He's the kindest, most polite person I've ever met.

He's tall and bright, a shining star. He clicks with my family. I've been so scared that Julian, with his gender-bending fashion choices, might be too much for them, that he's not the "right kind of gay" and that they'd disapprove of our relationship for fear of losing votes, that I'd forgotten they're human beings who care about me. They should be good with this.

My stomach unclenches.

When we sit down to dinner in my grandparents' formal dining room, Jules takes the seat next to me, his legs spread so his knee touches my thigh. It's comforting and arousing.

Kurt has never given me this kind of support. Kurt's a friend and confidant but not a true lover or partner.

With Jules, it's real.

Julian unfolds his napkin and puts it in his lap. And that reminds me of a different napkin I rubbed all over his lap. Now that I know what's under his clothes … And those are not thoughts I should be having at a family dinner.

"Tell us more about yourself," my mom says, as she unfolds her napkin and holds up a dainty fork.

"Well, I'm a singer," Julian starts.

Everyone chuckles. "I think they know that," I stage whisper.

"Cheers. Yeah. I've been doing it professionally for about ten years now. Before that, I just sang at church."

Pop-Pop perks up. Dammit. Religion performs well. "What church do you go to?"

I've been watching my grandfather's reactions, searching for anything from hostility to a desire to use Jules. He's been quieter than usual, but this has gotten his attention.

"I don't go to one anymore, but my family were C of E. Church of England."

Julian's lack of interest in organized religion isn't a plus in my grandfather's mind. But I'm starting to not think that the future of queer politics rests on my shoulders, so what's a plus for him or his campaign doesn't matter as much as my feelings for Jules.

"Do you think you'll ever become an American citizen?" my grandfather asks.

"Pop-Pop," I chide.

Jules puts a hand on my shoulder. "I don't mind him being curious. And no, I don't think so. If I did, it would be to vote, but I'm not really sure that's fair. I vote back home, and that's enough."

"Isn't home here?" my mother asks.

"These days, yes. Part of me will always consider London home, though, and I do have a residence there." He turns to me. "Want to go there with me sometime?"

"Absolutely," I murmur. "And sorry about the questions."

"I truly don't mind."

"Well, we're all for LGBT rights in this house," Pop-Pop says. "Even if dealing with it in real life takes some getting used to."

Dealing with it. I open my mouth to tell him he's being insensitive, but Mom pipes up. "So many rockers are gender-bending." She smiles at Jules fondly. "You're just one in a long line."

Pop-Pop nods. "Right. You're flamboyant to get attention. I understand."

"The truth is," Jules says, "I dress the way I do because I like to. I'm actually not fond of the attention it draws to my private life."

"Surely you wouldn't wear something feminine like those bracelets if you didn't want to press buttons. You're challenging men being men." Pop-Pop sips his wine.

"That's an interesting way to put it," Jules says.

"Pop-Pop," I say, "can we change the subject?"

"I don't mind talking about it," Jules says quietly. He meets my grandfather's gaze, his voice clear. "Many people think my clothing choices, gender expression, and sexuality are all the same thing. But they aren't."

"Since you're here as Sam's partner, I assume you're gay or bisexual," Pop-Pop says placidly.

Jules presses his lips together and tilts his head. "I don't have a label for my sexuality. I am into Sam, yes. Very much so. But don't confuse my sexual orientation and clothing choices. Or my gender expression." He leans forward, elbows on the table. "I'm cisgender. I just happen to not like to be constrained by gender norms when I dress. It's … fun. More than that, it makes me feel, well, more me."

My grandfather looks confused. Mom, meanwhile, is watching Jules with glowing eyes. I think she's still bowled over by the fact that she's having dinner with Julian Hill.

Jules continues, not missing a beat. "Let me put it this way. Have you ever met a cisgender heterosexual woman who hates traditional femininity? She doesn't wear dresses or cosmetics and can't stand flowers, that sort of thing."

"Of course." Pop-Pop clears his throat.

"Her sexuality and her gender identity are what the world would consider 'normal,' while her clothing choices are androgynous, or what some might call masculine. Expressing one's femininity or masculinity—or a combination thereof—doesn't mean one is gay or straight."

Pop-Pop furrows his brows and takes a sip of his wine.

"My point is that, in today's society, women can wear a wide range of clothes and have a wide range of interests without being assumed to be gender nonconforming. Yet many people still believe that a man who dresses as I do, for example, or who enjoys romantic films, must be gay. But that whole concept is heteronormative." Jules smiles, calm and easy. "We have these things mixed up, and they need to be separate. My gender is male. Wearing a dress doesn't make me male or female, gay or straight. It just means that's what I wanted to wear on that given day. And the way I express my sexuality is in my bedroom." He pauses, and I'm sure he's thinking, "… or elsewhere."

"Hmm." Pop-Pop sits back in his chair and looks to my dad, shrugging. "You learn something new every day."

"I see," my mom says.

My dad nods. "I guess we haven't had to consider these things, since Sam is, well, Sam."

"Since I wear traditional menswear?" I say.

"And you look handsome in it, honey," Mom says.

"Have you ever thought that I might wear suits and have pursued a traditionally male profession to make up for the fact that I'm gay?" I can't believe I said that out loud.

There's a sharp inhalation around the table, and Jules takes my hand, squeezing it and pressing a kiss to the back.

"Sweetheart!" my mom says. "You don't have to make up for anything. We love you just the way you are."

"Thanks," I say. "But can you see how Jules is braver than me? Because he doesn't give a, uh, flying frick what anyone thinks of who he is. He does what he likes because it's truly him."

Although he does care about public opinion in some regards. And that's the problem.

My mom eyes both of us. "Yes, I can see that. Oh, honey, perhaps your true self is more buttoned up, though."

I shrug. "Perhaps."

"Or perhaps I can get you to loosen up a little," Jules murmurs in my ear, his lips tickling my skin.

A shiver runs through me. "Perhaps."

Pop-Pop smiles. "You explained all that very well. Do you want to write my next speech for me?"

Jules shrugs. "Sorry, I only write songs."

"Good ones," I note. And I lean over and kiss his stubbled cheek.

The rest of the meal is less fraught, with my father—in a gender-conforming display that amuses me after Jules's commentary—turning the subject first to sports and then to the biography he's been reading. Later that evening, though, as we go to leave, my grandfather pulls me to the side again, voice low. "I trust you know how to behave. Don't rock the boat until the election's over. Everyone is counting on you."

I nod, tightly. "It's not up to me, though—"

"It's up to all of us. We can't afford any scandal."

And he's right. Julian could be a scandal.

But I look at Julian, all smiles and charm and kindness, and my chest grows tight. He was so kind to my family tonight, even when he could have snapped at them. I watch the way he's grinning at my mother and charming her. He's just so easy to be around. His impish sense of humor makes everything he says seem both naughty and nice at the same time.

I will fight to be with him.

Jules

"I have an idea," I say, my voice low, mouth close to Sam's ear as we walk out the back door at Gucci in Beverly Hills. I scrape my hand through my hair and glance around. My heart starts thudding erratically in my chest, but I want this. It's been a few weeks since Sam's family dinner, and I've been thinking about doing something like this more and more every day.

We're in a service alley—nicer than most, but still a public place, albeit shielded from the main street. My driver is waiting.

I've just taken some publicity pictures for the new collection, and they closed the store for the duration. Sam came along on his lunch break, because I asked him to. Now that I'm done, he and I are escaping.

Putting an arm round him, I tug him to me. He shivers and smiles. "Okay."

"I love that you seem genuinely into whatever I suggest," I murmur, and he trembles again.

"That's because I am." He flushes.

Studying him for a moment, I step back and reach out a hand. It's not very steady. "Come for a walk with me."

Sam stares at me, blinking. "You mean that?"

I nod and bite my lip.

"In public?" He lifts an eyebrow.

I nod again. This is on my terms.

He swivels his head, studying our surroundings, then returns his gaze to me. "With you?"

"Yes, Sam." I grin gently, but my mouth is dry.

Sam sighs. "I can't. I've had meeting after meeting with the PR people and my grandfather. And they keep telling me to put it off until after the election."

His words feel like the worst possible feedback, delivered straight to my brain via an in-ear monitor. It's taken a lot for me to get to where I want this, and now he's shutting me down.

"Do you really think your grandfather will lose an election just because you get photographed on Rodeo Drive with me?"

He twists the skull ring of mine he's wearing. "Well, when you put it that way, no." He swallows. "They asked me not to be photographed, though."

Ugh. It pisses me off that other people have a say in our relationship. I fold my arms across my chest and narrow my eyes. "So that's it, is it?"

Sam licks his lips and blinks rapidly. "What's it?"

A mirthless laugh bursts out of me. "I'm asking if I can be out in public with you—really and truly out—and you're saying no. Even though all I'm suggesting is an innocent walk, and you've been asking me to be more open practically since we met."

He blows out a noisy breath and lowers his voice. "I very, very much do not want to say no. It makes me incredibly proud that you're willing to come out in this way. I'm just worried about the campaign. I don't want to ruin anything."

Shoving my hands in my pockets, I lean in and say, "All I want to do is hold your hand while going for a walk. We can do it fast, if you want."

Sam starts to say something, then considers it and stops. His brows pull in, and he looks at his feet, then looks back at me, scratching his cheek.

I stand firm, widening my feet and lifting my chin. "What do you say? I'm coming out. No press release. Nothing like that. We're just walking. Two men, together."

There's another moment, during which I can feel him hovering on the edge. I want to say the perfect thing, *will* him to choose me, choose us. All I can do is wait. And then, "Okay," he whispers, mirroring my posture, standing steady, his jaw set.

I beam at him. "Hold that thought." I take the few steps to my waiting driver, Tom. "Hey, we're going to go for a short walk. Meet you in a little bit?"

"As you wish, Mr. Hill."

"Cheers." Without any further preamble, I grab Sam's hand.

He looks down at our joined fingers and then back up at me. "Like this?"

"That okay?" My heart is beating so fast it worries me, and my insides go all fluttery.

Sam takes a deep breath and squeezes my hand. His is dry and warm. "We're gonna get photographed."

"That's what I want. But let's be fast."

He giggles. "This is the worst idea ever, but I'm sick of doing everything for everyone else." He steps into my personal space. "I want to do something for us. For me. For you."

I kiss him lightly, then tug him, and we start running. I drag him with me down the alley, around the corner, and we burst out onto Rodeo Drive.

The famous part of Rodeo Drive is short, with shiny storefronts and this utter sense of decadent luxury. All the major designers have boutiques here, with security guards outside—a few of whom I know by name.

Sam and I zigzag down the street, laughing as we dodge people strolling, families with kids, people talking on their phones or texting. We pass two convertible Bentleys stopped in the middle of the road—going opposite directions—so the drivers can chat, heedless of the traffic they're holding up. In all likelihood, it's intentional, so everyone will notice their $300,000 vehicles.

Thankfully, they're diverting pedestrian attention and keeping gawkers from focusing too much on us. Sam and I get a few pointed fingers and shouts of "Hey!", and I see a few cameras raised, but we keep going until we get to the end of the next block and double over laughing.

Then we slip into an alcove between two stores, and I press him against the wall and kiss him.

We're breathless from running, and our chests are heaving, and I don't care, because I feel so alive with him in my arms. With his clean-cut look mussed up for me and his lips all soft and sweet … he's irresistible.

Our tongues slip into each other's mouths, and I'm where I want to be, kissing Sam and holding him. Being part of his world.

I'm captivated by him. How he tastes and how he smells. The feel of him and the noises he makes, simultaneously soothing and arousing. The way I react when I'm with him, like I'm lit up from the inside.

Sam is the missing piece I didn't know I was missing, and when he's around, everything is better.

And I took a small step—a fast run down a short street—but it feels like I ran a marathon and crossed some great divide, hand in hand with my boyfriend.

Sam makes this low sexy noise in the back of his throat, and I know it's because he wants more and he won't let himself do it in public.

This feels slightly dangerous because, well, we are outside. Someone could walk by and catch us. I don't think they will—we're hidden—but it's still daring.

We break apart, panting, and laugh again.

"Jules!" Sam says. "You make me do things I never thought I'd do."

"Like break the rules?"

"Yes."

"Like have fun?"

"That, too."

I kiss his nose. "I hope you have fun with me all the time. Life's too short not to."

The searing noise of a siren passes by, and we step back from one another. He runs his hands along his thighs and adjusts himself. Then he gives me a sheepish grin. "I seem to always get carried away with you," he murmurs.

"Good," I reply.

"Do you think anyone got a picture of us?"

"I'm sure of it."

Sam nods and swallows, tidying his hair. I love the way his hair gets disheveled when he's with me, and then he puts himself together, all polished like a penny. "Okay, then. I'm proud of you."

"Thanks. And you—are you okay dealing with your family?"

"They'll be pissed. But I'll deal with them, because you're right. About everything. If you're ready to be out, I'm ready to be out with you. This won't be the end of my grandfather's career or the end of gay rights nationwide."

I tilt my head. "Shall we find Tom?"

"Let's."

When we're seated in the back seat of my limo, I look at Sam and think:

Well …

I mean …

I am …

I am so much …

I'm in love with him.

I *love* this golden man with his plump lips and an arse designed to be grabbed. I love how foppish he is. I love how calm, caring, and stubborn he is. I love him when he's proper and when he's naughty. I don't love him for anything in particular that he does. It's *who he is* … and how I feel when I'm with him.

Like I'm allowed to be myself—that's all he wants from me. I don't have to perform or put on a show … but if I want to, he'll watch.

There's nothing I wouldn't do for him. Even change the way I talk about my private life with others.

I love him.

I tug him into me, welcoming his soft, sweet-smelling weight.

He puts his head on my shoulder and smiles. "Hey," he says.

"Hey." I kiss him lightly, tucking a knuckle under his chin so he looks at me. "You're wonderful, you know that?"

"Thanks." He gives me a bashful smile. "So are you."

Forty-Two

Jules

WE DROP SAM OFF AT WORK, AND MY DRIVER TAKES ME home. Not long after I get there, Loren stops by, a weird expression on their face. "I saw the pictures from Beverly Hills."

I shrug. "So?"

Truthfully, I don't feel nonchalant. Part of me wants to vomit. I've been dreading this coming-out moment for … my entire life. Except now that it's happening, I feel a tremendous sense of freedom. Like I'm finally living my truth. I'm suddenly giddy, and tears well up behind my eyelids.

My only worries are for Sam. I hope his family doesn't yell at him, but if they do I'll go there and talk with them myself. I want to show him off to the world.

I study the photo Loren shows me on their phone screen. It's of me laughing and holding Sam's hand. It's a sweet picture, actually. And it means so much. "Send it to me, please."

They take the phone back and fiddle with it. "I guess you're moving forward with a public relationship?"

I shrug again. "Yeah, kinda. I'm still figuring out how I want to present myself. But I'm going to show that I'm in a same-sex relationship. Little by little …"

They sit down next to me on the couch, scroll, then frown.

"What?"

"You're trending on Twitter."

"That's nothing new," I say, and pull out my own phone. The first tweets don't bother me.

OH MY GOD I KNEW IT

JULIAN HILL IS SO GAY

All of the ships were real!

He's one of us!!!!!!! No wonder he flew the rainbow flag <3 <3

He should be with someone else. This guy's not good enough for him.

Even greater than my fear of losing fans is my fear of them hurting Sam. Unfortunately, I can't control that.

"These aren't so bad. I can get used to them calling me gay," I say.

Loren nods, looking fairly resigned.

We both stare at our phones, checking the public reaction. I click over to top tweets, and I'm surprised that what I see isn't a photo.

It's a *Guardian* article. "Julian Hill's Brother to Tell All."

I gasp. "Wait. *What?*"

"What is it?" Loren says. They come closer, looking over my shoulder, and do a double take. "What the hell?"

"Fucking Colin," I mutter, and start reading.

Julian Hill, gender-bending rocker and longtime champion of gay rights, has finally gone public with a same-sex relationship.

"Okay," I say, taking a calming breath. "That's okay."

However, photographs of the mega pop star cavorting with another man are the tip of the iceberg. Julian's younger brother, Colin, has reportedly signed a seven-figure deal for a candid book about his brother, their childhood tragedies, and "the unvarnished truth" about Julian's life and relationships.

"Oh my fucking hell," I say bitterly.

It's a gut punch.

This betrayal—after all I've done for Colin—feels like he's taken everything I promised to my mother and ground it into the dust.

I keep scrolling.

Sam Stone, prominent gay rights advocate and the grandson of California gubernatorial candidate Fred Stone, was photographed today with Julian Hill in circumstances that suggest a romantic relationship. But according to Colin Hill, that relationship is fraught with falsehoods. For years, Sam Stone has been photographed with his supposed boyfriend, Kurt Delmont, and the two have appeared together in numerous political advertisements and at LGBTQIA+ events. But apparently the two were never truly dating. This calls into question the elder Stone's ethics and campaign platform as well as the veracity of Julian Hill's public persona.

No.

It's bad enough that my brother's a weasel. But my sweet Sam. He can't have this on his shoulders. His family will be livid, and it has nothing to do with the photos and everything to do with my brother, who can't keep his fucking mouth shut.

Speak of the devil.

The front door opens, and I storm to the entryway. "Colin," I yell. "What the fuck were you thinking?"

He has the absolute indecency to look embarrassed. "It's a ton of money, Jules. I've been sponging off of you. I don't want to do that anymore."

"And you think telling my secrets is *less* sponging off of me?" I'm still yelling.

I've never raised my voice like this with anyone. And it's fulfilling in a way I never thought possible. Even though I'm pissed as all get-out, I also feel relief at finally letting myself show negative emotions, not just positive ones.

Colin sneers. "What's the big deal? I'm not going to tell them anything they don't already know. It's a way for me to get back on my feet—have enough that I won't need to ask you for help ever again—and it's not going to hurt you. Any publicity is good publicity, right? You'll end up making even more money from it. You always do."

My eyes roll heavenward, and my hands clench into fists. "There's so much wrong with that, I don't know where to start. Did you ever think that selling me out to the highest bidder might just end our relationship as brothers? Or my relationship with Sam? That there are things more important than money—like family?" My voice lowers. "Or did you forget how I'm the one who kept us together all these years. How I'm the one who made sure you were never on the streets. And then you fucking betray me."

"That's not what this is," he insists. "It's just a quick way to make a few quid."

"Get the fuck out of my house, Colin. I don't ever want to see you again." *I'm sorry, Mum.* Tears form in my eyes, and I squeeze them tight.

"Fine," he spits. "I'll leave."

He tears away from me and pounds down the stairs to the guest room. I hear his door slam, and I can only assume he's packing the bags he brought with him. With the advance from his book, he can find a different place to stay.

I'm itchy and anxious, and I need to call Sam, although he's at work right now. I have to move, to get out some of this energy. Normally, I'd go running on the beach, but as I look at the balcony, I see a line of boats on the ocean with lenses trained on my house. I close the blinds and let out a bark of laughter. I'm trapped. If I get in my car, they'll just follow me. I'm sure there are paps on the street, too.

Loren's feet sound heavy behind me. My voice is a croak. "I don't think I can keep him from going forward with the book."

"That book is the least of your worries," they say, and my stomach clenches.

"Why? Did something happen to Sam?"

"No. Something happened to you. Lighthouse rejected your album. They're demanding you return the advances and compensate them for the studio musicians' time."

Somehow, on some level, I'd been expecting this. After the long days of silence and that awkward phone call with the VP. At some point, I'd gone into worst-case-scenario mode—at least with regard to the studio. I hadn't seen the shit with Colin coming.

So my response is measured. "I can do that." I pause. "Right? I have enough."

"You do." They sigh. "But that's not all. Apparently Lighthouse isn't amused by today's revelations about your relationship with Sam Stone. They're asking a lot of questions. Of him."

"I can't let that happen. I can't have him get in trouble because of me."

"Might be too late for that."

"What can I do?" I ask.

They shake their head. "I'm not sure, but sit tight. We'll do what we can."

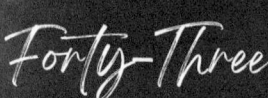

Sam

After running around Beverly Hills with Jules on my lunch break, I return to the office. Being seen with him like that was perhaps not my smartest move, but I've been wanting to go public with him so badly. And him wanting the same made my heart sing in ways I didn't know it could. I'm so proud of him.

I wonder what the pictures look like. I wake up my computer to search.

But before I click into a search engine, I see an email that makes me cold to my core.

Dear Mr. St. Martin and Mr. Stone:

After much deliberation, Lighthouse Records has made the decision to reject Julian Hill's submitted album. It doesn't fit his brand. The public wants to be entertained, not explore their fears or failings. And they're not going to be inspired if he won't claim it as an "own voices" album, which he has declined to do.

Thus, unfortunately, we want you to proceed with a formal demand for rescission of the contract and restitution of the sums paid in advance.

I wasn't supposed to get this email. I recused myself. I'm not supposed to know about any of this.

Didn't Terrill tell them?

I'm going to be sick. I'm about to hurl, hands shaking, utter dread in the pit of my stomach. I automatically reach for my phone to call Jules.

But, *shit*.

This is confidential client information. I can't tell Jules any of this.

My professional duty is to Lighthouse, not Jules. Even though I shouldn't have received this email—Terrill should have informed them of the staffing change—I did. And now I have to deal with it.

And it's not just Jules who is affected, but his whole band. What a clusterfuck.

Standing up, I hurry down the hall to Terrill's office to find out how to resolve this ethically.

Unfortunately, the client representative for Lighthouse Records is standing in his office when I burst in.

Terrill looks up. "Sam, there's a problem."

"I know," I say. "But I shouldn't have received that email. I should go."

The client rep—Kendra—steps forward. "You can stay."

"No, he can't. He's off this matter."

She glares at Terrill. "What? You made no mention of a staffing change. And we need attorneys, since we're prepared to litigate if we can't resolve Julian Hill's matter out of court."

My mouth opens and closes, but no words come out. My knees buckle, and I have to clutch the doorframe for support. I can feel all the blood drain from my face.

Kendra narrows her eyes. "Are you okay?" she asks.

"I can't," I whisper. "I can't do this. I'm recused."

"Why?" Kendra asks.

I turn to her. "I have a conflict of interest. I've been dating Julian Hill."

Terrill waves a hand. "We took him off the case. We just hadn't sent you notice yet. I'll get someone else to do the demand letter."

Kendra's hands fly to her hips, and she whips around to face Terrill. "Are you serious?" she says in a low voice. "You're just going to drop this bombshell of how your associate was screwing our artist and wave it off as nothing?"

He makes a placating gesture. "Now, calm down. Sam did nothing wrong."

"I didn't," I say, and I know I'm pleading. "I didn't have sexual relations with him until after he turned in the recording. Before that, I was just helping him to write it."

"Well, the executive team isn't satisfied with the album at all. They don't want to release it because it isn't marketable. And now it looks like we need to investigate what happened. This is extremely unprofessional."

"I'm sorry," I say, so embarrassed I want to crawl out of my skin. "I thought my recusal had been communicated to you."

"Why didn't you disclose this?" she asks Terrill. "As the managing partner, you had a duty to tell us if a conflict arose."

His grin overstays its welcome. "Press of business. My apologies. There's nothing to worry about. We can handle this." He holds out his hand to her.

But she's typing furiously on her phone. "Um, no. You can't. I'm going to recommend we take our business to a different law firm."

No. No, no, no.

While Terrill is an asshole, I didn't want to lose the client.

She storms out.

I hold up my hands. "Before you say anything, I quit. I'll turn in my badge."

"Get the fuck out of here," he says, rage barely contained. "We'll deal with you later."

Fuckity. Fuck.

I turn and run.

"You did *what?*" my mother screeches.

I'm on the phone, pacing around my living room, twisting the skull ring on my finger. Julian's ring. It's giving me some comfort, but I'm still a wreck.

"I got photographed with Julian Hill," I repeat.

And I quit my job. The one that I spent my entire life working toward. I only hope I can beg my way into a job at Weston & Ramirez and don't end up working god knows where.

"When we specifically told you not to."

"Mom," I protest. "It's not that big a deal."

It's a big deal.

"It very much is," she says. "Particularly given that there's an article in the *Guardian* saying Julian's brother claims the campaign has been making up your relationship with Kurt all along."

Which it has been, but that is definitely not what she wants to hear right now.

"We are fully in damage control mode. I have a car bringing Kurt over to pick you up. You and he are going to go for a walk on the Santa Monica Pier and get photographed at Muscle Beach. You are going to tell the press that the photographs from earlier today were just fun with a friend and that your relationship with Kurt is very real and as strong as ever."

"What? No!" I sweep my free hand out.

Her sharp voice stops me in my tracks. "Your grandfather's slipping in the polls, and this story could be catastrophic. We all have to do what we can to help. If you get this campaign derailed, you'll regret it for the rest of your life."

My throat aches. "Mom. Have some perspective. I'm not that important to the campaign." Though a story about the relationship being fake isn't good news. Mom's right; that's the sort of thing that might blow up. "I think there might be a silver lining here. Julian is such a big name, the bigger story as far as the press is concerned has to be him coming out as being in a same-sex relationship." I'm reaching, but hey—it's worth a try to get her to calm down a bit.

"I thought everyone already assumed he was gay."

"That's what I said originally," I admit. "But there's a difference between suspicions and fact. It's a big deal for him to confirm it."

"It's not too late for him to deny it, though. He could say it's a misinterpretation, like the *Guardian* article."

"He's not going to do that."

"Well, we need to do what we can on our end, anyway."

My stomach hurts.

There's a knock on my door. I cringe.

"Is he there yet?" my mom asks.

"Hold on." I open the door and Kurt is standing there, looking grim. "Yes," I say into the phone. "Kurt's here. Yes, I'll go out and take fake pictures one last time. But no more." I hang up on her.

"You ready?" Kurt asks, his smile forced.

Checking my hair in the mirror, I nod, grab my keys, and follow him out to the waiting car.

"Look," Kurt says, "I know you don't want to do this. But we can't have that bigot in charge. One last photo op should take the heat off."

"Yeah." I sigh. "Okay." I think he's wrong; if Colin really told the press we've been faking this relationship …

Oh god. Does Julian know about the article? He must. What is he thinking? What is he *feeling*? My chest feels heavy, and there's a sour taste in my mouth. I text Julian.

> **Sam**: We have a lot to talk about. I quit my job, and there's some article? Colin?
>
> **Jules**: Call me
>
> **Sam**: I can't right now. Too much going on.
>
> **Sam**: My family have basically ordered me to go on a public date with Kurt right now.
>
> **Jules**: What?
>
> **Sam**: I'm in a car, headed to go, like, hold hands or kiss or be affectionate in public.
>
> **Sam**: It's making me sick.

And it is. My chest is tingling, and my stomach is rolling.

> **Sam**: I'm so sorry.
>
> **Jules**: What do you want to do?

I sniff in annoyance, my fingers flying over the screen.

> **Sam**: It doesn't matter what I want. Politics is all that matters right now. We can't have Fred Stone lose because of me.

As we drive toward the beach, images from the past few weeks flood my brain. Julian in my office, offering me my pocket square back. Dancing with me under the twinkle lights. Taking time to hang out with me after his concert. Being vulnerable with me, letting me see his rational and irrational fears. And our time at the cabin. On the beach. In his bedroom.

Jules has never lied to me. He's always been honest about how he's not exactly straight, but he wants his privacy.

And today he gave up that privacy for me.

My phone buzzes.

> **Jules**: I'm livid with Colin. But if he goes forward with this story, won't it be better if at least we can show we're in a genuine relationship now? And that your family supports us? Wouldn't that maybe help shift the tone of the coverage?

He's right.

And the thought of going out with Kurt, holding his hand for the cameras, kissing him, when I'm in love with Jules—yes, I'm so in love with him—is filling me with dread.

This isn't how I want to live. I want to be in charge of my life. I want to be honest. I don't want to do things because of the way they look. I want to do them because of the way they *feel*.

The way I feel when I'm with Julian—when he tilts my head up with his knuckle and kisses me. When he's a solid and comfortable presence at my family dinner.

My brain goes blank, and my hands start to tremble. At first I think I'm panicking the way Jules did in the elevator. But then I realize I'm pissed off. Pissed at my family, pissed at myself, pissed at the world.

A hot tear slides down my cheek, and I bat at it with the back of my hand.

A voice that sounds suspiciously like my mother tells me I'm overreacting. That this is a charade I've played for years now, and what's one more time in the grand scheme of things?

Especially when I've dedicated my life to the LGBTQIA+ rights movement.

Without my old firm's backing, I won't be able to work on the initiatives I was hired to champion. Even if I can get a job with Weston & Ramirez, they probably don't have the same clout—or the budget to support that kind of pro bono commitment. Fuck. I'm hurting the cause. Maybe I should just keep everything the way it's been. That's what everyone wants me to do—my family, the campaign. Probably Julian's fans. They want him to stay single.

I know I'm spiraling, or seesawing, or maybe my brain is on a Tilt-A-Whirl. I'm going back and forth and feeling sick, but I can't get my thoughts to slow down long enough to think anything through.

I look at Kurt. He's a friend. I've been affectionate with him for years.

But the thought of kissing him … I can't. Everything's changed. I've fallen in love with Julian, and I can't do this to him.

I go hot all over, and I feel like I'm going to faint.

Kurt looks at me and calls to the driver, "Stop the car. Pull over, please."

He puts an arm around me, but I shy away from him.

"Sorry," he says. "Shh, Sam. It's okay. Hey, I'm here."

His voice sounds like it's coming from somewhere hollow.

"Take a deep breath," he continues. "When's the last time you went to yoga?"

I think about it. "A while," I say in a hoarse whisper.

"Do you need me to call someone?"

"Julian. Please." I hand him my phone, unlocking it. I vaguely hear Kurt's muffled voice—even though he's sitting right next to me, I can't make out his words through the buzzing in my ears. Then he's asking the driver something, and I notice the car moving again.

I'm not sure how long we drive, but when we slow down, I recognize the gates in front of Julian's house.

And for the first time since I got that email back in my old office, I feel at peace. Jules comes running up to the car and flings open the door before we've stopped moving. I stumble out into his arms.

Forty-Four

Jules

"Hey," I whisper into the top of Sam's head as I embrace him. "I'm here. It's okay. Whatever it is, we can work it out." I look over his shoulder at Kurt Delmont. We've never met before, and I haven't thought particularly kindly of him over the past couple of months, but I'm grateful he's brought Sam here now. I raise my eyebrows to ask what happened.

Kurt shrugs. "I'll let him explain. Just tell him I've got his back."

I study him, and he seems sincere. I nod. "Thanks."

Backing away from me, Kurt returns to his seat in the car, and it takes off. I urge Sam along and escort him inside.

It's getting near sunset, and I hope the flotilla outside has dissipated. I peek out through the closed shades, but seeing a few intrepid paparazzi in boats, I keep them shut.

I have a door open, though, and the fresh breeze makes me feel not so trapped.

We curl up on a couch, me stroking Sam's hair. He doesn't say anything, and I don't make him talk. I just hold him until his breathing regulates and he loosens his grip on me.

"Want some water?" I ask.

He nods and wipes at his eyes with the backs of his hands. I get up and bring him a glass of cold water and a damp cloth for his face, then snuggle in behind him. He drains the water, then sags against me. "Tell me what happened," I murmur.

"I couldn't do it," he whispers.

"Couldn't do what?"

"Kiss Kurt." His words make my gut twist. "My family ordered me to go be seen with him, to counter the pictures of you and me and the article and everything. But I didn't want to. I can't pretend anymore that I want to be with anyone other than you. Because I don't. You're the only one I want."

His words leave me breathless and excited. I shift around so we're facing each other. His eyes are red, his face is puffy, his hair's a mess, and he's never looked more beautiful.

Lifting his chin up with my knuckle, I murmur, "Sam Stone, I need you. I need you like I need to breathe. Like I need to sing. If I couldn't have you, I don't know how I could go on. I mean—that's not some manipulative 'You can't ever leave me or I'll die' bollocks, but … I'd feel like part of me was missing. You're it for me. Do you understand?"

"Yes," he whispers.

"Good. Because I am totally, completely, outrageously, head over heels in love with you," I say. "Fearlessly, thoroughly in love with you."

"I love you, too," he says. "So much that it hurts."

My smile just might break my face.

He keeps talking, sniffling between words. "I never believed in love—not for myself. I never thought I'd find anyone who cared for me the way you do. Everything seems clearer when you're around. I feel stable and settled. You make me feel like I matter. Like what I think means something. And you make me feel like I'm not second best, a person who ends up getting left behind. I feel like, together, we can handle anything—the public, my family, whatever comes at us."

"We can." I hug him, and he feels so right in my arms. Because he's supposed to be there. Because he's my Sam.

We sit together quietly for a few minutes before I tell him about Colin, and then he gets agitated again.

"Today has been the wildest day," he says. "Apparently Terrill never communicated to the Lighthouse rep that I had recused myself, so she was outraged when I said I had a conflict."

"And you quit."

"I did."

"They rejected my album," I say.

He noticeably relaxes. "They told you. I found out this afternoon, too, but I didn't know if you knew, so I felt caught in the middle."

"I'm sorry about that. They won't have to sue me. I'll just repay everything." I press my lips together in a hard line. "Easy come, easy go. Loren's going to see if we can find another label to contract with once this is done."

My phone buzzes for the millionth time today, and I pull it out. "It's James," I say to Sam. "Do you mind?"

"Not at all." He tucks an arm around me.

> **Winterthorn**: So you decided to cause a scandal?
>
> **Jules**: Hello to you too
>
> **Winterthorn**: When do I get to meet him?
>
> **Jules**: Soon
>
> **Winterthorn**: Excellent. I want to threaten him.
>
> **Jules**: Why?
>
> **Winterthorn**: Because if he hurts you, he'll have to answer to me.

I look up at Sam. "My best mate says you're not allowed to hurt me."

He bursts out laughing. "Em said the same thing. Have you seen the response to you being out with me?"

"It's ... not horrible, last time I looked," I say.

I open Twitter, where I'm still trending high, with most tweets supportive, and we read some together.

Sam is great for him. If it was worth it for him to come out because of Sam, I think by definition that means Sam is wonderful.

We should all just leave him alone. Give him some privacy

Tell me all the juicy gossip. I want to know every last bit.

Can you picture those two in bed? Oh god I hope they have a sex tape. It would be so hotttt.

"That's better than I thought," he says, smiling. "So ... what do we do about my grandfather's campaign?"

"We tell the truth. Let me talk with Loren."

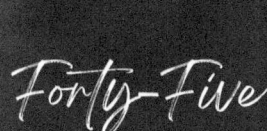

Forty-Five

Sam

A FEW DAYS LATER, LOREN HAS ARRANGED A PRESS conference. Julian's still not speaking with Colin. And my work has given me my last paycheck.

I'm unemployed, but I have an interview next week. And my old job isn't the only way I can work on advocacy.

For now, I have something else to do.

My pulse is spiking and skittering all over the place, with sharp peaks and deep valleys. And I'm not even the one who has to do the public speaking today. Jules and I talked about it, and while I'm willing to *not* just stand around and look pretty, let's be real: his fans don't want to hear from me. I'm merely Exhibit A.

His adoring public wants to hear *him*.

The Stone and Delmont campaigns issued a joint press release stating that they were supportive of my relationship with Julian and that Kurt and I are longtime friends whose romance had cooled but who remained close. I'm fine with that. Not everyone needs to know my business.

I hold Julian's hands tightly, like he's a sail in the wind and I'm the carabiner holding him by a grommet. He's in full rock god glory, wearing black leather pants and a black net blouse that shows off his tattoos, his hair artfully untidy. I note the tip of my pocket square peeking out of his back pocket. I'm in a dark gray pinstripe suit with a pink bow tie. We don't match, but I think we work.

Leaning over, I whisper in his ear, fingering the skull ring he gave me. "Don't forget, I love you."

His grin when he whips his head my way almost makes me stumble, it's so dazzling. He's got a dimple in his cheek that sometimes shows, sometimes hides. I get a glimpse of it, and it makes my heart happy. We eye each other, silent communication that says:

I believe in you.

I trust you.

I know you can do this.

And:

We fucking rock.

We belong together.

"I love you, too," he murmurs. Then, a little louder, "Shall we?"

He radiates more confidence than I feel, which makes sense—he feeds off the energy of a crowd. Though, to be fair, this is different from his concerts.

More exposed. Less produced. All real.

We're off to the side of a hotel stage, a stand bristling with microphones in the center. Peeking out into the crowd of reporters, I'm not sure if I'm anchoring him or vice versa.

"I'm glad we're doing this together," he says.

Holding hands, we walk out onto the stage, and the cameras immediately start snapping, flashes going off like fireworks. It's disorienting for a moment, but we navigate to the podium.

I drop his hand and take a step back. We discussed what degree of PDA we'd give them, and, well, some things are private.

While I can't see Jules's expression from where I stand, I can see the reaction of the crowd, and they're rapt, quieting down immediately as he opens his mouth to talk. Old-school reporter notebooks with pencils, iPhones, professional video setups, and everything in between are set to record what Julian Hill is going to say.

Julian speaks directly into the microphones. "Hey," he says in his gorgeous voice. "Thanks for coming today." I can see his shoulders rise and fall, and I want to squeeze his hand. "I've been feeling the need to say something publicly that I've never said before." He takes another deep breath. "It's about who I love. Who I choose to be with.

"I've always said in the past that this was private, because it was. It is. Some people took my desire for privacy as an indication I was ashamed of my sexuality or that I was trying to hide. I wasn't. I just didn't want to bring the whole world into my bedroom.

"But now I want to share with you two things. First, I am in a committed relationship with Sam Stone. So, second, yes, at least a facet of my sexuality is that I'm not straight. I don't have a label beyond that. Don't ask. I don't know. None of the terms I've heard has ever felt right for me.

"However, I want to talk directly to those who might not be in this room. If you're questioning the gender you are attracted to, or whether you're interested in sex or romance at all, I want you to know that it's okay to take the time to figure it out. You don't owe anyone a definition. And you don't have a responsibility to label yourself in some way to make someone else happy."

A shiver races through me. I'm so glad he's doing this. I'm so glad he's stepping out and being the leader he is.

Jules continues, "But not defining yourself can make it more difficult to find community. And sometimes community is the most incredible thing you'll ever know. If you feel comfortable identifying with a community, then do it. You don't need my permission to be who you are."

He looks at me and smiles. "I don't ever want my partner here to think I think less of him because I don't tell you about him. Quite the contrary: I want to keep him to myself because he's so special. Some things need to be just ours. So, there's a balance. I want you to know that I'm with Sam, and I'm overjoyed about that, and I hope you'll be happy for us—or, at least, respectful of what we share with the world and what we keep private. Next, I recognize that as a public figure I have a responsibility. I have a leadership role, even if I didn't totally intend it. And as part of that, I want to tell you that it's okay to be you. Whoever you are. If you are comfortable identifying as a particular label, I am proud of you. If you don't know what label fits you, I'm proud of you. If you don't ever want to find out, I'm proud of you. Wherever you are on your journey to claim or reclaim your own body, just as you are, you are worthy of love and respect.

"I've gone a long time thinking you don't need to hear this from me. Having some bloke say you're gorgeous just the way you are isn't going to solve anything. But maybe you *want* to hear it from me. Maybe me saying this to you can help.

"So. You are wonderful just the way you are. If it makes you happy to find a group to be a part of, go find them. And if you feel more comfortable blazing your own path, go do it. We don't have to fight for space. There's room for everyone.

"I wish you much love and light. And I wish you find someone who makes you feel as good as Sam makes me feel. Thank you."

He takes a step back, and the room explodes with noise from people standing up, waving hands, asking questions.

But he's not answering reporters' questions today. Although I think he's answered a few for himself.

He looks around for me and grabs my hand. His palm is clammy. That's the first indication I've had that this got to him at all.

You'd never know he was stressed, though, from the way he smiles.

Drawing our clasped hands to his mouth, he kisses my knuckles. I'm sure the pictures will show me gazing at him adoringly.

Well, they should.

With a bow of his head, he waves, and we walk off stage together.

"I've never been more proud," I whisper in his ear in the wings. "And when we get home, I have ideas of things I want to do with you that don't involve any politics or labels. Or clothes."

"That's an excellent plan."

My phone buzzes.

Emily: OMG OMG OMG

Sam: He's brave, isn't he?

Emily: When can I have the "don't hurt my best friend" talk with him?

Sam: I'll ask.

Emily: It will be the new highlight of my life.

Forty-Six

Jules

After my press conference, Sam and I are walking along the beach when he starts humming a song.

"What is that?" I ask.

"It's a song by this indie band I like." He pulls out his phone and plays it for me, the noise somewhat muffled by the crash of the waves.

"That's what I should do. Just post my songs direct," I say. "I made the music. I've cut checks to repay the label and the band." I paid Lighthouse back for everything they requested: all the studio time and the fees for the producers and studio musicians. The whole advance. I didn't want to owe them anything.

"Have they signed over the rights to the tracks?"

"They have." I trace a half circle in the sand with my toe. "If Loren can't find a smaller label to go with, I'm gonna do this on my own."

"I believe in you," is all he says.

I grab him in my arms, electricity buzzing all over my skin, and kiss him.

I have nothing to hide anymore.

A few months later, early in the morning, my phone rings. I mute it, not wanting to disturb the beloved man in my arms. He snuggles in closer, and I sigh.

But I can't ignore the call, much as I want to. Only a few people ever call me, and one of them is lying next to me. So it must be important.

Yawning, I hit the button to return the last call. "Hey, Loren."

"Have you seen the latest streaming numbers?"

I rub my face. "No."

"Check them. Because you're number one in so many categories right now they may have to create a new category just for you. Everyone on social media is talking about your album. They love it. The Hillions are starting to create all these 'Face your fears with love' things. You did it."

Blinking, I stare at my phone. "Are you telling me that the album Lighthouse said would never sell is selling?"

"It's selling faster than anything we've seen in decades. And people are so excited about the cover art that they're preordering the vinyl."

"Wow." We struck a deal with Kurt to use his painting of two men embracing, the one I first saw hanging in Sam's office, as the cover.

"And they're loving the video at the mini-golf place. It looks like it was shot on an iPhone with you just having fun."

"That's 'cause it was."

"I know. Still, it's got a great look."

"What's up?" Sam asks sleepily.

I kiss his lips. "It seems your boy here may be doing rather well for himself with his new album."

"Seriously?" He sits up, the blanket dropping from his shoulders, exposing his torso. His body radiates heat. He's all hard planes combined with soft, drowsy pleasure, and I can't get enough of him.

"Seriously."

"Lighthouse must be kicking themselves right now. Serves them right for being so narrow-minded."

"There's my champion." I pull over my laptop and log into a few music sites, seeing that yes, indeed, my new release is trending everywhere. Not one or two songs. The whole album. And not just in one place, but in various categories.

Because my songs transcend labels.

It's nice to be validated like this, but I'm more heartened that people are connecting with the music, which is all I really ever wanted.

"We need to celebrate," he says. "Once we're awake, I mean."

"Do you have any ideas of celebratory things we could do before we wake fully?"

"I have lots of ideas," he says. He carefully sets the laptop aside and then tackles me to the bed.

I kiss his shoulders, brushing my lips along his skin, watching the tiny hairs stand up. Watching the way he shivers and reacts. Feeling his low moans. I chuckle. "That good?"

"So good."

I ghost my hands over him, and he lets me. I love this part. When he lets me touch him. When it's just us and I know what we both want.

I feather my fingers over his nipples and listen to his breath, indulging, enjoying him. I let myself feel him, my lips caressing his skin.

He squirms under me. "Get a move on, Hill. I need you."

"Need?"

"Definitely need."

"I feel the same way," I murmur.

I trail my fingers down and reach his hard cock. I scratch my nails through his happy trail and over his balls, and he groans. Then I grasp the base of his cock and slide my hand up to the head, where I know he likes to be tugged.

His groan is guttural, feral. It's nothing like his buttoned-up public persona. Knowing I can do this to him—turn him inside out—is one of my favorite things.

I kiss him hard and then somehow end up licking his cock. Oops.

Well, since I'm here, I might as well take a big suck. My mouth floods with precome, and I'm lost in him. I'm falling and our bodies are crashing and everything is so amazing and he's right here and it's too much to handle except that it's not. And then the tables are turned and he's holding me. He's kissing me.

When Sam kisses me, the world falls away and all I focus on is him. I get this way when singing. Or writing. But with Sam, like this, I feel more myself than I do at just about any other time.

And I love everything about it.

Forty-Seven

Sam

I walk around a different floor of the same Century City building I worked in for years.

The construction padding has moved on to another elevator by now, but this floor is put together and gleaming—though, on the whole, this firm feels more like a place where people work than one designed to impress clients.

"And this is your office," Shelby says.

Shelby is the receptionist at Weston & Ramirez. He's a chatty, slim, twinkish kid.

The office is small but functional, with a desk, a laptop computer and docking station, a credenza, an empty bookcase, and a few chairs.

It'll do. It will totally do.

Lighthouse dropped any talk of an ethics complaint against me when Jules's indie album took off. I expect they decided the PR would've been too negative if they were seen to be attacking his partner—especially since their opinion of his album was so dramatically overruled by the public.

And, to my and Jules's surprise and relief, Colin Hill pulled out of the book deal and went back to college to study business. While that didn't fix everything between him and Jules, it helped. They're still not speaking, but maybe they'll get there eventually.

"If you need any office supplies, I can show you where to get them, or you can just ask me." Shelby claps his hands. "Let me show you the rest of the place, and then I'll leave you to get settled."

I nod. "Sounds good."

He points out the names of the partners on the ream of letterhead waiting on my desk. "Everyone here is either LGBT+ or an ally."

We walk down a hallway on the side of the building with the nicer views. "August Ramirez has his office here," he gestures, "and Noah Weston is here." He grins. "They founded the firm and have been best friends—and no more than friends—since they were kids. There's an office pool on how much longer it will take them to get together." He claps his hand over his mouth. "Sorry, that was inappropriate. But really, everyone sees it but them. My god, when will they just kiss?"

"Odds are never," a tall man in a suit says.

"This is Danny Villaseñor," Shelby says. "He's one of our litigators."

Danny and I shake hands. "Nice to meet you. I'm Sam Stone. I do transactional work."

"Welcome." Danny's super handsome, with a look about him that's more Miami clubster than LA cool. "You're the one dating Julian Hill, right?"

"He's my boyfriend, yes."

"Cool. Invite him to happy hour."

"That's a thing we do," Shelby says. "Every Friday at 4:30, we close up and go into the break room with beer and wine ... or, if you don't drink, there's soda and water and snacks. August and Noah think it's good for firm morale. It's not required, but they're a lot of fun."

I hook my fingers in my belt loops. "I look forward to it."

The vibe at this place is a million times better than my old firm. I can't wait to get started. After giving me the tour, Shelby drops me back at my office, where I'm visited by partner after partner until I finally am left alone to settle in.

I think I'm gonna like it here.

Sam

MY MAN STANDS ON STAGE, CRADLING THE MICROPHONE, his husky, rich voice magnificent. It's modulated and expansive, precise and messy in turn, full of emotion yet clear on the lyrics.

The crowd is hushed, listening attentively. We're at an outside amphitheater, and the stars twinkle overhead, looking magical.

And Jules is singing a song he wrote for me.

I can't help the tears that stream down my face. Fuck toxic masculinity. I'm moved.

My boyfriend—my life partner—my other half is telling the world that he loves me.

And by sharing that truth, he's encouraging them to go and love, too.

It's a beautiful circle he's created, and I'm lucky to be a part of it.

The crowd below him sings along with every word. And I feel like somehow they are adding to our love. Their love for him and for each other—for the people in their lives—commingles until all there is is love. The way it was always supposed to be.

And thank Rihanna, since my grandfather won the governor's race, it might stay that way.

"I want to introduce to you all my partner, if you'd like to meet him," Jules says after the song ends.

I grin and walk slowly out to him, and the applause is thunderous.

He's shirtless, his new octopus tattoo winking at me. I'm wearing my usual bow tie and slacks, although with suspenders and no jacket. Rather casual for me. I walk up to him and take his hand.

"This is Sam Stone, everyone."

I wave.

"I've come to realize something," Jules says. He raises my hand to his lips and kisses my knuckles.

I grin and say into the microphone, "What's that?"

It's not an exaggeration to say the crowd goes wild.

He lets go of my hand and holds his hands out in front of him. "I'm not afraid of anything anymore. My childhood fears, like octopi, are gone. I can face my adult fears. I feel … whole."

Again, a massive cheer.

"Me, too. Especially when I'm with you," I say, hearing my words amplified throughout the stadium.

Jules looks at me as he says into the mic, "It amazes me that, out of all of the souls on the planet, we found each other."

"You're so romantic," I chide, and the crowd says, "Aww."

He shrugs. "Sometimes. Maybe my next album will be full of sappy love songs. With you accompanying on piano."

"Can they be sappy if they're true?"

The crowd says "Aww" again and then starts chanting, "Kiss! Kiss! Kiss!"

Jules smiles at me. "Up to you. Do you want to give them what they want?"

"We could," I say.

"Then, perfect." He reaches out and tucks a knuckle under my chin. And then he kisses me. In front of smartphones and social media. In front of an audience of thousands, and millions watching at home. In front of the whole world, Jules claims me as important to him. I shiver with joy and gratitude.

He smiles against my lips. "I know one thing for certain."

"What's that?"

"Me and you. We're together. Unambiguously."

Bonus Ambiguous Scenes

Note from Leslie:

I don't write books in chapter order i.e., starting from the beginning and working my way to the epilogue. Instead, I start with the scene I really want to write—usually the one that sparked the idea for the book—then continue writing chapters in random order, based on what sounds like the most fun or what feels best to me. When I have enough scenes written, I rearrange them … hopefully in an order that makes sense. With this method, I'm usually starting the writing process somewhere in the middle of the story. That said, even though I start in the middle, I usually have a strong idea of the opening scene.

Not so with *Ambiguous*. The problem was I had *too many* ideas on how to start it.

The very first draft began with the scene where Karen interviews Jules. I changed it to Sam going to work—what eventually became Chapter 2. Then I wrote Jules waiting backstage to sing at a concert. The final version uses a portion of that chapter, but I cut all but the very end of the original draft. While the interview and Sam going to work both ended up in the book in different places, the full story of Jules backstage did not. So … here is the original beginning:

One

Jules

The warm, syrupy tea coats my throat as I drink it down. I'll work my throat ragged and raw by the end of tonight's show, so I take good care of it. Based on stories of rockers from the '70s and '80s, it's obvious the hedonistic rock 'n' roll lifestyle isn't sustainable, so I've tried to learn from their mistakes.

Even through the thick walls of the arena, a low thrum of bass and drums is audible. Our opening band—Ivy—should be on their last number. When they finish, the crew will quickly switch the stage over for me and my band.

And then I go on to face … *everyone*. My goal? To keep my fans happy.

That's not as effortless as it seems.

"Hungry?" Stu looks up as I pace in the greenroom, his mouth full of sandwich.

"No, thanks." I can't stomach much before performing. A few sips of soup and some crackers are all I can handle. I'll have a proper meal after the show.

My trusty guitar sits in the corner. I'm rarely without one backstage. This one is an old friend, and it keeps my nervous fingers company.

And, yes. I get anxious. Quite. Even though this isn't my first time playing this large a crowd.

Not for the first time, I wish someone were here just for me.

Obviously, everyone—literally everyone—is here for me, since I'm the show. All I'm saying is, I wish I had a partner I could confide in. Someone to hug before I go on.

I don't. But I have my touring band, which counts for something, I suppose.

Looking around, I see I'm not the only one who can't stay still. While Mitch, the drummer, sits to the side playing on his phone, he's twitchy, tapping out a rhythm with his toes. Like me, a few of the backup singers sip hot tea and move about the room, full of pre-performance jitters. The only members of the band staying still are Lizzie and Janice, my guitarists, who lie on a couch, Lizzie's head in Janice's lap.

I'm keyed up. Energy courses through me as I complete another circuit of the cluttered space, and I'm dying for a way to let that energy out. I'll do it on stage.

Greenrooms always feel sticky. Each one has a soul, like they're imbued with the ghosts of past performances … as well as metric tons of past jitters. It's an interesting vibe, but I don't want to think about everyone who's sung at Staples Center before—including myself—or I'll feel intimidated. Right now, I'm going a bit out of my skin, even though I know when I get out on stage I'll feel the power and the rush of the moment.

Some people skydive or take drugs. I sing for thousands.

Taking a deep breath, I work on getting in the headspace to perform, doing my best to ignore any distractions and tamp down the rising nerves. With my eyes closed, I hum the first tune, my thumbs tapping against the cup, and focus on what I have to do.

I'm a singer. I have to not only hit the notes but *perform* them. I must tap into that deep, emotional place where what I'm feeling and what the song means come across to the audience.

Oh, and it needs to sound bloody brilliant.

I'll never be associated with something less than the best it can be. Ever.

Which is why my next album is so late. I've been stuck, needing it to be perfect.

I suppose that's what has separated me from all the rest. From my previous bandmates and the supposed competition. It isn't talent or any one thing. I pay attention to dozens or even hundreds of little things and make sure they're all amazing, because the cumulative effect can blow away an audience.

As I hope to do tonight.

Ivy ends, and minutes tick by while our roadies set up. The buzz in the greenroom increases.

"Five minutes, Julian," Loren says, poking their head in, and I nod and toss my cup.

Time to go.

I don't believe in making people wait for me. They've already waited for the day of the show and then through the opening bands at this concert. I don't need to be a tosser and make them stand around a half hour beyond when we're scheduled. Besides, some of the audience are quite young. I'm not going to keep a bunch of tweens or teenagers up until two in the morning. As much as I curse in private, I try to keep it a family show when I'm behind a microphone because I like having mums and their kids and their nans all in the audience at once.

The band files out before me, wishing me luck, and I smile and wave at them as they leave, my legs still restless. After they take their places, after Mitch settles into his drum kit and everyone else checks their instruments, *that's* when I show up.

That's when I step out front and face down thirteen thousand people—thirteen thousand people who are now chanting my name.

I can hear them begin, a dull sound muffled by the walls, but inescapable.

"Jules! Jules! Jules!"

Note from Leslie:

I originally had Jules and Sam being a bit naughtier than they were in the book and not keeping their ethical resolve to avoid having an intimate relationship while Sam was working for Lighthouse Records. An example of that is in this cut scene. When I edited the book, I realized what I really wanted was for Jules to sing to Sam. I kept that in but put it in a different chapter. At any rate, here's them being a little naughtier, while Sam is still working for the record company.

Thirty-Nine

Sam

Jules: Almost done. Producers working on mixes. I need a night off. Come dancing with me

Sam: I'm sorry, what are you talking about? Where do you want to go?

Jules: I want to dance with you

Jules: Will you come dancing with me? In a gay club

Jules: Does it violate lawyer ethics to dance?

Sam: No, of course not.

I've been to a few clubs before. But I'm wondering where Julian Hill would go. Probably some exclusive place.

Jules: I'll pick you up

That evening, a dark car pulls into my underground parking garage, and a driver opens the door to let me in.

Julian's outfit causes a physical reaction in my core. He's wearing tight black pants with very thin gray pinstripes, a white eyelet shirt with a Peter Pan collar, and a dark blue granny sweater, and it's so *him*. My fingers itch to touch him, but he doesn't get out, likely not wanting to be seen on security cameras. When I step into the car, he slides an arm behind me and I snuggle into his warmth.

Snuggling the enemy is fine, right?

Not that Julian's the enemy.

"You look wonderful," I say. And sweet Sheeran, he smells good.

He lifts his chin and gives me a once-over. "You look fantastic as well."

I shrug. I'm wearing a dress shirt, tie, and dark slacks. Not particularly trendy, but it is particularly me. "Where are we going?"

Julian smiles and gives my shoulder a squeeze. "Club One."

Excitement courses through me. "I've never been there. How are you planning on getting in without a million photos?"

He grins. "You'll see."

Here, behind the tinted car windows, he and I are in our own world. With the privacy screen up, not even the driver can see us.

I like being with him. Even though we're tempting fate by going out in public, to a gay club, no less.

I'm not concerned solely for him, though. I don't want to hurt the campaign.

But what's the worst that can happen? We get photographed? We can say we're friends. Being seen with someone, especially when I'm working with him, is not enough to lose me my job, my grandfather his election bid, or Jules his fans, especially when Jules is so vocally supportive of LGBTQ+ rights. It'll be fine.

I hope.

His hand hovers over my arm, but he pulls it back, once again practicing restraint.

I'm not sure anyone but us will ever know we've not had more of a physical relationship yet, but it makes me feel better knowing if I got called on it, I could say all there have been are a few consensual kisses, and it hasn't affected my judgment.

Not much, at least.

The driver takes us to the club with a long line outside the front, pretty boys in everything from elegant designer wear to next to nothing, and then down an alley. You'd expect dumpsters and graffiti in an alley, but the elegant secondary entrance has a black-clad bouncer, who nods as Julian walks up, letting us in with a, "Welcome, Mr. Hill."

Clearly, this place is known for its discretion. No wonder Jules chose it.

We go up a flight of stairs, and a server ushers us to a room at the top. It's curtained off, with a balcony looking over the dance floor. The music is thumping, but we can still hear each other in this private room. There's a plush couch, a few scattered chairs, a low table, and an area where we could dance if we wanted to, along with two TV monitors that alternate between shots of people on the dance floor and music videos. A small leather menu sits on the table, and the server waits quietly for our order.

Julian sits next to me on the couch, closer than he normally would in public, I think. But because one, this is a gay club, and two, no one knows he's here, he can get away with it. "What would you like to drink, love?" His lips brush my ear as he asks. The touch makes me shiver, the little hairs on the back of my neck rising from the pleasure of being near him.

I couldn't care less what we drink. With his dark hair all messy-perfect and those lips so close to my skin, I wish I could drink *him* up.

I turn to reply and accidentally almost kiss him. We grin at each other and scoot back, aware of our audience. "Maybe just a beer."

"Two lagers," he tells the server, over my shoulder.

"Thanks," I say. I can see why he brought me here. "This place is ... seductive. Both private and public. I bet a lot of people get up to a lot of naughty things in this room."

His grin turns lascivious as he rakes his gaze over my body. "We can't be proper *all* the time."

"I suppose not. Even if the circumstances are inconvenient."

"Sam, if I'd written the album two years ago, I'd never have met you. A wee breach of contract would be well worth it for that outcome. Not that I'm saying I did that."

His words pull me up short, because that is exactly the kind of thing I could use against him on Lighthouse's behalf. "Julian. We still have to be careful."

"Sorry. We do." Nevertheless, he rests a hand on my thigh and keeps it there, even when the server comes back with our drinks.

It's all I can do to stave off an erection. Because having Julian Hill this close to me? Having his undivided attention? It's dizzying.

This is a fuckton of temptation.

We're hidden from view, but we can see downstairs and get glimpses of the dancers on the TV screens. I trace the tattoos on Julian's fingers, then take off one of his silver skull rings and try it on.

It fits.

"Keep it," he says.

I shake my head. "I can't wear one of your rings."

"Why not?"

A laugh comes out of me, and I gesture down at myself. "Skulls and preppy don't mix."

"I think they do." He leans forward. "Keep it."

The warmth of the heavy ring on my forefinger reminds me of him. "Okay," I say. Then I rub the design it had covered on his hand.

With his head cocked, he asks, "Would you ever get a tattoo?"

I take a sip of my beer. "How do you know I don't already have one?" His startled look makes me laugh.

"Oh, this I have to see. You've been holding out on me?"

"No, I'm just kidding. I don't have one. And no, I'd never get one."

He raises an eyebrow. "You say that so fast."

"There's nothing I want permanently drawn on me. Do you ever want to get any of yours removed? Do you regret any of them?"

"Not a one. Even the ones that symbolize things long past. They're my history. Life is so digital, and digital can easily be erased after a few automated 'Are you sure?' messages. I like having the scars. I like having a record of things that happened." Jules sips his own beer. "There are probably hundreds of thousands of photos of me out there, and I have heaps of memories, but if an event or thought or symbol made it onto my body, I know it's important." He sets his drink down. "What would you get? I mean, if you had to."

I pause, thinking about it. "I don't know. Obviously something meaningful."

"That's what I'm asking. What means something to you? A symbol of an event or something you use or love?"

"My P-touch."

"Your what?"

"My label maker."

He laughs. "That is a *whole* lot less interesting than what I thought a 'p-touch' would be." Then he sobers, taking in the look on my face. "You're serious, aren't you?"

I shrug. "What can I say? I told you I like things to be organized."

"That's cute." He drains his beer and scoots back a bit, studying me.

"Why are you looking at me like that?"

"I like you." Jules tugs on my tie, pulling it loose, and the act is somehow erotic and innocent at the same time. Because we know we can't do anything.

But when we *do* get a chance to get together …

I smile. And the temptation to kiss him is almost irresistible.

Instead, I finish my drink. I need to tone this down, otherwise I won't survive tonight.

But a moment later, Jules tugs me up. "Dance with me."

His voice makes me tingle. He pulls me into his arms and starts moving. We're dancing so close, it feels like sex. It feels like lust and all the overwhelming emotions I've been feeling for him.

He feels right in my arms. Like he's supposed to be there. Like when we danced before.

Only it's worse, because we're pressed together instead of doing a formal box step.

The music pulses, and as we dance—helped by a tiny bit of alcohol—things get messier. Our dancing becomes raw and hedonistic, pelvises grinding, chest to chest, hands on each other's asses.

Why do I even care about the ethical issues? Is anyone going to believe me? Can I prove that we didn't have sex? That I didn't ignore the best wishes of my client?

I suppose the only person I really have to prove these things to is myself. Because if asked, I'll be truthful. I've kissed Julian Hill a few times, and I am sort of beginning a relationship with him. But nothing has happened that I think will hurt my client.

Faint justification for my actions.

But one of his songs comes on, and I almost laugh. I open my mouth to say something about it, when he starts singing in my ear. Quietly, but harmonizing along with himself. It gives me goose bumps. It makes my mouth water. It makes my dick leak. It makes me *want him* more than *anything*.

I *want* this man. I like how he pays attention to me and how he respects my reserve.

But my reserve is shattering.

Fuck it.

We've already kissed. One more time won't hurt anything, and no one, absolutely no one can see us back here. It's as private as we can get in a dance club.

I kiss him, my lips crashing into his and my hands gripping the back of his neck. He tastes like beer and sweat, but he smells so, so good and his body is warm under my fingers. Jules grunts at the press of my lips and then opens his mouth, slips his tongue between my lips and takes over the kiss like he's in charge.

And I'm lost. In the music, in him. I've lost the ability to process. I've lost the floor. The ground has dropped out, and the ceiling is limitless. All I am is held by Julian.

When we stop for breath, I come to my senses, if only a bit. "I'm sorry," I gasp. "We can't. I know I'm the one who started it. But I had to."

"Shh, love," Jules murmurs, his lips along my neck making me groan. He kisses the bolt of my jaw, his mouth soft against my stubble.

"Fuck." I look at him. "I am about thirty seconds away from dropping to my knees in front of you."

"Bloody hell. You can't say things like that and expect me to care about your lawyer ethics." There's no trace of mockery in his voice. He's completely serious. "But I know I mustn't let you do something you'll regret."

"How long until you finish the album?" I ask it against his ear, while sucking on it—because I'm only human. His skin is warm and salty.

"It's getting very close. A few days, perhaps. I will meet that deadline."

I step back. "I can wait that long. Can you?"

He gulps. "I can. Barely. But yes, I can."

Note from Leslie:

When Jules went to meet Sam's parents, I originally had him wearing a sexy dress. My editor pointed out that Jules would have a sense of time and place and probably wouldn't wear something so bold to meet Sam's parents. So I dressed Jules in an outfit my friend Johan wore. She also didn't like Sam's indecision about inviting Jules and then wanting to leave. Still, I like Jules in a dress, so here it is.

Fifty-Two

Sam

"Are you ready for this?" I ask, as Jules and I walk up to my grandfather's midcentury modern showcase home, which isn't all that far from Jules's house. "Because we don't have to go in." I stop on the walkway. "You know what? We can leave. We should go. We can just do this over the phone."

Jules stops me, turning to face me and put two hands on my shoulders. "I'm ready. They're your family. Of course I want to meet them. I only wish I had family to share with you. I mean, apart from Colin."

I stare at Julian and relax at the gentle look in his eyes. Then I brace myself. "It might take them a while to come around, since for years I've only been with Kurt. And also, well …"

"They may have heard of me before," Jules supplies.

"Right."

I bite my lip. Jules is wearing a long black tank dress in thick jersey fabric, tight to his body, and soft gray sneakers. The dress clings to all the bumps of his muscles and the dip of his hips, and it doesn't hide the bulge at the front. Or the jockstrap he's wearing underneath.

Fuck, he looks sexy.

"That's a dangerous dress to wear," I murmur. "I bet I could make you hard."

He winks at me. "If I cared about people seeing me stiff, I'd wear something else."

"Fuck, now you're making me all …" I gesture to my crotch. "And this is not the way to be when I am seeing my grandparents."

"Would you rather I'd worn something else?"

"Never," I say fiercely. "You look hot. It might provoke them, but that's on them."

He studies my expression and nods, then leans in and gives me the lightest brush of a kiss. "Okay."

We walk up to the glass doorway, and I knock and open the door, our usual protocol.

Everyone's gathered in the living room, chatting and drinking wine.

"Mom, Dad, Pop-Pop, Grandma?" I say, as we walk in holding hands, "This is my new boyfriend, Julian."

Their jaws drop. They look like fish. Or some big-eyed animal from *Star Wars*.

Acknowledgments

About a year ago, my friend Cory Stierley (the cover photographer) sent me a link to the Harry Styles "Falling" video, because he thought I'd like it. I now blame him for this whole book (Cory, not Harry). Basically, I'd never listened to him before (Harry, not Cory, although Cory can sing), but I thought the video was gorgeous, with a soaking wet Harry playing the piano while wearing a ruffled shirt. After I saw it, I took a shower and had one of those moments where the entire story came to me like a creative download from the universe. I wrote the initial outline to this book dripping wet and wearing a towel. That's probably TMI. So, is this book Harry Styles fanfic? IDK. He certainly started it, and my thanks to some YouTubers out there who compiled videos of him … but I think Jules is his own person. Up to you to decide. If you're wondering about my personal musical tastes (likely you aren't), my favorite musicians are Beck (I've seen him more than a dozen times in concert over a few decades) and twenty one pilots (the lead singer shook my kid's hand, and I'm still not over it—video on my TikTok), but I used to be a college radio deejay and nowadays I listen to just about anything, Harry included. If you ask me if I like a type of music, I'll most likely say yes, and most likely it influenced some part of this book. At any rate, thanks, Cory, for the initial inspiration and the cover photo of Brock Grady. Side note: Cory told me when he began his photo shoot with the 'Brock star,' the first song that came on—randomly—was "Falling." <shivers> Big thanks as well to Garrett Leigh for the lovely cover design.

Thank you to the most wonderful editor, Alicia Z. Ramos. Because of her, I have a fighting chance of getting a comma in the right place and a book that makes sense. She is also so very thoughtful and so very kind. I also thank Megan Dischinger for beta reading early drafts and Virginia Tesi Carey for proofing the final version.

Lots and lots of people gave me useful feedback and support, and I'm very scared I'm going to forget someone, but here goes: Kristy Lin Billuni, Mary Carr (hero support), Deb Markanton (nice to meet you in person finally!), Lex Martin, Julia Heudorf, Phala Theng, and Katy Cuthbertson.

Jerica MacMillian always has my back as does Heather Roberts. Thank you.

Special thanks to JR Gray, who helped me through the book when I was very stuck and who sent me Harry Styles stickers, because he's awesome like that. (Gray, not Harry. Although Harry too…)

Extra thanks to Karen Cundy for making sure Julian didn't sound too American and for video-interviewing more than a dozen UK teenagers to tell me that "aftershave," not "cologne" is what he'd say. Also for sending me the best Pinterest board ever.

Special edition cover design by RJ Creatives and interior design by Champagne Book Design.

Thanks to my family for understanding my need to spend lots of time with fictional characters.

And thanks to you for reading.

I love you all.

Also by
LESLIE McADAM

Sarina Bowen's World of True North (m/m)
Undone
Unmanageable

IOU Series (m/m)
Ambiguous
Studious
Oblivious
Curious

With J.E. Birk and Rachel Ember (m/m/m)
ILYBSM

Contemporary Romance (m/f)

All American Boy Series
Boy on a Train

Romantic comedies with Lex Martin
All About the D
Surprise, Baby!

The Giving You … series
The Sun and the Moon
The Stars in the Sky
All the Waters of the Earth
The Ground Beneath Our Feet

Love in Translation series
Sol
Sombra

Standalone novella
Lumbersexual

About the Author

Leslie McAdam is a California girl who loves romance and well-defined abs. She lives in a drafty old farmhouse on a small orange tree farm in Southern California with her husband and two children. Leslie's first published book, *The Sun and the Moon*, won a 2015 Watty, which is the world's largest online writing competition. She's gone on to receive additional literary awards and has been featured in multiple publications, including Cosmopolitan.com. Her books have been Top 100 Bestsellers on both Amazon and Apple Books. Leslie is employed by day but spends her nights writing about the men of your fantasies.

Website: www.lesliemcadamauthor.com
M/M-only newsletter: http://eepurl.com/hD9a4r

www.ingramcontent.com/pod-product-compliance
Lightning Source LLC
LaVergne TN
LVHW020409070526
838199LV00054B/3573